WITHDRAWN

EILEEN

ALSO BY OTTESSA MOSHFEGH

McGlue

EILEEN

OTTESSA MOSHFEGH

PENGUIN PRESS | *New York* | 2015

PENGUIN PRESS
An imprint of Penguin Random House LLC
375 Hudson Street
New York, New York 10014
penguin.com

ISBN 978-1-59420-662-7

Printed in the United States of America
7   9   10   8   6

Designed by Gretchen Achilles

For X.

EILEEN

1964

I looked like a girl you'd expect to see on a city bus, reading some clothbound book from the library about plants or geography, perhaps wearing a net over my light brown hair. You might take me for a nursing student or a typist, note the nervous hands, a foot tapping, bitten lip. I looked like nothing special. It's easy for me to imagine this girl, a strange, young and mousy version of me, carrying an anonymous leather purse or eating from a small package of peanuts, rolling each one between her gloved fingers, sucking in her cheeks, staring anxiously out the window. The sunlight in the morning illuminated the thin down on my face, which I tried to cover with pressed powder, a shade too pink for my wan complexion. I was thin, my figure was jagged, my movements pointy and hesitant, my posture stiff. The terrain of my face was heavy with soft, rumbling acne scars blurring whatever delight or madness lay beneath that cold and deadly New England exterior. If I'd worn glasses I could have passed for smart, but I was too impatient to be truly smart. You'd have expected me to enjoy the stillness of closed rooms, take comfort in dull silence, my gaze moving slowly across paper, walls, heavy curtains, thoughts never shifting from what my eyes identified—book, desk, tree, person. But I deplored silence. I deplored stillness. I hated almost everything. I was very unhappy and angry all the time. I tried to control myself, and that only made me more awkward, unhappier, and angrier. I was like Joan of Arc, or Hamlet, but born into the wrong life—the life of a nobody, a waif, invisible. There's no better way to say it: I was not myself back then. I was someone else. I was Eileen.

And back then—this was fifty years ago—I was a prude. Just look at me. I wore heavy wool skirts that fell past my knees, thick stockings. I always buttoned my jackets and blouses as high as they could go. I wasn't a girl who turned heads. But there was nothing really so wrong or terrible about my appearance. I was young and fine, average, I guess. But at the time I thought I was the worst—ugly, disgusting, unfit for the world. In such a state it seemed ridiculous to call attention to myself. I rarely wore jewelry, never perfume, and I didn't paint my nails. For a while I did wear a ring with a little ruby in it. It had belonged to my mother.

My last days as that angry little Eileen took place in late December, in the brutal cold town where I was born and raised. The snow had fallen for the winter, a good three or four feet of it. It sat staunchly in every front yard, rolled out at the lip of every first-floor windowsill like a flood. During the day, the top layer of snow melted and the slush in the gutters loosened a bit and you remembered that life was joyful from time to time, that the sun did shine. But by afternoon, the sun had disappeared and everything froze all over again, building a glaze on the snow so thick at night it could hold the weight of a full-grown man. Each morning, I threw salt from the bucket by the front door down the narrow path from the porch to the street. Icicles hung from the rafter over the front door, and I stood there imagining them cracking and darting through my breasts, slicing through the thick gristle of my shoulder like bullets or cleaving my brain into pieces. The sidewalk had been shoveled by the next-door neighbors, a family my father distrusted because they were Lutheran and he was Catholic. But he distrusted everyone. He was fearful and crazy the way old drunks get. Those Lutheran neighbors had left a white wicker basket of cellophane-wrapped waxed apples, a box of chocolates, and a bottle of sherry by the front door for Christmas. I remember the card read, "Bless you both."

Who really knew what happened inside the house while I was at work? It was a three-story colonial of brown wood and flaking red trim. I imagine my father sucking down that sherry in the spirit of Christmas, lighting an old cigar on the stove. That's a funny picture. Generally he drank gin. Beer, occasionally. He was a drunk, as I said. He was simple in that way. When something was the matter, he was easy to distract and soothe: I'd just hand him a bottle and leave the room. Of course his drinking put a strain on me as a young person. It made me very tense and edgy. That happens when one lives with an alcoholic. My story in this sense is not unique. I've lived with many alcoholic men over the years, and each has taught me that it is useless to worry, fruitless to ask why, suicide to try to help them. They are who they are, for better and worse. Now I live alone. Happily. Gleefully, even. I'm too old to concern myself with other people's affairs. And I no longer waste my time thinking ahead into the future, worrying about things that haven't happened yet. But I worried all the time when I was young, not least of all about my future, and mostly with respect to my father—how long he had left to live, what he might do, what I would find when I got home from work each evening.

Ours was not a very nice home. After my mother died, we never sorted or put her things away, never rearranged anything, and without her to clean it, the house was dirty and dusty and full of useless decorations and crowded with things, things, things everywhere. And yet it felt completely empty. It was like an abandoned home, its owners having fled one night like Jews or gypsies. We didn't use the den or the dining room or the upstairs bedrooms much. Everything just sat there collecting dust, a magazine splayed over the arm of the couch for years, candy dish full of dead ants. I remember it like those photos of homes in the desert ravaged by nuclear testing. I think you can imagine the details for yourself.

I slept in the attic, on a cot purchased by my father for some summer camping trip he never took a decade earlier. The attic was unfinished, a cold and dusty place I'd retreated to when my mother had gotten sick. Sleep in my childhood bedroom, which was next to hers, had been impossible. She had wailed and cried and called my name throughout the night. The attic was quiet.

Not much noise traveled up there from the lower floors of the house. My father had an armchair that he'd dragged from the den into the kitchen. He slept there. It was the kind of chair that shuttled backward at the pull of a lever, a charming novelty when he'd bought it. But the lever no longer worked. The thing had rusted into permanent repose. Everything in the house was like that chair—grimy, ruined, and frozen.

I remember it pleased me that the sun set so early that winter. Under the cover of darkness, I was somewhat comforted. My father, however, was scared of the dark. That may sound like an endearing peculiarity, but it was not. At night he would light the stove and the oven and drink and watch the blue flames whir under the weak overhead light. He was always cold, he said. And yet he barely dressed. This one evening—I'll begin my story there—I found him sitting barefoot on the stairs, drinking the sherry, the butt of a cigar between his fingers. "Poor Eileen," he said sarcastically when I walked through the door. He was very contemptuous of me, found me pathetic and unattractive and had no qualms about saying so. If my daydreams from back then came true, one day I'd have found him splayed out at the bottom of the stairs, neck broken but still breathing. "It's about time," I'd say with the most bored affect I could muster, peering over his dying body. So I loathed him, yes, but I was very dutiful. It was just the two of us in the house—Dad and me. I do have a sister, still alive as far as I know, but we haven't spoken in over fifty years.

"Hi, Dad," I said, passing him on the stairs.

He was not a very large man, but he had broad shoulders

and long legs, a sort of regal look about him. His thinning gray hair stood up high and bowed over the crown of his head. His face appeared to be decades older than he really was, and bore in it a wide-eyed skepticism and a look of perpetual disapproval. In retrospect he was much like the boys in the prison where I worked—sensitive and angry. His hands shook all the time no matter how much he drank. He was always rubbing at his chin, which was red and drawn and wrinkled. He'd tug at it the way you'd rub the head of a young boy and call him a little rascal. His one regret in life, he said, was that he'd never been able to grow a real beard, as though he could have willed it, but he had failed to. He was like that—regretful and arrogant and illogical at once. I don't think he ever really loved his children. The wedding band he continued to wear years after her death suggested that he'd loved our mother to some degree at least. But I suspect he was incapable of love, real love. He was a cruel character. Imagining his parents beating him as a child is the only path to forgiveness that I have found so far. It isn't perfect, but it does the trick.

This isn't a story of how awful my father was, let me be clear. Bemoaning his cruelty is not the point of this at all. But I do remember that day on the stairs, how he winced when he turned to look up at me, as though the sight of me made him ill. I stood on the landing, looking down.

"You're going out again," he croaked, "to Lardner's." Lardner's was the liquor store across town. He let the empty sherry bottle slip from his fingers and roll down the staircase, step by step.

I'm very reasonable now, peaceful even, but back then I was easily enraged. My father's demands that I do his bidding like a maid, a servant, were constant. But I was not the kind of girl to say no to anyone.

"All right," I said.

My father grunted and puffed on the short butt of his cigar.

When I was disturbed, I took some comfort in attending to my appearance. I was obsessed with the way I looked, in fact. My eyes are small and green, and you wouldn't—especially back then—have seen much kindness in them. I am not one of those women who try to make people happy all the time. I'm not that strategic. If you'd seen me back then with a barrette in my hair, my mousy gray wool coat, you'd have expected me to be just a minor character in this saga—conscientious, even-tempered, dull, irrelevant. I looked like a shy and gentle soul from afar, and sometimes I wished I was one. But I cursed and blushed and broke out in sweats quite often, and that day I slammed the bathroom door shut by kicking it with the full sole of my shoe, nearly busting the hinges. I looked so boring, lifeless, immune and unaffected, but in truth I was always furious, seething, my thoughts racing, my mind like a killer's. It was easy to hide behind the dull face I wore, moping around. I really thought I had everybody fooled. And I didn't really read books about flowers or home economics. I liked books about awful things—murder, illness, death. I remember selecting one of the thickest books from the public library, a chronicle of ancient Egyptian medicine, to study the gruesome practice of pulling the brains of the dead out through the nose like skeins of yarn.

I liked to think of my brain like that, tangled up in my skull. The idea that my brains could be untangled, straightened out, and thus refashioned into a state of peace and sanity was a comforting fantasy. I often felt there was something wired weird in my brain, a problem so complicated only a lobotomy could solve it—I'd need a whole new mind or a whole new life. I could be very dramatic in my self-assessments. Besides books, I enjoyed my issues of *National Geographic* magazine, which I got delivered to me in the mail. That was a real luxury and made me feel very special. Articles describing the naive beliefs of the primitives fascinated me. Their blood rites, the human sacrifices, all that needless suffering. I was dark, you might say. Moony. But I don't think I was really so hardhearted by nature. Had I been born into a different family, I might have grown up to act and feel perfectly normal.

Truth be told, I was a glutton for punishment. I didn't really mind getting bossed around by my father. I'd get angry, and I loathed him, yes, but my fury gave my life a kind of purpose, and running his errands killed time. That is what I imagined life to be—one long sentence of waiting out the clock.

I tried to look miserable and exhausted when I came out from the bathroom that evening. My father groaned impatiently. I sighed and plucked the cash he held out. I buttoned my coat back up. I was relieved to have somewhere to go, a way to pass the evening hours other than to pace the attic or watch my father drink. There was nothing I loved more than leaving the house.

If I had slammed the front door hard on my way out, as

I was tempted to, one of those icicles overhead would have surely cracked off. I imagined one plummeting through the hollow of my collarbone and stabbing me straight through the heart. Or, had I tilted my head back, perhaps it would have soared down my throat, scraping the vacuous center of my body—I liked to picture these things—and followed through to my guts, finally parting my nether regions like a glass dagger. That was how I imagined my anatomy back then, brain like tangled yarn, body like an empty vessel, private parts like some strange foreign country. But I was careful shutting the door, of course. I didn't really want to die.

Since my father had become unfit to drive it, I drove his old Dodge. I loved that car. It was a four-door Coronet, matte green, full of scrapes and dents. The floorboards had rusted through from years of salt and ice. I kept in the glove box of the Dodge a dead field mouse I'd found one day on the porch frozen in a tight ball. I'd picked it up by its tail and swirled it through the air for a moment, then slung it in the glove box with a broken flashlight, a map of New England freeways, a few green nickels. Every now and then that winter, I'd peek at the mouse, check on its invisible decomposition in the freezing cold. I think it made me feel powerful somehow. A little totem. A good luck charm.

Outside I tested the temperature with the tip of my tongue, sticking it out into the biting wind until it hurt. That night it must have been down close to single digits. It hurt just to breathe. But I preferred cold weather over hot. Summers I was restless and cranky. I'd break out in rashes, have to lie in cold baths. I'd sit at my desk in the prison whipping a paper fan furiously at my face. I did not like to sweat in front of other people. Such proof of carnality I found lewd, disgusting. Similarly, I did not like to dance or do sports. I did not listen to the Beatles or watch Ed Sullivan on TV. I wasn't interested in fun or popularity back then. I preferred to read about ancient times, distant lands. Knowledge of anything current or faddish made me feel I was just a victim of isolation. If I avoided all that on purpose, I could believe I was in control.

One thing about that Dodge was that it made me sick to drive it. I knew there was something wrong with the exhaust, but at the time I couldn't think of dealing with such a problem. Part of me liked having to roll down the windows, even in the cold. I thought that I was very brave. But really I was scared that if I made a fuss over the car, it would be taken away from me. That car was the one thing in my life that gave me any hope. It was my only means of escape. Before he'd retired, my father had driven it on his days off. He'd wheeled it around town so carelessly—parked up on curbs, screeched around corners, stalled out on no gas at the dead of night, scraped it alongside milk delivery trucks, the side of the AMP building, and so forth. Everybody drove drunk back then, but that was no excuse. I myself was a decent driver. I never sped, never blew through red lights. When it was dark out, I liked to drive slowly, foot barely on the pedal, and watch the town roll by like in a movie. I always imagined other people's homes to be so much nicer than mine, full of polished wood furniture and elegant fireplaces and stockings hung for Christmas. Cookies in the cupboards, lawn mowers in the garages. It was easy to think of everyone having it better than me back then. Down the block, one illuminated vestibule made me feel particularly disparaged. It had a white bench and a blade by the door like an upturned ice skate to scrape the snow from your boots and a garland of holly hung on the front door. The town was a pretty place, quaint, you'd call it. And unless you've grown up in New England, you don't know the peculiar stillness of a coastal town covered in snow at night. It is not like in other places. The light does something funny at sunset. It seems not to wane but to recede out toward the ocean. The light just gets pulled away.

I'll never forget that bright jangle of the bell over the liquor store door since it rang for me nearly every evening. Lardner's Liquors. I loved it there. It was warm and orderly, and I wandered the aisles for as long as I could, pretending to browse. I knew, of course, where the gin was kept: center aisle on the right if you're facing the cashier, a few feet from the back wall, and just two shelves of it, Beefeater on top and Seagram's below it. Mr. Lewis, who worked there, was so gentle and happy, as though it had never occurred to him just what all that liquor was for. That night, I got the gin, paid, and went back to the car, laid the bottles on the passenger's seat. How odd it is that liquor never freezes. It was the one thing in that place that simply refused the cold. I shivered in the Dodge, turned the key, and drove slowly home. I took the long and scenic route as the darkness fell, I remember.

My father was in his chair in the kitchen when I got back to the house. Nothing special happened that night. It's just a place to begin. I set the bottles down within his reach on the floor and crumpled the paper bag in my fist, threw it at the pile of trash by the back door. I walked up to the attic. I read my magazine. I went to bed.

So here we are. My name was Eileen Dunlop. Now you know me. I was twenty-four years old and had a job that paid fifty-seven dollars a week as a kind of secretary at a private juvenile correctional facility for teenage boys. I think of it now as what it really was for all intents and purposes—a prison for children. I will call it Moorehead. Delvin Moorehead was a terrible landlord I had years later, and so to use his name for such a place feels appropriate.

In a week, I would run away from home and never go back. This is the story of how I disappeared.

FRIDAY

$\mathcal{F}$riday meant a noxious aroma of fish was wafting up from the basement cafeteria and through the cold quarters where the boys slept, down the linoleum halls and into the windowless office where I spent my days. It was a smell so pungent and punishing I could detect it even outside in the parking lot when I arrived at Moorehead that morning. I had built up the habit of locking my purse in the trunk of my car before I went in to work. There were lockers in the break room behind the office, but I didn't trust the staff. My father had warned me when I'd started there at age twenty-one, naive beyond reproach, that the most dangerous individuals in a prison are not the criminals but the very people who work there. I can confirm this to be true. Those were perhaps the wisest words my father ever told me.

I'd packed a lunch consisting of two squares of Wonderbread, buttered and packaged in tinfoil, and a can of tuna fish. It was Friday and I didn't want to go to hell, after all. I did my best to smile and nod at my coworkers, both awful middle-aged women with stiff hairdos who barely looked up from their romance novels unless the warden was around. Their desks were littered with yellow cellophane wrappers from caramel candies which they each kept in fake crystal bowls on the corners of their desks. As awful as they were, the office ladies ranked low on the list of despicable characters in my life over the years. Working day shifts in the office with them, I really didn't have it so bad. Having a desk job meant I rarely had to interact with one of the four or five terrifying and pig-nosed correctional officers whose job it was to mend the wicked ways of Moorehead's young residents. They were like army sergeants, rapping boys with batons on the backs of their legs as they shuffled around, restraining them in schoolyard-style choke holds. I tried to look the other way when things got hairy. Mostly I looked up at the clock.

The overnight guards would get off shift at eight, when I arrived, and I never knew them, though I remember their exhausted faces—one was a loping idiot and the other a balding veteran with tobacco-stained fingers. They're not important. But one daytime guard was just wonderful looking. He had big hound-dog eyes, a strong profile still softened with youth and what I thought, of course, was some sort of magical sadness about him, and hair that gleamed in a high ducktail—Randy. I liked to watch him from my desk. He sat in the hallway that connected the office to the rest of the facility. He wore the standard starched gray uniform, well-oiled motorcycle boots, a heavy set of keys clipped to his belt loop. He had a way of sitting with one flank on the stool, one off, a foot hanging midair, a posture which presented his crotch as though on a platter for me to gaze at. I was not his type, and I knew so, and that pained me though I never would have admitted it. His type was pretty, long-legged, pouty, probably blond, I suspected. Still, I could dream. I spent many hours watching his biceps flick and pump as he turned each page of his comic book. When I imagine him now, I think of the way he'd swerve a toothpick around in his mouth. It was beautiful. It was poetry. I asked him once, nervous and ridiculous, whether he felt cold wearing just short sleeves in winter. He shrugged. Still waters ran deep, I thought, nearly swooning. It was pointless to fantasize, but I couldn't help imagine one day he'd throw stones at my attic window, motorcycle steaming out in front of the house, melting the whole town to hell. I was not immune to that sort of thing.

Though I didn't drink coffee—it made me dizzy—I walked to the corner where the coffee pot was because there was a mirror on the wall above it. Looking at my reflection really did soothe me, though I hated my face with a passion. Such is the life of the self-obsessed. The time I languished in the agony of not being beautiful was more than I care to admit even now. I rubbed a crumb of sleep from my eye and poured myself a cup of cream, sweetened it with sugar and Carnation malted milk, which I kept in my desk drawer. Nobody commented on this strange cocktail. Nobody paid any attention to me at all in that office. The office women were all so soured and flat and cliquish. I suspected at the time they were secretly homosexual for each other. Such persuasions were more and more on one's mind back then, townsfolk ever watchful for the errant "latent homosexual" on the prowl. My suspicions about the office ladies weren't necessarily disparaging. It helped me to have a little compassion when I imagined them going home at night to their disgusting husbands, so bitter, so lonely. On the other hand, to think of them with their blouses unbuttoned, hands in each other's brassieres, legs spread, made me want to vomit.

There was a small section in a book I'd found in the public library that showed casts of faces taken of figures such as Lincoln, Beethoven, and Sir Isaac Newton after they'd died. If you've ever seen a real dead body you know that people never die with such complacent grins, such blankness. But I used their plaster casts as a guide and practiced very diligently in the mirror, relaxing my face while keeping an aura of benign resilience, such as I saw in those dead men's faces. I mention it because it is the face I wore at work, my death mask. Being as young as I was, I was terribly sensitive, and determined never to show it. I steeled myself from the reality of the place, this Moorehead. I had to. Misery and shame surrounded me, but not once did I run to the bathroom crying. Later that morning, delivering mail to the warden's office, which was within the complex of chambers where the boys studied and had recreational activities, I passed a corrections officer—Mulvaney or Mulroony or Mahoney, they all seemed the same—twisting a boy's ear as he knelt down in front of him. "You think you're special?" he asked. "See the dirt on the floor? You matter less than a speck of that dirt between those tiles." He pushed the boy's head down face first into his boots, big and steel-toed, hard enough to club someone to death. "Lick it," said the officer. I watched the boy's lips part, then I looked away.

The warden's secretary was a woman so steely-eyed and fat she appeared never to be breathing, her heart never beating. Her death mask was impressive. The only sign of life she ever gave was when she lifted a finger to her mouth and a centimeter of pale lavender tongue came out to wet its tip. She leafed through the stack of envelopes I handed her robotically, then turned away. I lingered for a minute or two, pretending to count days on the calendar hanging on the wall by her desk. "Five days till Christmas," I said, trying to sound cheerful.

"Praise God," she replied.

I often think of Moorehead and its laughable credo, *parens patriae,* and cringe. The boys at Moorehead were all so young, just children. They frightened me at the time because I felt they didn't like me, didn't find me attractive. So I tried to cast them off as dunces and wild animals. Some of them were grown, tall and handsome. I was not immune to those boys either.

Back at my desk, there was plenty I could have pondered. It was 1964, so much on the horizon. In every direction something was getting torn down or built up, but I mostly pondered myself and my own misery while I arranged my pens in the cup, crossed off the day on my desk calendar. The second hand on the clock shook and bolted forward like someone at first terrified with anxiety, then, bolstered by desperation, jumping off a cliff only to get stuck in midair. My mind wandered. Randy, more than anywhere else, was where it liked to go. When my paycheck came that Friday, I folded it and slipped it into my bosom, which was hardly a bosom. Just small, hard mounds, really, which I hid beneath layers of cotton underthings, a blouse, a wool jacket. I still had that pubescent fear that when people looked at me, they could see through my clothes. I suspect nobody was fantasizing about my naked body, but I worried that when anyone's eyes cast downward, they were investigating my nether regions and could somehow decipher the complex and nonsensical folds and caverns wrapped up so tightly down there between my legs. I was always very protective of my folds and caverns. I was still a virgin, of course.

I suppose my prudishness did its duty and saved me from a difficult life such as my sister's. She was older than me and not a virgin at all and lived with a man who was not her husband a few towns over—"whore" is what our mother had called her. Joanie was perfectly nice, I suppose, but she had a dark, gluttonous streak beneath her buoyant, girlish exterior. She once told me how Cliff, her boyfriend, liked to "taste" her as she woke up in the mornings. She laughed as my face contorted in perplexity, then turned red and cold when I caught her drift. "Isn't that funny? Isn't that the most?" she tittered. I envied her plenty, sure, but I never let on. I didn't really want what she had. Men, boys, the prospect of coupling with one of them seemed ridiculous. The most I desired was a wordless affair. But even that scared me. I had my crush on Randy and a few others, but they never went anywhere. Oh, those poor nether regions of mine, swaddled like a baby in a diaper in thick cotton underpants and my mother's old strangulating girdle. I wore lipstick not to be fashionable, but because my bare lips were the same color as my nipples. At twenty-four I would give nothing to aid any imagining of my naked body. Meanwhile, it seemed, most young women were intent on doing the opposite.

There was a party at the prison that day. Dr. Frye was retiring. He'd been the very elderly man in charge of doling out gross amounts of sedatives to the boys for decades as the prison's psychiatrist. He must have been in his eighties. I'm old now myself, but when I was young I really didn't care for elderly people. I felt their very existence undermined me. I couldn't have cared less that Dr. Frye was leaving. I signed the card when it crossed my desk with precise, schoolgirl cursive, wrist bent high in sarcasm: "So long." I remember the image on the front was a black ink drawing of a cowboy riding off into the sunset. Good grief. Over the years at Moorehead, Dr. Frye would come occasionally to observe the family visits, which it was my duty to administrate on a daily basis, and I'd watched him stand at the open doorway to the visitation room, nodding and clacking his gums and hmming, and now and then interjecting with long, wobbling fingers to point for the child to sit up straight, answer the question, apologize, and so on. And he never once said "Hello," or "How are you, Miss Dunlop?" I was invisible. I was furniture. After lunch—I think I left that can of tuna in my locker, uneaten—they called the staff to the cafeteria for cake and coffee to bid Dr. Frye adieu, and I declined to participate. I sat at my desk and did nothing, just stared at the clock. At some point I got an itch in my underwear, and since there was nobody to see me, I stuck my hand up my skirt to get at it. As swaddled as they were, my nether regions were difficult to scratch. So I had to dig my hand down the front of my skirt, under the girdle, inside the underwear, and when the itch had been relieved, I pulled my fingers out and smelled them. It's a natural curiosity, I think, to smell one's fingers. Later, when the day was done, these were the fingers I extended, still unwashed, to Dr. Frye when I wished him a happy retirement on his way out the door.

Working at Moorehead, I wouldn't say I was sheltered, exactly. But I was isolated. I did not get out much at all. The town where I lived and had grown up—I'll call it X-ville—had no tracks of which there could be a wrong side per se. There were grittier areas, however, for the blue-collar and troubled people, a bit closer to the ocean, and I'd driven past their ramshackle houses with yards littered with children's toys and garbage only a few times. Seeing the people on the roads, so forlorn and angry and uninterested, delighted me and scared me and made me feel ashamed not to be so poor. But the streets in my neighborhood were all tree lined and orderly, houses loved and tended to with pride and affection and a sense of civic order that made me ashamed to be so messy, so broken, so bland. I didn't know that there were others like me in the world, those who didn't "fit in," as people like to put it. Furthermore, as is typical for any isolated, intelligent young person, I thought I was the only one with any consciousness, any awareness of how odd it was to be alive, to be a creature on this strange planet Earth. I've seen episodes of *The Twilight Zone* which illustrate the kind of straight-faced derangement I felt in X-ville. It was very lonely.

Boston in all its brick and ivy gave me hope that there was

intelligent life out there, young people living as they pleased. Freedom was not so far away. I'd gone there only once, a trip I took with my mother to see a doctor when she was dying, a doctor who couldn't cure her but who did prescribe medicine that would make her "comfortable," as he called it. Such an excursion felt glamorous to me back then. It's true that I was twenty-four. I was an adult. You'd think I could have driven anywhere I wished. Indeed, my last summer in X-ville, toward the end of one of my father's longer benders, I took a trip down the coast. My car ran out of gas and I was stranded on a country road just an hour from home until an older woman stopped and gave me a dollar and a ride to the filling station and told me to "plan ahead next time." I remember the wise woggle of her double chin as she steered the car. She was a country woman, and I respected her. That was when I began to fantasize about my disappearance, convincing myself bit by bit that the solution to my problem— the problem being my life in X-ville—was in New York City.

It was a cliché then and it's a cliché now, but having heard "Hello, Dolly!" on the radio, it seemed wholly possible for me to show up in Manhattan with money for a room in a boardinghouse and have my future roll out automatically, without my having to think too hard about it. It was just a daydream, but I fed it as best I could. I started saving my own money in cash hidden in the attic. It was my responsibility to deposit my father's pension checks, which the X-ville police department sent at the beginning of each month, at the X-ville Bank, where the tellers called me Mrs. Dunlop, my mother's name, and, I thought, would have no problem emptying the account and handing me an envelope of hundred-dollar bills from the Dunlops' savings if I lied and said I was buying a new car.

I never once discussed my desire to leave X-ville with another person. But a few times, during my darkest hours—I was so moody—when I felt impelled to drive off a bridge or, one particular morning, had a compulsion to slam my hand in the car door, I imagined what relief I might feel if I could lie on Dr. Frye's couch just once and confess like some sort of fallen hero that my life was simply intolerable. But, in fact, it was tolerable. I'd been tolerating it, after all. Anyway, that young Eileen would never lie down in the company of a man who was not her father. It would be impossible to keep her little breasts from sticking up. Although I was small and wiry then, I believed that I was fat, that my flesh was unwieldy. I could feel my breasts and thighs swinging sensuously to and fro as I walked down the hall. I thought everything about me was so huge and disgusting. I was crazy in that way. My delusion caused me much pain and confusion. I chuckle at it now, but back then I was the bearer of great woes.

Of course nobody in the prison office had any interest in me and my woes, or my breasts. When my mother died and I'd gone to work at Moorehead, Mrs. Stephens and Mrs. Murray had kept their distance. No condolences, no kind or even pitying looks. They were the least maternal women I've ever met, and so they were very well suited for the positions they held at the prison. They weren't severe or strict as you'd imagine. They were lazy, uncultured, total slobs. I imagine they were as bored as I was, but they indulged themselves in sugar and dime-store paperbacks and had no problem licking their fingers after a donut, or burping, or sighing or groaning. I can still remember my mental pictures of them in sexual positions, faces poised at each other's private parts, sneering at the smell as they extended their caramel-stained tongues. It gave me some satisfaction to imagine that. Perhaps it made me feel dignified in comparison. When they answered the phones, they would literally pinch their noses shut and speak in high-pitched whines. Perhaps they did this to entertain themselves, or perhaps I'm misremembering it. Either way, they had no manners.

"Eileen, get me that new boy's file, that brat, what's his name," said Mrs. Murray.

"The one with the scabs?" Mrs. Stephens clanked her caramel, spat as she spoke. "Brown, Todd. I swear they get uglier and dumber every year."

"Be careful what you say, Norris. Eileen's likely to marry one of them someday."

"That true, Eileen? Your clock ticking?"

Mrs. Stephens was always bragging about her daughter, a tall, thin-lipped girl I'd gone to school with. She'd married some high school baseball coach and moved to Baltimore.

"One day you'll be old like us," Mrs. Stephens said.

"Your sweater's on backwards, Eileen," said Mrs. Murray. I pulled up my collar to check. "Or maybe not. You're just so flat, I don't know what side I'm looking at—front or back." They went on and on like that. It was awful.

I suppose my manners were just as bad as theirs. I was terribly grim and unaffected, unfriendly. Or else I was strained and chipper and awkward, grating. "Ha-ha," I said. "Coming or

going, that's me—flat." I'd never learned how to relate to people, much less how to speak up for myself. I preferred to sit and
rage quietly. I'd been a silent child, the kind to suck my thumb
long enough to buck out my front teeth. I was lucky they did not
buck out too far. Still, of course, I felt my mouth was horselike
and ugly, and so I barely smiled. When I did smile, I worked
very hard to keep my top lip from riding up, something that
required great restraint, self-awareness and self-control. The
time I spent disciplining that lip, you would not believe. I truly
felt that the inside of my mouth was such a private area, caverns
and folds of wet parting flesh, that letting anyone see into it was
just as bad as spreading my legs. People did not chew gum as
regularly then as we do now. That was considered very childish.
So I kept a bottle of Listerine in my locker and swished it often,
and sometimes swallowed it if I didn't think I could get to the
ladies' room sink without having to open my mouth to speak. I
didn't want anyone to think I was susceptible to bad breath, or
that there were any organic processes occurring inside my body
at all. Having to breathe was an embarrassment in itself. This
was the kind of girl I was.

Besides the Listerine in my locker, I always had a bottle of
sweet vermouth and a package of mint chocolates. I stole the
latter regularly from the drugstore in X-ville. I was a fabulous
shoplifter, gifted in the fine art of snatching things and
squirreling them up my sleeves. My death mask saved me from
trouble many times by hiding my ecstasy and terror from clerks
and shopkeepers who must have thought I looked very strange
in my huge coat, trolling around the candies. Before visiting

hours began at the prison, I'd take a long swig of vermouth and throw back a handful of mint chocolates. Even after several years, having to receive the pained mothers of the imprisoned boys made me nervous. Amongst my deadly boring duties, part of my job was to ask visitors to sign their names in a ledger and then tell them to sit down on molded orange plastic chairs in the hallway and wait. Moorehead had an insane rule that only one visit could take place at a time. Perhaps this was due to the small staff or Moorehead's limited facilities. Either way, it created an atmosphere of interminable suffering as for several hours mothers sat and waited and wept and tapped their feet and blew their noses and complained. In an attempt to fend off my own hard feelings, I fashioned meaningless surveys and handed out the mimeographed forms on clipboards to the most antsy of the mothers. I thought having to fill them out would give the women a sense of importance, create the illusion that their lives and opinions were worthy of respect and curiosity. I had questions on there such as "How often do you fill your gas tank?" "How do you see yourself in ten years?" "Do you enjoy television? If so, what programs?" The mothers were usually pleased to have a task to handle, although they'd pretend to look impinged upon. If they asked what it was all about, I told them it was a "state questionnaire," and that they might leave their names off of it if they preferred to remain anonymous. None of them did. They'd all write their names on these forms much more legibly than in the visitors' ledger, and answered so ingenuously, it broke my heart: "Once every Friday." "I will be healthy, happy, and my children will be successful." "Jerry Lewis."

It was my job to maintain a file cabinet full of reports and statements and other documents for each of the inmates. They stayed at Moorehead until their sentences ran out or they turned eighteen. The youngest boy I'd ever seen in my time at the prison was nine and a half. The warden liked to threaten to have the bigger boys—tall or fat or both—transferred to the men's prison early, especially the ones who made trouble. "You think it's rough here, young man?" he said. "One day in state would make any of you bleed for weeks."

The boys at Moorehead actually seemed like nice people to me, considering their circumstances. Any of us would be ornery and disgruntled in their place. They were forbidden to do most things children ought to do—dance, sing, gesture, talk loud, listen to music, lie down unless they were given permission to. I never talked to any of them at all, but I knew all about them. I liked to read their files and the descriptions of their crimes, the police reports, their confessions. One had stabbed a taxi driver in the ear with a pen, I remember. Very few of them were from X-ville itself. They came to Moorehead from across our region, Massachusetts' finest young thieves and vandals and rapists and kidnappers and arsonists and murderers. Many of them were orphans and runaways and were rough and tough and walked with swagger and aplomb. Others were from regular families and their demeanor was more domestic, more sensitive, and they walked like cowards. I liked the rough ones better. They were more attractive to me. And their crimes seemed far more normal. It was those privileged boys who committed the per-verse, really twisted crimes—strangling their baby sisters or

lighting a neighbor's dog on fire, poisoning a priest. It was fascinating. After several years, however, it had all become old hat.

I remember this particular Friday afternoon because a young
woman came to visit her perpetrator—her rapist, I assumed.
She was a pretty girl who had a tortured flamboyance, and at
the time I thought all attractive women were loose, sex kittens,
tramps, floozies. Such a visit was strictly forbidden, of course.
Only close relatives were allowed visits with inmates. *Kin* was
the word we used. I told the girl as much, but she demanded to
see the boy. She was very calm at first, as though she'd been
practicing what to say. I can't believe my audacity when I asked,
death mask on, whether she was demanding to become the
boy's kin. I said, "Do you mean to say you're engaged to be
married?" was my question. She seemed to lose her mind when
I asked that, and turned to the weepy mothers with their
clipboards and questionnaires and cursed them and threw the
ledger to the floor. I don't know why I was so cold to her. I
suppose I may have been envious. No one had ever tried to rape
me, after all. I'd always believed that my first time would be by
force. Of course I hoped to be raped by only the most soulful,
gentle, handsome of men, somebody who was secretly in love
with me—Randy, ideally. Once the girl had left and I had a free
moment, I pulled her rapist's file. The photograph showed a
pimpled, sleepy black boy. His rap sheet included stealing
laundry off a neighbor's line, smoking marijuana cigarettes,
vandalizing a car. He didn't seem so bad.

Another part of my job during visiting hours was to tell the
guards which boys were being summoned for visits, one by one.

The two guards I remember most clearly were Randy, of course, and James. I think James must have had brain damage or some sort of nervous condition. He was always agitated, sweated constantly, and seemed utterly uncomfortable in anyone's company. The job became very difficult for him when he had to interact with the boys or appear in front of the weeping mothers. When he was alone he had an ominous kind of stillness, like a slingshot being pulled back too hard. He seemed to sit like that, rigid, about to explode, for hours at a time when it was his turn to guard the hallway. This was a ridiculous waste of man-hours in retrospect, since there was another guard farther down the hall who sat by the door to the residential facility, or whatever we called the place where the boys lived and slept and paced around and read the Bible, or whatever they were supposed to do.

What was also ridiculous—I'm just remembering this now— was how I was put in charge of administering the security test for the women visitors. Since there were no female guards or officers, I suppose, it was my duty to pat the mothers down, lazily tapping around their shoulders and hips, a small pat on the back. It was the most intimate moment of my day, tapping these sad women. Randy would be there, too, usually standing guard at the door of the visitation room, and sometimes as I touched those women I imagined it was Randy I was touching, Randy, who like those women, seemed to barely even notice me. I was just a pair of hands flashing nervously through the air. These were all very sad women, passive and remorseful, and never violent. Of course in all my pathetic pat-downs, I never once came across a concealed knife or gun or vial of poison in a skirt pocket of any of those sad mothers. The guards hardly seemed concerned either. Men rarely visited. Most likely that had to do with work schedules, but I think many of the boys in the prison lacked fathers, which was part of the problem, I suppose. It was all pretty grim.

The bright spot in the misery of visitation hours was the chance to be close to Randy. I remember the peculiar scent of his sweat. It was strong, but not offensive. A good-natured smell. People smelled better back then. I am certain this is true. My eyesight has deteriorated over the years, but my sense of smell is still quite keen. Nowadays I often have to leave a room or walk away when a person near to me smells bad. I don't mean the smell of sweat and dirt, but a kind of artificial, caustic smell, usually from people who disguise themselves in creams and perfumes. These highly scented people are not to be trusted. They are predators. They are like the dogs who roll around in one another's feces. It's very disturbing. Although I was generally paranoid about how I smelled—if my sweat stank, if my breath was as bad as my mouth tasted—I never wore perfume, and I always preferred the scentless soaps and lotions. Nothing calls more attention to one's odor than a fragrance meant to mask it. At home alone with my father, I was in charge of the laundry, a duty I inherited by default and which I rarely honored. But when I did, the aroma of his soiled garments was so distressing, I often gagged and coughed and dry-heaved when I sniffed them. It was the smell of something like soured milk, sweet and laced so strongly with the perfume of gin, it turns my stomach just to think of it now.

Randy smelled completely different—tart like the ocean, brawny, warm. He was very attractive. He smelled like an honest man. Mrs. Stephens had told me that the guards were all hired through the employment office of the county correctional facility. So they were all ex-convicts, I suppose. They all had tattoos. Even James had one. A swastika, I believe. Randy's tattoo was a fuzzy portrait of a girl—his mother, I hoped. One early morning during my first months at Moorehead, when the office ladies were setting up the Easter crèche, I read Randy's employee file, which included a list of his adolescent offenses—sexual misconduct, breaking and entering. He had been an inmate at Moorehead as a teenager, a fact which only endeared him to me more.

You know me. I spent many hours wondering who might have been the recipient of Randy's sexual misconduct. I guessed some young teenage girl who got in trouble with her parents for breaking curfew or getting pregnant. Randy didn't seem like the violent type to me, but I'd seen him use force in restraining the boys from time to time. He'd have been great in a fistfight, I imagined. One of my favorite daydreams went like this: Randy would wait for my shift to end and ask to escort me to my car. He would offer his arm as I stepped across the black slate of ice in the parking lot, but I would refuse it, and he would feel jilted and abashed. But then I would slip on the ice and be forced, despite my prudence, to take his thick arm in my gloved hands, and he would look deeply into my eyes, and maybe we would kiss. Or instead, he'd take hold of me by the shoulders and steer me up against the Dodge, press my face into the frosted window, reach up my skirt to rip my stockings, my underpants, then around my leg to feel my caverns and folds with his fingers as he pushed into me, his breath hot at my ear, saying nothing. In that fantasy, I wore no girdle.

This is not a love story. But just one last bit about Randy before the real star of my story appears. It's funny how love can leap from one person to another, like a flea. Until Rebecca showed up a few days later, it was the constant thought of Randy that kept me afloat. I still remember his address, since on weekends I would drive past his apartment one town over and sit low in the Dodge trying to see whether or not he was home, alone, awake. I wanted to know what he was doing, what he was thinking, whether I ever even crossed his mind. A few times, without planning, I'd bumped into him in X-ville just walking down Main Street. Each time, I'd raised my gloved hand, opened my mouth to speak, but he just sauntered past me. My chest nearly caved in on itself. One day he would see me, the real me, and he'd fall in love, I told myself. Until then, I pined and moped and did whatever I could to understand his gestures and habits and expressions, as though a fluency in the language of his body would give me a leg up when it came time to please him. He wouldn't have to say a word. I thought I'd do anything to make him happy. But I wasn't a fool. I knew Randy had been with girls sexually. Still, I could not imagine him in the act of copulation, which is what I called it in my head at the time. I couldn't even begin to picture his bare nether regions, despite having seen a picture of some in one of my father's pornographic magazines. I could imagine, though, in a postcoital moment, Randy laughing casually across a mussed bed at an invisible female figure. I held him in such high esteem. Just a glance in my direction had my pulse quick for hours. But that's enough of him. Good-bye for now, Randy, good-bye.

Here's what I looked like that Friday: brittle, fake alligator loafers with thick, worn heels and chipping gold buckles; white stockings which made my thin legs look wooden, doll-like; large yellow bouclé skirt that hung past my knees; gray wool jacket with sharp shoulders over a white cotton blouse; small brass-colored cross; hairdo several days old by now; no earrings; lipstick of a shade the store called Irreparable Red. I must have looked nineteen going on sixty-five in that foppish approximation of decency, that adult costume. Other girls were married by my age, had children, settled. To say I didn't want all that would be too generous. All that simply wasn't available to me. It was beyond me. By all appearances I was a homebody—naive, disinterested. If you'd have asked me, I would have told you I believed that a person had to be in love to make love. I'd have said I thought anyone who does, and isn't, is a whore.

In hindsight, I don't think I was so off-base in my desire for Randy. A union wouldn't have been completely preposterous. He was employed, in good health, and it wasn't completely unfeasible, I don't think, that he might date me. I was a live young woman in his vicinity, after all. Despite my paranoia, there wasn't anything outright offensive about the way I looked back then. I was unattractive in temperament most of all, but many men don't seem to care about things like that. Of course Randy must have had other women to turn to. I wouldn't have known what to do with him if I'd actually snagged him anyhow.

By the time I turned thirty I'd learned how to relax, wink in the mirror, fall charmingly into the arms of countless lovers. My twenty-four-year-old self would die from shock at the quick death of my prudence. And once I left X-ville and filled out a bit, bought some clothes that fit me right, you might have seen me walking down Broadway or Fourteenth Street and thought I was a graduate student or maybe the assistant to some famous artist, on my way to pick up his check from the gallery. What I mean to say is that I was not fundamentally unattractive. I was just invisible.

That afternoon the mothers came and went. Sheaves of completed questionnaires got tossed in the trash along with glittering piles of caramel candy wrappers like heaps of dead insects. "Do you believe there is life on Mars? What qualities do you value most in your state officials?" Every day I picked up a dozen snot-filled tissues marked with lipstick like fat, dead, pink-tipped carnations. "Can you speak a foreign language? Do you prefer canned peas or canned carrots? Do you smoke?" A bell rang to signify that someone, one of the boys, had done something that would result in heavy punishment. James got up off his stool and mechanically walked down the corridor, wringing his hands. I squeezed the used tissues in my fists, added them to the papers and wrappers in the garbage.

"Take out that trash, Eileen," said Mrs. Stephens, looking up at me from behind her armpit as she reached down to her desk drawer to retrieve a fresh box of candies.

"If there was life on Mars, it's dead now," one mother wrote.

"A man should be broad-shouldered and have a mustache."

"A little French."

"Peas."

"Six packs a week. Sometimes more."

*B*efore I left Moorehead that Friday, Mrs. Stephens asked me to decorate the Christmas tree which the janitor had dragged into the prison waiting room, empty now that visiting hours were over. I remember it was a voluptuous pine and the needles were thick and waxy and its sap filled the air with a stunning tang. There was a storage closet where all the seasonal decorations were kept—Easter cutouts of bunnies and golden eggs, Independence Day flags, Labor and Memorial Day banners, Thanksgiving turkeys and pumpkins. One Halloween we hung garlands of garlic over the office doorway, and in an assembly after lunch the warden gave a ghoulish recitation of the Lord's abominations in Deuteronomy. It was ridiculous.

The Christmas tree ornaments were just as I'd left them the year before, haphazardly packed back into their sagging cardboard box. The metal balls encrusted with glitter and gold were chipping and fading, each year fewer of them to stuff back into the nests of old newspaper, but they were charming and filled me with longing. I had hard feelings around the holidays, the one time of year I couldn't help but fall prey to the canned self-pity Christmas prescribes. I'd mourn the lack of love and warmth in my life, wish upon stars for angels to come and pluck me from my misery and plunk me down into a whole new life, like in the movies. I was a sucker for the spirit of Christmas, as it was called. Growing up, I learned I'd be praised and rewarded for my suffering, for my strong efforts to be good, but every year God smote me. No presents, no miracles, no holy night. I pitied myself for that, too. I tried to keep a straight face as I unpacked the decorations. There were garlands of holly made of shiny plastic that smelled like strong antiseptic chemicals, which I liked. And at the bottom of the box there were tinsel and old paper snowflakes the boys had snipped from white construction paper many Christmases ago, some as old as twenty years, probably. When I unfolded them, they were disturbed and angry geometries, little acts of violence, but the names written in the corners were in controlled, regular penmanship in pale silver pencil. I remember names like Cheyney Morris, age 17. Roger Jones, 14. I was supposed to stick them on the painted brick wall in the waiting area, but I'd used up all my Scotch tape fixing the hem of my coat when the stitching had unraveled the week before, so I stuffed the snowflakes deep between the branches of the tree. They looked like snow there. I liked methodical work like hanging ornaments and so I lost myself in the task quite easily. That was good. I felt wistful. I saved a portion of the decorations for the top third of the tree, which was too high for me to reach without extending my arms above my head. If I did that, anyone would be able to see the darkened stains of sweat beneath my arms. Heaven forbid.

"Can you bring a ladder?" I asked James when he returned to his post.

I remember the smell of his pomade—a sad, lanolin smell— from when he placed the ladder gingerly beside the tree and held it for me while I climbed it, drops of sweat sitting like dew on his balding forehead.

"Don't look," I said, although I knew he would never dare glance up my skirt. He nodded. I so rarely got to act important, I relished that exchange.

When I had finished with the ornaments and put the empty cardboard box back in the storage closet, Mrs. Stephens looked up from her paperwork. The tree looked beautiful—I was proud of it—but she hardly noticed. She had powdered sugar on her nose and a smear of raspberry jelly on her sweater, no sense of decorum, seemed to care nothing what people thought of her. She'd been the office manager at Moorehead for decades.

"Eileen," she said. Her voice was a vicious monotone. "You'll work the lights Monday at the pageant. I can't do the lights any-more. I don't want to."

"Fine," I said.

One day I'd be gone, I hoped, never to have to look at her or think of her again, so I tried to hate her with all my might, squeeze our encounters for every last drop of disgust she could ever inspire in me. I knew better than to mouth off or cause any fuss, but I tried to send her violent messages with my mind. She'd hired me as a favor to my father. To my great embarrassment, on occasion I had mistakenly called her "Mom." Mrs. Stephens rolled her eyes then and chimed sarcastically— gums glistening, bubbles of saliva popping in a broad grin, that damn caramel candy clanking against her back teeth—"Of course, dear, whatever makes you happy."

I'd laughed and cleared my throat and corrected myself. "Missus Stephens."

I doubt she deserved the amount of hatred I directed at her, but I loathed just about everybody back then. I recall driving home that night, imagining what her body looked like under all that paisley print and gray wool. I pictured the flesh hanging from her bones like cold flanks of pork swinging from hooks at a butcher shop—thick, clammy, orange-hued fat, meat tough and bloodless and cold when the knife hacked through it.

I can still see the twenty-minute drive from Moorehead to X-ville. The long expanse of snow-filled pastures, the dark forest and narrow dirt roads, and then houses, first sparse, homesteads, then smaller and closer together, some with white picket fences or black iron posts, then the town with the ocean glinting on the horizon from atop the hill, then home. There was, of course, a sense of comfort in X-ville. Imagine an old man walking a golden retriever, a woman lifting a bag of groceries from her car. There was really nothing so very wrong with the place. If you were passing through, you'd think that everything was fine there. Everything was wonderful. Even my car with the broken exhaust and the biting cold at my ears was fine and wonderful. I hated it, and I loved it. Our house sat one block from an intersection where a crossing guard directed traffic in the mornings and afternoons for the children who went to the elementary school up the block. Oftentimes stray mittens or scarves were placed on the spokes of the neighbors' fences, or in winter spread out on the high banks of snow like a lost-

and-found. That night there was a boy's knit wool hat on the snow by our driveway. I inspected it under the lamplight and tried it on. It was tight enough to make a seal around my ears. I tried saying something, "Randy," and my voice vibrated, an echo inside of me. It was weirdly peaceful there inside my head. A car passed silently through the slush.

As I walked up the narrow path to the front porch, a car door opened across the street and a uniformed cop crossed the murky ice toward me. The wind was strangely still, a storm brewing. A light went on inside the house, and so the cop stopped in the middle of the road.

"Miss Dunlop," he said, and motioned for me to come near. This was not out of the ordinary. I knew most cops in X-ville. My father did his best to prompt their visits. That night Officer Laffey told me the school had called to complain that my father was lobbing snowballs at children from our front porch. He handed me a letter of warning, bowed his head, and walked back to his car.

"You can come inside," I said, voice booming between my ears. "Talk to him?" I held the letter out.

"It's late," he said, and got back in his car and on his radio.

Those icicles hanging above the front door must have grown by several inches while I'd been gone, since I remember reaching up and touching the tip of one and being disappointed by its bluntness. I could have swung my purse up and broken them all off if I'd wanted to. But I just shut the door gently and kicked off my shoes.

Here's the house. The front hall was wallpapered in dark

green and blue stripes and had golden wood moldings. The stairs were bare because I'd broken the vacuum cleaner that summer, then ripped out all the rugs. It was too dark in the house to see the layer of dust over everything. The lights in the front hall and the living room had burned out. Every once in a while I collected my father's cans and bottles, his disordered newspapers which he read, or pretended to read, at the top of the stairs, letting page after page sail over the banister and drift down into the front hall. That night I snatched up a few pages— we got the *Post*—crushed them into tight balls, and threw them at his back while he stood at the sink.

"Hi, Dad," I said.

"Smart ass," he said and turned and kicked the crumpled newspaper across the floor. In all my twenty-four years of knowing him, I don't think he ever said "Hello" or asked how I was. But some nights when I looked particularly tired he might have asked me, "How are your boyfriends? How are all your boys?" I really only ever sat down at the kitchen table long enough to eat some peanuts and listen to him complain. We ate a lot of peanuts, Dad and I. I warmed my hands on the stove. I remember I wore these thin black gloves with green flowers stitched along the fingers. In my ridiculous self-denial I did not buy proper winter gloves for myself. But I liked those black ones with the flowers. Women still wore gloves then. I didn't mind the custom. My hands were thin-skinned, sensitive, and always ice-cold anyway, and I didn't like touching things.

"Anyone new they drag in?" Dad asked that night. "Polk's boy faring all right?" Polk had been in the news recently, an

X-ville cop killed by his own son. My father had known him. They'd been on the force together.

"Paying for his sins," I replied.

"Good riddance," said my father, wiping his hands on his robe.

The mail sat in a pile on the counter by the stove. The *National Geographic* was rather lackluster that month. Several years ago I found that same issue in a used book store—December 1964—and have it here somewhere between all my books and papers. I doubt a thing like that is valuable fifty years later, but to me that magazine feels sacred, a snapshot of the world before everything in it changed for me. It was nothing special. The cover shows two ugly white birds, doves maybe, sitting on a cast-iron fence. A holy cross looms out of focus above them. The issue includes profiles of Washington, D.C., and some exotic vacation destinations in Mexico and the Middle East. That night, when it was new and still smelled of glue and ink, I opened it briefly to a picture of a palm tree against a pink sunset, then slapped it down on the kitchen table, disappointed. I preferred to read about places like India, Belarus, the slums of Brazil, the starving children in Africa.

I handed my father the letter of warning from Officer Laffey and sat down for a few peanuts. He waved the letter in front of his eyes and tossed it in the trash. "Just for show," he said. The delusions he suffered from were the most effective kind—everyone played a role in his conspiracy theories. Nothing was as it appeared. He was haunted by visions, dark figures—"hoodlums," he called them—that moved so fast, he said, he could only see their shadows. They'd duck under porches and hide in dark spots and in bushes and up in trees, and they watched him and taunted him, he said. He'd thrown some snowballs out the window that day just to let on that he knew what they were up to, he explained. The police had to admonish him to make it look like there was nothing fishy going on—just an old man losing his mind.

"They're in here, too," he said about the hoodlums, waving his finger around at the house. "Must be getting in through the basement. Walk around like they own the place. I've heard them. Maybe they're living in the walls, like rats," he said. "They sound just like rats, in fact. Black ghosts." He was tortured by them day and night, so his only recourse was to drink, naturally. He sat down at the kitchen table. "It's the mob who's sent them," of course. "Why do you think the cops are always here? They're here to protect me. After everything I've done for this town?"

"You're drunk," I said flatly.

"I haven't been drunk in years, Eileen. This," he held up his can of beer, "is to calm my nerves."

I opened a beer for myself, ate a few more peanuts. When I looked up I asked, "What's so funny?" because he was laughing. He could do that—turn on a dime from terrorized to cruelly hysterical.

"Your face," he replied. "You have nothing to worry about, Eileen. Nobody's going to bother you with a face like that one."

That's it. To hell with him. I recall catching my reflection in the dark glass windows of the living room later that evening. I looked like a grown-up. My father had no right to bully me.

Joanie stopped by that night wearing a white faux-fur jacket and a miniskirt and snow boots, her hair coiffed and bouncy, eyes lined in thick black liner. She was a blonde, pouty and light-hearted, back then at least. My guess is she went on to be soured—that pout was on its way somewhere, after all—but I hope she's healthy and happy and with someone who loves her. Here's to hoping. She was a special kind of girl. When she moved, she seemed to throw her flesh around as though it were a fur coat, so relaxed and comfortable, I couldn't understand her. She was charming, I suppose, but so critical, always with this naive way of asking me things like, "You don't feel funny wearing your dead mother's sweater?" And sometimes it was more sisterly, such as "Why is your face like that? What's your problem now?"

That night I just shook my head, made a ham sandwich. Bread, butter, ham. Joanie clapped her compact shut and came up from behind to poke me in the ribs. "Sack of bones," she said, grabbing my sandwich off the plate. "I'll see you," she said, kissing Dad in his chair. I never saw her again.

I went up to the attic to lie on my cot with my magazine. Would I miss my sister if she died? I wondered. We'd grown up side by side, but I barely knew her. And she certainly didn't know me. I pulled chocolates from a tin and chewed and spat them out one by one into the crinkly brown paper they came in. I turned another page.

SATURDAY

By noon on Saturday a good six inches of fresh snow had fallen on top of the knee-high blanket already standing. Such mornings were quiet, all sound dampened by the new snow. Even the cold seemed to back off, everything insulated and hushed. Before the furnaces began to roil, logs in fireplaces smoked and burned, and the houses of X-ville all covered in snow and ice started to melt and drip like wax candles, it was peaceful. Cold as it was in my room in the attic, I felt there was nothing to be gained by getting out of bed. Enough of the world could be explored by simply sticking my arm out from under the covers. I lay on my cot, dreaming and thinking for hours. I had a large mason jar for such circumstances and for when my father's moods forced me to hole up in the attic. It made me feel I was camping, living close to nature and far away from home when I squatted over that jar in my mother's pilly night-gown and an old Irish wool sweater, breath dribbling out my nose like white smoke from a witch's boiling cauldron. My pee steamed and stank, a honey-colored poison I poured out the attic window and into the snow-filled gutter.

The movements of my bowels were a whole other story. They occurred irregularly—maybe once or twice a week, at most— and rarely without assistance. I'd gotten into the gross habit of gulping down a dozen or more laxative pills whenever I felt big and bloated, which was frequently. The closest bathroom was one floor down and I shared it with my father. Moving my bowels there never felt quite right. I worried that the smell would carry downstairs to the kitchen, or that my father would come knocking while I sat there on the toilet. Furthermore, I'd become dependent on those laxatives. Without them my movements were always pained and hard and took a good hour of clamping down and kneading my belly and pushing and praying. I often bled from the effort, digging my nails into my thighs, punching my stomach in frustration. With the laxatives, my movements were torrential, oceanic, as though all of my insides had melted and were now gushing out, a sludge that stank distinctly of chemicals and which, when it was all out, I half expected to breach the rim of the toilet bowl. In those cases I stood up to flush, dizzy and sweaty and cold, then lay down while the world seemed to revolve around me. Those were good times. Empty and spent and light as air, I lay at rest, silent, flying in circles, my heart dancing, my mind blank. In order to enjoy those moments I had to have complete privacy. So I used the toilet in the basement. My father must have assumed I was just doing the laundry down there. The basement was safe and private territory in my post-toilet reverie.

Other times, though, the basement bore the grim tinge of memories of my mother and how much time she spent down there—doing what for so long? I still don't know. Coming up with a basket of clean clothes or linens on her hip, sniffling, grunting, she would tell me to get going, clean my room, brush my hair, read a book, leave her alone. The basement still held whatever secrets I guess she had stewing down there. If my father's dark ghosts and hoodlums sprang from anywhere, it was from there. But somehow when I went down to use the toilet, I felt fine. Memories, ghosts, dread can be like that, in my experience—they can come and go at their own convenience.

That Saturday I stayed in bed as long as I could until my thirst and hunger forced me into a robe and slippers and I shuffled downstairs. My father was curled up in his chair in front of the open oven. He seemed to be sleeping so I shut the oven door, drank some water out of the tap, filled my robe pockets with peanuts and put some water to boil. Outside it was bright, blinding, and the light filled the kitchen like a flood lamp on a crime scene. The place was filthy. Later, in certain particularly unkempt subway stations or public restrooms, I'd be reminded of that old kitchen and gag. It was no wonder I barely ever had an appetite. Grime and grease and dust coated every surface. The linoleum floor was freckled all over with drips and spills and dirt. But what use was there in cleaning? Neither my father nor I cooked or cared much for food. From time to time I'd rinse out a sink full of cups and glasses. Generally I ate bread, drank milk straight from the carton, only occasionally cranked open a can of green beans or tuna or fried a slab of bacon. That day I ate the peanuts standing out on the front porch.

Neighbors were digging out their cars—something I hated doing myself. I preferred to wait for one of the boys on the block to come around and do it for a quarter. I was always glad to pay. I threw the peanut shells into the snow-filled bushes, as close as I would get that year to decorating my own Christmas tree.

"Quiet!" yelled my father when the kettle started its high whine. "At this hour?" he mumbled, eyelids dragging open, wincing at the sunshine. "Pull the blinds," he said. "Dammit, Eileen." There were no blinds. He'd taken the old curtains down years earlier, claiming the shadows they made distracted him from what was real. He wanted a clean view of the backyard and anyone who might be trespassing through it. That morning he ground his fists into his eyes, then looked at me as I made a cup of tea. "Somebody might see you in that getup. You look like a bum." He rolled on his side, rubbed his face along the rough and dusty upholstery. The chair creaked and ticked like a resting locomotive under the shifting weight of his body.

"Are you hungry?" I asked him. "I could boil eggs."

"I'm parched," he said, words slurring, saliva popping between his lips. "No eggs. No rotten eggs." I watched his foot shake beneath the thin blanket. "It's cold," he said. I sipped my tea and stared at his face, his drawn eyelids a curtain of wrinkled skin. He seemed to have no eyelashes, barely any color in his cheeks. "For Christ's sake, Eileen." He suddenly bolted upright, wrenched the oven door down, letting the heat blast out. "You're trying to kill me. Think you're so smart. This is my house." He snatched his blanket back over his legs, tucked his feet in. "My house," he said again, and curled up like a baby in a bassinet.

My father had been a police officer at the county precinct, one of just a handful of local cops who rarely had more to do than scare cats out of trees or drive drunk guys home from the VA hospital one town over. They were a tight bunch, the X-ville police. My father was always well respected, of course, dear to all who knew him on the beat, and his cold blue eyes and charming moralism earned him the nickname Father Dunlop. He never lost the cutting brininess of being a marine. He loved his police uniform. While he was on the force, he slept in it most nights, with his gun. He must have thought he was really something, prepared for the middle-of-the-night call to come and catch the bad guy. Such calls for heroism never came. I have to put it one way, so I'll put it my way: He loved only himself and was full of pride and wore his badge like a gold star affixed to his chest by God himself. If he sounds trite, he was trite. He was very trite.

I didn't think there was anything strange about my father's drinking until my mother died. He'd been a run-of-the-mill beer drinker, I'd thought, whiskey just in the colder mornings. He'd gone with his friends on the police force to O'Hara's regularly, nothing unusual. O'Hara's was the town pub, which I'll name after the poet whose work I always felt shut out of, even after I'd learned to read like a grown-up. Dad became persona non grata at O'Hara's after he'd pulled his gun on the owner. Once my mother got sick—"fell ill" is an expression I like for its prissiness and, hence, its irony with respect to her violent demise—my father started taking time off work, drinking at home, wandering the streets at night, falling asleep on neighbors' porches. And then he drank more—in the mornings, on the job. He totaled a squad car, and then fired his gun by accident in the locker room. Because he had seniority and was beloved by the whole department for reasons I'll never understand, these indiscretions were never discussed openly. He was simply encouraged into an early retirement, replete with pension and constant surveillance and babying as the time went on and he got into more and more trouble. For some mysterious reason he switched to gin once my mother died. The most I can make of it is that perhaps gin reminded him of her perfume—she wore a stringent, flowery but bitter eau de toilette called Adelaide—and maybe imbibing the very fragrance of the dead was somehow soothing to him. But maybe not. I've heard a sip of gin will make you immune to mosquitoes and other pests. So perhaps he drank it with that logic in mind.

I spent the early afternoon shoveling snow. No boy ever did come asking if I'd pay him to do it for me. In the past I'd always gotten a little thrill when one of the neighborhood boys would ring the doorbell after a storm. They couldn't have been more than twelve or thirteen years old, mittens and hats on, smelling like pine and candy canes. One boy in particular was just adorable. Pauly Daly, name sing-song and a face like an angel—big rosy cheeks and sapphire eyes. Whenever I saw him I wanted to embrace him, snuggle him in his thick wool coat. Pauly did a perfect job cleaning the snow off the car and out from under the tires, shoveled the drive well enough that I could open the driver's side door, something I always forgot to do when I shoveled myself. It seemed so thoughtful. It proved, I imagined, that he really cared for me. One time I invited Pauly Daly inside while I looked for change to pay him. He shook off his boots before stepping into the front hall, removed his little hat. He was very well trained. Hair soft and tousled, I had to stop myself from putting my hands in it.

"Want a hot chocolate?" I asked him. I could tell he didn't have the wherewithal to judge me as the odd, stiff and stone-faced girl everyone else saw me as, or so I thought. He sniffled and looked down at the dirty carpet, twisted one foot behind the other, then put his hat back on.

"No, thanks," he said softly, blushing.

I kissed him on the cheek then. I meant nothing by it. He was a sweet boy and I liked him. But then he blushed and wiped away the clear mucus glistening between his nose and top lip. He looked utterly dismayed. I skidded away and dug through the pockets of coats hanging in the front closet. "Sorry," I said after an awkward silence. I dumped all the change I could find into his cupped hands.

He nodded, called me "Mrs. Dunlop," left, and never came around again.

When I'd finished clearing the snow off the car that Saturday, I rolled down the windows and let the Dodge run to warm up and defrost a bit. It was early afternoon by then and I wanted to drive over to Randy's. I felt I had to. He lived in the upstairs of a split-level house not far from the interstate. I held tight to the magical notion that as long as I kept close tabs on him, he wouldn't fall in love with anybody else. As far as I could tell, he spent most of his time alone in his apartment. But I rarely stalked him at night—I was afraid to—so who knows how many female visitors Randy entertained in the dark. From time to time a second motorcycle appeared next to his, parked in front of his snow-filled driveway. I guessed he had a best friend or brother who came to see him, and even that made me jealous. I generally parked across the street, huddled down behind the steering wheel, and watched his house in my side-view mirror. There was no real use in hiding, though. I doubt Randy would have recognized me if he'd found me camped out back there, surveilling him. I doubt he even knew my name. Still, I prayed for the perfect occasion to win him over. I spent hours sitting there scheming how I'd impress him with my feminine wiles. My daydreams of fingers and tongues and secret rendezvous in the back hallways of Moorehead kept my heart beating, or else I think I would have dropped dead from boredom. Thus, I lived in perpetual fantasy. And like all intelligent young women, I hid my shameful perversions under a facade of prudishness. Of course I did. It's easy to tell the dirtiest minds—look for the cleanest fingernails. My father, for example, had no discretion about his pornographic magazines. They were behind the toilet, under the bed he'd shared with my mother, piled on shelves in the cellar, in a drawer in the den, in a box in the attic. And yet he was so staunchly Catholic. Of course he was. My own hypocrisies paled in comparison to my father's. I've never had any guilt for what I did to him. I've been lucky in that regard.

Before I left for Randy's that afternoon, I put on my mother's old sunglasses—big, funny, petal-shaped lenses with tortoise-shell frames.

"Who do you think you're fooling?" my father hollered, awake now and bent over the table, it seemed, to catch his breath. He wore the blanket over his back like a cape. "Going out with your pals? Happy happy?" He rolled his eyes, grabbed the back of the kitchen chair and rattled it. "Sit down, Eileen."

"I'm late, Dad," I lied, edging closer to the front door.

"Late for what?"

"I'm meeting a friend."

"What friend? What for?"

"We're going to the movies."

He squinted and snorted and rubbed his chin and leered at me, up and down. "That's what you wear on a date?"

"I'm meeting my girlfriend," I told him, "Suzie."

"What's wrong with your sister? Take her to the movies, why don't you?" He gestured widely with his skinny arm and the blanket fell away. He winced, as though the cold at his back were a knife stabbing him.

"Joanie couldn't come." Lies like this one were common. He never knew the difference. I turned the knob and opened the front door, looked up at those icicles. If I plucked one, I thought, maybe I could throw it at my father, aim for his head, hit him dead between his eyes.

"That's right," he said, "because your sister has a life of her own. She's made something of herself. Not a hanger-on like you, Eileen." He bent stiffly at the waist to pick up the blanket. I watched from down the hall and through the kitchen doorway as he struggled to tie the belt of his robe with his shaky hands, adjust the blanket, wobble back to his chair with a new bottle of gin in his hand. "Get a life, Eileen," he said. "Get a clue."

He knew how to hurt me. I understood, nevertheless, that he was a drunk, that whatever cruel words he had for me were the nonsensical mumblings of a man who had lost his mind. He was convinced he'd need witness protection from all the work he had done "pinning down the mob." He seemed to think of himself as some kind of imprisoned vigilante, a saint forced to contend with evil from the confines of his cold abode. The shadowy pranks of those ghostly hoodlums, he complained, tormented him even in his dreams. I tried to reason with him. "It's in your mind," I said. "Nobody's out to get you." He'd scoff and pat my head like a small child's. We were both a bit crazy, I suppose. Of course there was no mob in X-ville. In any case, my father had hardly done more as a cop there than pull a car over for a broken taillight. He was terribly confused.

Soon after my father retired, the chief of police took his license away. He'd been caught driving in the wrong direction on the freeway one night, and parked his car in the public cemetery the next. So he stayed at home. On foot, he was nearly as menacing. He'd wander outside in a blackout, knock on neighbors' doors to perform invented investigatory searches, pull his gun out at shadows, lie down in the gutter or in the middle of the road. Cops dropped him off quietly at the house with a pat on the back, and one of them would scold me for letting him get so out of hand, always with an apologetic sigh, sure, but it still filled me with spite. Once, after a good six-day absence, a bender of greater proportions than I had ever seen my father go on, I got a call from a hospital two counties over and drove out there to pick him up. That persuaded me to gather up all his shoes and keep them locked in the trunk of the car from then on. He did stay indoors for the most part after that, at least in the winter. I wore the car key like a pendant around my neck. I remember the weight of it dangling there between my measly bosoms, thudding around, sticking to my hard and sweaty breastplate, scraping against my skin as I walked out the door.

Before I go on describing the events of that Saturday, I should mention the gun again. When I was growing up, my father would sit at the kitchen table after dinner and clean it, explain all of its mechanics and the necessity of its upkeep. "If you don't do this and that"—I don't recall his exact words—"the gun will mis-fire. It could kill someone." He seemed to tell me this not as a way of inviting me into this intimate procedure, his life and work, but as a warning, to say that what he had to do was so important, sacred in fact, that if I should ever distract him, or if I should ever touch his gun, God forbid, I would die. I tell you this simply to put the gun into the scenery. It was there, from childhood until the end. It frightened me the way a butcher knife would frighten me, but that was all.

Outside, the yard was filled with exhaust and windblown snow and already dwindling sunlight. I got in the Dodge and drove toward Randy's, biting my chapped lip in anticipation of catching a glimpse of him through his bedroom window—he didn't have curtains either—or, better yet, on his way out, so I could follow him secretly through the X-ville streets, led by the heavenly roar of his motorcycle engine. Then I could imagine what he did when he was not at home. If there was a woman in his life, I would know, once and for all. And I could find a way around her, I reasoned. There was a limit to the lengths I would go to win Randy's affection—I was lazy, after all, and shy—but my obsession with him had become such a habit, I really lost all good sense. Who knows what I would have done had I found him French-kissing some Brigitte Bardot type? I don't know that I was really capable of real violence. I probably would have punched myself in the head and rolled the windows up in the Dodge, prayed to die. Who knows?

But Randy wasn't home when I got there. His bike wasn't parked out front. So, for whatever reason, I decided to make good on my lie to my father and go to the cinema. Seeing movies has never been a favorite pastime of mine, but that afternoon I craved company. I didn't like movies for the same reason I don't like novels: I don't like being told how to think. It's insulting. And the stories are all so hard to believe. Furthermore, beautiful actresses always made me feel terrible about myself. I burned with envy and resentment as they smiled and frowned. I understand that acting is a craft, of course, and I have great respect for those who can toss themselves aside and assume new identities—as I have done, one might say. But generally speaking, women on-screen have made me feel ugly and lackluster and ineffectual. Back then especially, I felt that I had nothing to compete with—no real charm, no real beauty. All I had to offer were my skills as a doormat, a blank wall, someone desperate enough to do anything—just short of murder, let's say—simply to get someone to like me, let alone love me. Until Rebecca showed up a few days later, all I could pray for was some kind of fluke or miracle wherein Randy would be forced to need and want me, like if I happened to save his life in a fire or a motorcycle accident, or if I wandered into the room with a handkerchief and a shoulder to cry on the moment he heard his mother had died. Such were my romantic fantasies.

There was a small cinema in X-ville that played only the most tasteful, childish movies. If I wanted to see *Contempt* or *Goldfinger,* I'd have had to drive ten or more miles south where the X-ville Women's League's clout ran out. I can't say I was relieved or disappointed that my plans to stake out Randy's place for the few remaining hours of sunlight fell to the wayside, but I do remember a sense of impending doom descending upon me as I drove toward the cinema. If I lost Randy to another woman, I'd have to kill myself. There'd be nothing else for me to live for. As I parked the car outside the cinema and rolled up the windows, it struck me again how easy it would be to die. One snagged vein, one late night skid on the icy interstate, one hop off the X-ville bridge. I could just walk into the Atlantic Ocean if I wanted to. People died all the time. Why couldn't I?

"You'll go to hell," I imagined my father would say, busting in on me as I slit my wrists. I was afraid of that. I didn't believe in heaven, but I did believe in hell. And I didn't really want to die. I didn't always want to live, but I wasn't going to kill myself.

And anyway, there were other options. I could run away as soon as I had the courage, I told myself. The dream of New York City beckoned like the twinkling lights of the cinema marquee—a promise of darkness and distraction, temporary and at a cost, but anything was better than sitting around.

I bought a ticket to *Send Me No Flowers* and padded down the black and red diamond carpet leading to a studded leather door. An acned teenage boy guided me inside the theater with a small flashlight. The movie had already started. In the warmth and darkness and aroma of cigarettes and burnt butter, and despite Doris Day's squawking, I could barely keep my eyes open. And when I could, what I saw bored me to tears. I vaguely remember the film. I slept through most of it, but it had something to do with a housewife whose husband becomes consumed by hypochondria, or perhaps just a paralyzing general fear of death. Doris was already an old lady at that point—a paper doll now frayed and haggard, hairdo like an infant's, a wardrobe fit for a maid. Rock Hudson couldn't have cared less for her charm. As it turned out, even Doris Day could barely get a man to love her.

Once the credits were rolling, I shuffled out of the theater amongst the crowd of X-villers, young and old, each of them wrapped in brightly colored wool coats and hats and mufflers. The cold evening air refreshed me. I didn't want to go home. Across the street, Christmas lights in the window of the donut shop caught my eye. I went in and bought a Boston cream, ate it in one gulp, as I was wont to do, and walked out immediately remorseful. I didn't want to be like the woman behind the counter—greasy and fat, body like a sack of apples. In a storefront window of a boutique next door I saw my reflection clear as day. I looked ridiculous in my huge gray coat, alone and stunned in the headlights of a passing car like a dumb and frightened deer. I tried to fix my hair, which had gotten messed up while I'd slept. I looked up. The awning over the door spelled the name of the boutique in canned girlish cursive: Darla's. My eyes rolled as I went inside.

"Yoo-hoo," said a voice when the bell over the door chimed. The shopgirl came out from the back room. "I'm closing soon but take your time and look around. Anything you need, just holler."

My death mask didn't seem to perturb her at all. It always peeved me when my flatness was met with good cheer, good manners. Didn't she know I was a monster, a creep, a crone? How dare she mock me with courtesy when I deserved to be greeted with disgust and dismay? My manly boots tracked dirty snow across the carpeted floor as I circled the racks and fingered the wool and silk crepe dresses. It was preposterous to think I could wear such fine garments, let alone afford them. I remember all the bright colors and bold prints, satin and wool, everything cute and tailored, big bows and pleats and all that nonsense. I was greedy, of course, turning over each tag, tallying everything I coveted but despised. It wasn't fair. Others could wear nice things, so why not me? If I did, certainly people would pay me the attention I deserved. Randy even. Fashion's for the fools, I know now, but I've learned that it's good to be foolish from time to time. It keeps your spirit young. I suspected as much back then, I suppose, since despite my contempt—or maybe because of it—I asked to try on the party dress in the window.

It was a gold shift dress with a high neck and lines of alternating gold and silver baubles patterned from the neck to the bust. It reminded me of photographs I'd seen of African village women with necks painfully extended by stacks of gold rings. The shopgirl looked at me wide-eyed when I pointed to it, then smiled and hopped to the window. It took her several minutes to unzip the garment, then scoot the mannequin to the side to tip it over so that the dress could be taken off. I casually sauntered to the back wall to have a look at the hosiery. Keeping one eye on the girl wrestling with the mannequin, I slipped four packages of navy blue hose into my purse with ease. I looked in the mirror on the glass jewelry display case, which was locked from the other side, removed my gloves and rubbed the chocolate off the corners of my mouth. I wiped my hands on a scarf hanging decoratively from a bamboo staff. The shopgirl carried the dress to the fitting room as though it were a sleeping child, arms extended, careful not to rustle the baubles. I followed her, folding my purse inside my parka as I took it off. I didn't care if the shopgirl judged my pathetic outfit. She herself wore a demure but ridiculous circle skirt which, I recall, had pompoms on it, maybe an embroidered kitten. "I'll be out front if you need anything," she said and shut the door.

I took off my sweater, blouse and brassiere and took an earnest look at my bust, assessing the heft and shape of my little breasts. I shook my shoulders vigorously at the mirror, just to horrify myself. When I menstruated, my breasts were sore to the touch and heavy, like lead, like rocks. I pinched and poked them with my fingers. I took off my pants, but didn't look at myself below the waist. My feet were fine, my ankles, my calves. That was all passable. But there was something so foreboding and gross about the hips, the buttocks, the thighs. And there was always a sense that those parts would suck me into another world if I studied them too closely. I simply couldn't navigate that territory. And at the time, I didn't believe my body was really mine to navigate. I figured that was what men were for.

The dress was heavy, like the hide of a strange animal. It was too big on top, buckling awkwardly between my arms and breasts, the baubles crashing against each other like a tribal instrument as I zipped up the back. And the whole thing was too long. In the mirror I looked tiny, frumpy, my hairy calves poking out at the bottom like the hind legs of a farm animal. The dress clearly did not fit me, and yet I wanted it. Of course I did. The tag said it cost more than I made in two weeks working at the prison. I thought to rip the tag off, as though that would make the dress free. I considered pulling one of the metallic baubles loose and slipping it in my purse along with the panty hose. But instead I used the sharp point of my car key to poke a hole in the inside lining around the hem and tore it a little. I pulled on my old clothes, which felt all the more old and stank of my sweat, the shirt under my sweater cold and wet in the armpits. I walked out back through the store.

"How'd you do?" I remember the shopgirl asked, as though I may have done well or poorly. Why was my performance always called into question? Of course the dress looked awful on me. The shopgirl must have predicted that. But why was it *I* who had failed, and not the dress? "How did the dress do?" is what she should have asked instead.

"Not my style," I said to her and walked out quickly, fat purse under my arm, wincing in the sudden cold but smiling in triumph. When I stole things I felt I was invincible, as though I had punished the world and rewarded myself, setting things right for once—justice served.

I drove around for a while that evening, passed by Randy's place again, clucked my tongue at the disappointing dark of his windows. Then I headed up 1-H to a lookout over the ocean where young lovers went to park. I pulled on my newfound knit hat as I drove. I wasn't looking for anything in particular. One needed a car to go there and neck, so there was no risk of running into Randy on his motorcycle with some girl, I supposed. Still, as I rolled up the steep, snow-filled drive, I tried to see through the fogged-up backseat window of every car to make sure he wasn't in any of them. I'd been up there many times before, just snooping. That night I parked and stared out at the black night over the ocean. I rolled up the windows for a few minutes and enjoyed myself, thinking of Randy. At my age, I'd still never been on a proper date. Later, once I'd left X-ville and had some romantic experiences behind me, I'd sit in parked cars with men—"the view is beautiful from up here," they liked to say—and I'd know the sweet thrill of opening my eyes in a moment of ecstasy to see the moon blazing and the stars like Christmas lights strung across the sky as if just for my own delight. I'd know, too, the delicious shame of being caught by highway patrol in a breathless moment of passion and love, dear God. But that night I just sat with myself and looked up and wondered where my life would lead if I chose not to drive off the cliff in front of me. Inevitably it led back down to Randy's place—still dark, maddening—and home again. Did I cry and pout with self-pity? I didn't. I was used to my loneliness by then. One day I'd run off, I knew. Until then, I would pine.

At home I gulped water from the tap and swallowed a handful of laxatives which I kept below the kitchen sink. Then I sat down and drank a beer. My father raised his hand, saluting me gravely, mocking my mood.

"Cops brought whiskey," he said, pointing to a bottle of Glenfiddich with a bow tied around its neck. It sat by the door to the cellar stairs. "How was the movie?"

He seemed calm, in a better mood. Gone was the cutting fury of earlier. He seemed to want to talk.

"It was dumb," I answered honestly. "Should I open it?" I went and picked up the whiskey.

"By any means necessary," my father said. I didn't always hate him. Like all villains, he had his good side, too. Most days he didn't mind that the house was a mess. He hated the neighbors, as I did, and he would rather have been shot in the head than admit defeat. He made me laugh now and then, like when he'd attempt to read the papers, bristling with contempt at any headline he managed to decipher, one eye shut tight, finger shaking at the words, drunk as he was. He still ranted about the Reds. He loved Goldwater and despised the Kennedys, though he made me swear I'd keep that a secret. He was a hard-liner about certain duties. He had a stern attachment to things like paying the bills on time, for example. He'd sober up once a month for that task and I'd sit next to him, opening the envelopes, licking the stamps, making out the checks for him to sign. "That's terrible, Eileen," he'd say. "Start again. No bank would accept a check written like that, like a little girl made it out." Even on his dry days he could barely hold a pen.

That night I poured us each a few fingers of whiskey and pulled my chair up next to his, stuck my frozen hands toward the burning oven.

"Doris Day's a fat hack," I said.

"Waste of time going to the movies if you ask me," he mumbled. "Anything good on the tube?"

"Some nice static, if you're in the mood," I said. The television had been broken a long time.

"Ought to have someone come take a look at it. Bulb's broken. Must be the bulb." We'd had the same exchange once a week for years.

"Everything's a waste of time," I said, collapsing a bit in my chair.

"Have a drink," my father grumbled, sipping his. "Cops brought me good whiskey," he said again. "That Dalton boy looks like some kind of weasel." The Daltons lived across the street. He stopped, paused. "You hear that?" He put his hand out, perked his ears. "Hoodlums are rowdy tonight. What day is it?"

"Saturday," I said.

"That's why. Hungry as rats." He finished his whiskey, absent-mindedly fumbled through the folds of the blanket spread across his lap, pulled up a half-empty bottle of gin. "How was the movie? How's my Joanie?" He was like that. His mind was not quite right.

"She's fine, Dad."

"Little Joanie," he said wistfully, somberly. He rubbed his chin, raised his eyebrows. "The kids grow up," he said. We stared into the hot oven like it was a crackling fireplace. I warmed my thawing fingers, poured myself more whiskey, pictured the moon and stars swirling as they would through the windshield if I'd sped off the side of that cliff and down onto the rocks earlier that evening, the glittering of broken glass over the frozen snow, the black ocean.

"Joanie," my father repeated, reverently. Despite her whorish ways, my father adored my sister, pined for her, it seemed—"my dear, sweet Joanie"—spoke of her with such admiration and decency. "My good little girl." Those last years in X-ville, I'd stay up in the attic most times she came to visit. I couldn't stand to watch how he'd give her money, eyes filling with tears of pride and honor, and how they loved each other—if love was what that was—in a way I could never understand. She could do no wrong. Although she was older than me, Joanie was his baby, his angel, his heart.

As for me, no matter what I did, he was certain it was the wrong thing to do, and told me so. If I came down the stairs holding a book or a magazine, he said, "Why do you waste your time reading? Go for a walk outside. You're pale as my ass."

And if I bought a stick of butter, he would hold it between his fingers and say, "I can't eat a stick of butter for dinner, Eileen. Be reasonable. Be smart for once." When I walked through the front door, his response was always, "You're late," or "You're home early," or "You've got to go out again, we're in short supply." Although I wished him dead, I did not want him to die. I wanted him to change, be good to me, apologize for the half decade of grief he'd given me. And also, it pained me to imagine the inevitable pomp and sentimentality of his funeral. The trembling chins and folded flag, all that nonsense.

Joanie and I were never really close growing up. She was always much more personable and happier than I was, and being around her made me feel stiff and awkward and ugly. At her birthday party one year, she teased me for being too shy to dance, forced me to stand and grabbed my hips in her hands, then squatted down by my nether regions and rotated my body side to side as though I were a puppet, a rag doll. Her friends laughed and danced and I sat back down. "You're ugly when you pout, Eileen," my dad had said, snapping a picture. Things like that happened all the time. She left home at seventeen and abandoned me for a better life with that boyfriend of hers.

I'm reminded of one Fourth of July when I must have been twelve, since Joanie is four years older and she'd just gotten her license to drive. We'd come home from an afternoon at the beach to find our parents hosting a barbecue in our backyard for the entire X-ville police department, a rare social event for the Dunlops. A rookie, whom I recognized from around town—his little sister had some sort of disability, I recall—was made to

sit next to me at the picnic table, a situation that afforded my
father a chance to joke to the boy that Joanie and I were "jail-
bait." The meaning of this term eluded me until years later, but
I never forgot him saying it, and I'm still resentful. I remember
it irritated my thighs to sit on the raw pine board set up on two
pails filled with rocks that served as a bench at this barbecue,
and when I went inside to change out of my swimsuit, the boy
followed me into the kitchen and tried to kiss me. I refused his
advance by steering my head back and away from his, but he
took me by the shoulders and spun me around, gripping my
wrists behind my back. "You're under arrest," he joked, and
reached his hand up my shorts and pinched me. I ran to the
attic, where I stayed for the rest of the night. Nobody missed
me. I know other young women have suffered far worse than
this, and I myself went on to suffer plenty, but this experience
in particular was utterly humiliating. A psychoanalyst may term
it something like a formative trauma, but I know little about
psychology and reject the science entirely. People in that profes-
sion, I'd say, should be watched very closely. If we were living
several hundred years ago, my guess is they'd all be burned as
witches.

Back then, on that Saturday night in X-ville, the whiskey
dwindled fast. My father was asleep and I was on my way down
to the basement toilet, burping up the liquor churning in my
stomach and about to explode out the other end from the laxatives. I was drunk, tripped and would have killed myself on the
steps had I not been gripping the splintery banister like it was
the handrail of a sinking ship. I'd tripped and fallen down those

stairs once before, when I was a child running from my mother who was chasing me with a wooden spoon and screaming, "Clean your room!" or something like that. I split my lip and bumped my head on the way down, scraped my hands and knees when I hit the hard dirt floor. I recall looking up at the yellow rectangle of light in the kitchen from the foot of the stairs, my mother's silhouette appearing like a paper cutout. She said nothing to me. She simply shut the door. How many hours did I spend down there, hurt and terrified? It was dark and full of dust and cobwebs and a dank, moist smell, gray steel tools, the boiler, an old-fashioned toilet with a yank hanging from the ceiling that smelled of old urine. Mice. I got over my childhood fear of the dark that day, I suppose. Nothing came at me—no angry spirits attacked me, no restless ghosts tried to suck out my soul. They left me alone down there, which was just as painful.

By midnight I was back on that cold cellar floor, panting with the effort that my body had exerted in emptying my innards, thanks to the laxatives. The toilet tank ran hard. Part of me, I remember, wished one of my father's dark angels would materialize from the musty shadows and yank me down into its underworld. Alas, no one came. The darkness spun and spun and then it stopped, and so I floated up the cellar stairs and through the cold kitchen and up to my attic and fell asleep, exhausted, pacified, and utterly miserable.

SUNDAY

That Sunday morning I woke up hungover on my cot in the attic, my father calling up to me to help him get ready for morning Mass. That meant buttoning his shirt, and holding the bottle to his lips because his hands were too shaky. I wasn't very well myself, of course, vision still blurred from the whiskey, my body a limp rag wrung hard by the laxatives the night before.

"I'm cold," my father said, shivering. He tugged at his unshaved jaw and winced, looked at me as if to say, "Get the razor." And I did. I lathered up the cream and shaved him right there in the kitchen, standing over the sink full of dirty dishes, a salad bowl full of cigar ash, moldy bits of bread green as pennies here and there. It may not sound all that bad to you, but it was pretty grim living there. My father's moods and explosions were exhausting. He was so often upset. And I was always afraid of displeasing him by accident, or else I was so angry that I would try to displease him deliberately. We played games like an old married couple, and he was always winning. "You smell like hell," he said to me that morning as I curved the razor around his jaw.

So of course I felt like killing him sometimes. I could have slit his throat that morning. But I said nothing: I didn't want him to know how much he displeased me. It was important to me that he not know he had the power to make me miserable. It was also important not to let on just how much I wanted to get away from him. The more I thought about leaving him, the more I worried he might chase after me. I figured he could rustle up his friends in the police department, call a statewide search for the car, plaster my face in "Wanted" posters up and down the eastern seaboard. But that was all just fantasy, really. I knew he'd forget all about me when I was gone. And it seems he did. Back then I reasoned that if I were to leave, someone would step up to take care of him. His sister could hire help. Joanie could make an effort for once. Not everything was my responsibility, I told myself. He'd be fine without me. What was the worst that could happen?

When my aunt arrived to pick him up that day, she beeped and we bustled out. Her name was Ruth. She was my father's only sibling. My father waited on the porch—oh, for one of those icicles to break off and lodge in his brain—while I walked around to the driveway, unlocked the trunk of the car and pulled out a pair of his shoes.

"Not those," he hollered. "Those have a hole."

I pulled out another and held them up.

"OK," he said. My aunt barely looked up at me, pinched face

squinting from the glare on the snow. I waved as I passed her car. She did not wave back. On the porch I tied my father's laces and sent him on his way.

What a good girl I was, in hindsight, buttoning my father's shirt and tying his shoes and all. I knew in my heart that I was good, I suppose. Here was the crux of my dilemma: I felt like killing my father, but I didn't want him to die. I think he understood. I'd probably told him as much the night before, despite my instinct toward secrecy. We'd stay up and drink together often, just my father and I. I have a vague memory from that Saturday night of laying my face down on the kitchen table and yawning, looking up at him with the bottle of whiskey in his one hand, gin in the other. "Not very nice, Eileen," he'd said, referring, I think, to my splayed legs, lipstick all smeared. This wasn't unusual for us. We weren't friendly, but we did talk sometimes. We argued. I'd wave my hands around. I'd say too much. I did the same thing later on in life, when I drank with other men, mostly stupid men. I expected them to find everything about me interesting. I expected them to see my drunken wordiness as a kind of coy gesture, as though I were saying, "I'm just a child, innocent to my own foolishness. Aren't I cute? Love me and I'll turn a blind eye to your faults." With those other men, this tactic earned me brief sessions of affection until I became soured and saw that I had defiled myself by appealing to them in the first place. I failed and failed with my father to win his affection in this way, blabbering on about my ideas, regurgitating barely read synopses from the backs of books at the kitchen table, talking about how I felt about myself, life, the times in which we lived. I could get very dramatic after just a few drinks. "People act like everything's OK all the time. But it isn't. Nothing is OK at all. People die. Children starve. Poor people are freezing to death out there. It's not fair. It isn't right. Nobody seems to care. La-dee-dah, they say. Dad. Dad!" I'd slap the table to make sure he was listening. "We're in hell, aren't we? This is hell, isn't it?" He'd just roll his eyes. It drove me mad.

Once he'd gone off to church that morning, I cooked myself scrambled eggs with ketchup and heated a beer on the stove, my hangover cure of choice. That doesn't work, of course. Don't bother trying it. But it did feel good to eat after having emptied my guts into the basement toilet the night before. I felt I had a blank slate, a clean beginning, though I don't think I showered that morning. I hated showering, especially in winter since the hot water was spotty. I liked to languish in my own filth as long as I could tolerate it. Why I did this, I can't say for sure. It certainly seems like a rather lame way to rebel, and furthermore it filled me with constant anxiety that others were sniffing my body and judging me by its odor: disgusting. My father said it himself: I smelled like hell. I dressed myself in my mother's old Sunday clothes—gray trousers, black sweater, hooded woolen parka. I put on my snow boots and drove to the library. I'd just finished looking through a brief history of Suriname and a book on how to tell the future from looking at the stars. The former had great pictures of nearly naked men and old topless women. I recall one photograph of a monkey suckling a woman's nipple, but perhaps I'm inventing. I liked twisted things like that. My curiosity for the stars is obvious: I wanted something to tell me my future was bright. I can imagine myself saying at the time that life itself was like a book borrowed from the library— something that did not belong to me and was due to expire. How silly.

I can't say I've ever really understood what it means to be Catholic. When Joanie and I were little, our mother would send us to church with our father every Sunday. Joanie never seemed to protest, but she'd just sit there during the liturgy reading Nancy Drew, chewing gum. She refused to kneel and stand along with the rest of us and said, "Blah blah blah" instead of the "Our Father," twirled her hair. She was pretty enough, aloof enough already at nine or ten for our father to overlook any flawed manners. But at five, I was still plump, pale, eyes small and squinty—I didn't find out I needed glasses until I was thirty—and I suppose my aura carried enough doubt and anxiety to fill my dad with shame. "Don't embarrass me," he'd mutter on our way up the church steps. He'd be greeted left and right by cheerful, brownnosing members of the congregation, X-villers who must have thought it advantageous to be in the good graces of a man in blue. Dad wore his uniform to church, of course. Or maybe they were all scared of him. He certainly scared me. I remember he'd leave his gun in the glove box while we were at Mass, perhaps the only time he spent without it those days. "Good morning, Officer Dunlop," someone would say. Dad would shake hands, put an arm around Joanie, a hand on my head, and stop to chat. If I was ever asked a question or received any attention at all, my father would leer down at me as though to say, "Be normal, look happy, act right." Inevitably I would disappoint him. I'd go mute or mess up my words, grimace and tear up when some friend of his tried to pinch my cheek. I hated church.

"Where is Mrs. Dunlop this morning?" someone always asked. The excuses my father would give were that she wasn't feeling well, that she was visiting her mother, but she sends her very best. My mother never once came to Mass. The only time I remember her setting foot in that church was for my grandfather's funeral. When we got home Sunday afternoons—Joanie and I sat through endless hours of Bible study taught by an elderly nun, none of whose teachings penetrated into my consciousness one bit—the house would be only slightly less disheveled, and our mother would be lying on the couch in the living room, reading a magazine, a bottle of vermouth stuck between her thighs, cigarette smoke floating above her head in the stuffy afternoon sunlight like a brooding storm cloud.

"Promise you'll visit me in hell, Eileen?" she'd ask.

"Go to your room," said my father.

My mother rolled her eyes at my father's superstitions, how he'd cross himself before eating, look up at the ceiling whenever he was hopeful or mad. "God is for dummies," she told us. "People are scared of dying, that's all. Listen to me, girls." I remember when she said this, pulling us aside one day after our aunt Ruth had come over and scolded us for being lazy, for being spoiled brats, or something like that. She and our mother didn't get along. "God is a made-up story," our mother told us, "like Santa Claus. There is nobody watching you when you're alone. You decide for yourself what's right and wrong. There are no prizes for good little girls. If you want something, fight for it. Don't be a fool." I don't think she was ever so caring as when she delivered this terrifying pronouncement: "To hell with God. And to hell with your father."

I remember sitting for hours on my bed after that, picturing all of eternity laid out before me. God was, in my mind, a white-haired old man in a robe—not unlike the man my father would later turn into—presiding over the world, marking papers with red pencil. And then there was my sad, mortal body. It seemed impossible that such a God could care what I did with my little life, but perhaps I was special, I thought. Perhaps He was saving me for good things. I pricked my finger with a safety pin and sucked the blood out. I decided I would only pretend to believe in God since that seemed just as good as real faith, which I didn't have. "Pray like you mean it!" my father would shout when it was my turn to say grace. I'm not as angry at my father for his idiotic moralism as I am for the way he treated me. He had no loyalty to me. He was never proud of me. He never praised me. He simply didn't like me. His loyalty was to the gin, and his twisted war against the hoodlums, his imaginary enemies, the ghosts. "Devil's spawn," he'd say, waving his gun around.

When I pulled up to the X-ville library that Sunday, I parked and slogged through the slush, but the big red door was locked. It was a small library in the town's old meeting house, and the one librarian—Mrs. Buell, I still remember her name—kept hours according to her personal schedule. I visited often enough to know all the books there by the look of their spines, the order they appeared on the shelves. In some books I'd even memorized the stains on their pages—spaghetti sauce spilt here, ant squashed there, booger smeared over here. I remember sensing something hopeful in the breeze that morning. I detected a hint of spring in it, although it was late December. My favorite part of drinking too much was the enthusiasm and vigor I felt at certain points of my hangover the day afterward. It sometimes carried a kind of blind excitement—mania, it's called now. The good feeling always petered out into gloom by noon, but in that bright light of Sunday morning, I pushed the books through the return slot for Mrs. Buell and decided to take a drive to Boston.

If I'd had any idea that this would be the last Sunday I'd ever spend in X-ville, I might have spent it packing a suitcase surreptitiously up in my attic, or darkly meditating on the house I'd never see again. I could have taken the time and space to weep at the kitchen table, mourn my entire youth while my father was at church. I could have kicked the walls, torn at the peeling paint and wallpaper, spat on every floor. But I got on the highway. I didn't know I'd soon be gone.

Roads were slick with melting ice, I remember. I rolled the windows down so as not to be poisoned by the exhaust fumes. I pulled on the knit hat I'd found a few nights previous, let the icy cold air freeze my face a little. Several times that winter with the car windows up I'd nearly fallen asleep at the wheel. One night on my way home from Randy's, I think, I veered off the road and into a snowbank. Luckily my foot had fallen off the pedal, so there was no great impact. On that Sunday drive out of X-ville, I thought about stopping at my old college on the way to Boston, but I couldn't summon the courage. I'd lived in that small college town barely over a year, in a dorm with other girls. I went to class, ate in the cafeteria, et cetera. It felt good to have a coffee percolator, a set of sheets of my own, and to be away, albeit not far, from home. Then I was pulled out of school halfway through my sophomore year and forced back to X-ville to care for my mother, though "care for" is not quite the right way to say it. I was terrified of my mother. She was a mystery to me, and by then I didn't "care for" her in the least. Since she was sick, I tended to her as a nurse would, but there was nothing warm or caring about what I did.

I was secretly glad that I had to leave school. I hadn't received very good grades in college, and the prospect of failing my classes, classes my father was paying for me to pass, had kept me up at night. I'd been in some trouble with the dean already since I'd chosen to "fall ill" and stay in bed instead of taking my quarterly exams. Of course, back home I blamed my parents for my misery, wished I was in school again learning to use a typewriter, studying the history of art, Latin, Shakespeare, whatever nonsense lay in store.

Even with that hat I wore, the whipping cold air was so severe that I had to roll the windows up. You can't imagine how cold it was driving down that frozen highway. I played the radio and drove fast for a while, but there was some traffic approaching the city—an accident up ahead, I think—and as I sat there waiting for the cars to move, the wooziness suddenly hit me. My eyelids began to droop and my head felt heavy. I was dead tired.

My brain ached. Those fumes get into the brain tissue. I believe I have permanent damage to this day. Still, I loved that car. I lay my head on the steering wheel for what couldn't have been more than a minute, and when I woke up, cars were streaming past me, honking their horns. So I drove, and I must have swerved out of my lane as I struggled to stay alert because then there was a police car behind me, a face in my rearview mirror, a black gloved hand motioning for me to pull over. In my confusion, I assumed it was my father's face in the mirror, that he'd somehow followed me out of town. I still had that picture of him as a cop in my head, in his uniform, laughing, ruddy cheeks and hands, an ominous glimmer in his eye. The man had never worn a coat as long as he was on the force. "You can't cover up your uniform with a coat," he said. And so he'd always been sick, his nose always dripping, his body tense, shoulders high up by his ears, shifting his weight from side to side. You can picture him. Of course, my father was sitting in Mass at this time, and he hadn't worn a uniform in years. But I always thought I saw him everywhere. Years after I left X-ville and still today I sometimes think I see him, swinging a baton at the park, coming out of a bar or coffee shop, slumped over at the top of the stairs.

I pulled onto the shoulder and rolled my window down. "I'm sorry, officer," I told the cop. "It gets stuffy in here, and my heating is broke."

I remember the policeman was young, thin faced with bags under his large pale blue eyes. He reminded me of a newscaster, asked the usual questions. I tried to speak with my mouth closed, worried he would smell the alcohol on my breath.

"Oh, my gosh," I said, rubbing my eyes. "I'm so, so sorry." I looked up at him imploringly. "My father is sick and I was up all night at his bedside. It's a very difficult time." This was the excuse I thought would solicit the most compassion. But as I said the words, my throat clenched like a fist and a well of tears rose to my eyes, as though I believed in my pathetic little story, as though I cared so deeply for my father and was just heartbroken that I might have to face life without him. I was just beside myself, barely able to steer my car straight. It was very dramatic. I ground the heels of my palms into my eye sockets and cleared my throat. The policeman looked unamazed.

"Tell you what," he said. He let me go once I promised to pull off at the next exit and get a cup of coffee. I assented. "I wouldn't want anything bad to happen right when your father needs you most." What a big heart he had. I put on my death mask and nodded. I have always hated the police. But I felt compelled to obey them then. So I did take the next exit.

I found myself on a street called Moody. Of course I did. A Christmas banner hung above the road, hitched between two electric poles. A woman in a bright red parka loped by me, pulled by a pair of German shepherds as though on a sled. I didn't like dogs. Not because they scared me—they didn't—but because their deaths were so much harder to take than people's. My dog since childhood, Mona, a Scottish terrier, the runt of its litter, passed away the week before my mother died. Without hesitation I can say my heart was broken as much over the loss of that dog as by the death of my own mother. I imagine I'm not the only person on Earth to feel that way, but for a long time the feelings seemed shameful. Perhaps had I a Dr. Frye to confess this to, I might have uncovered something which would have brought me relief, a new perspective, but I never did. Anyway, I don't trust those people who poke around sad people's minds and tell them how interesting it all is up there. It's not interesting. My mother was mean and that dog was nice. One doesn't need a college degree.

The coffee shop on the corner of Moody Street had windows dotted with cutout elves and a Santa face. Blinking Christmas lights and holly trimmed the door. I ordered a cup of hot tea and sat, still angry and worried about the car. It would not be a reliable getaway vehicle when I eventually chose to make my great departure, I realized. Given the cold and the drowsiness I'd felt just minutes after driving with the windows rolled up, I knew I would not get farther than Moody Street in that car without freezing or fainting when it came time to leave for good. So this little day trip had been something of a road test, a dress rehearsal. And the car had failed. I was demoralized, to say the least. I'd have to wait until spring. And even then, would I really go?

The waitress stood and fixed her apron strings and chewed her gum. Her uniform was mustard yellow with a white collar. Over it she wore a pink sweater with shiny black beads embroidered along the neck. They looked like busy ants swarming at her throat. I remember it well. My own sweater was a black wool cardigan, pilly and snagged. My pants were sprinkled with coffee stains across the lap. I pulled my parka back on, suddenly self-conscious and angry. Why should I have cared who saw me in a bad sweater, who might have judged my outfit in a nearly empty coffee shop? I didn't care. Let people stare at my shabbiness. Let them throw rocks at my unwashed hair. I was better than the lot of them. I'd leave them all behind to kiss the seat I'd sat on. I told myself these things, and to further convince myself, I ordered some chocolate ice cream. I watched the waitress labor with the scooper, arm deep in a freezer, pink sweater pushed up over her dainty elbows. She served it in an oblong metal dish with whipped cream, chopped nuts and a maraschino cherry on top. I spooned it into my mouth like a starving orphan, let the chocolate drip down over my chin. I didn't care. When I gulped the hot tea afterward my teeth screeched and my head nearly exploded. I don't remember what ration of whiskey my father had allowed me before he sucked the bottle dry the night before, but he must have been feeling generous. Even at my flimsy weight I could usually tolerate quite a bit of booze. Most weekends I wasn't nearly as shaky.

With the ice cream sloshing remorsefully inside my stomach, I paid and went outside, feeling very sorry for myself. I dragged my heel across a pane of ice while waiting at the crosswalk, then stomped the edge of my boot down on it. It cracked, turned milky, but didn't crumble. Funny the things one remembers. I spent most Sundays holed up at home or driving to and from Randy's house while my father was out communing with God or whatever he thought he was doing at church. Only occasionally did Aunt Ruth come inside when she dropped him off after Mass. When she did, she'd hold her purse tight, keep her gloves on, squinch her lips shut so hard they turned white. "Get

your father a cup of coffee" is the most she'd ever say to me. My
father would simply ignore me when Aunt Ruth was around.
"Hire someone to come and clean," she told him once. "Your
children are obviously busy doing other things." I was standing
in the doorway as they spoke, my father settling into his kitchen
recliner, Aunt Ruth sitting at the table, careful not to touch
anything.

"Eileen takes after her mother," my father had replied. "Good
for nothing."

"Charlie, don't speak ill of the dead."

"Don't be such a goody-goody," he snorted. "All that woman
ever did was spend my money and snore."

It was true, my mother had liked to shop. And she snored
so loudly sometimes it sounded like a locomotive chugging
through the house. As a child, I often dreamt of fast trains,
smoke tufting through black nights spangled with stars, sailing
across the country, away from X-ville, tracks rumbling beneath
me, nearly shaking me awake.

"Does the girl ever clean? Does she cook?" my aunt asked.

"I don't eat much," my father answered in my defense. "My
gout." When they finally saw me standing there, my aunt just
clucked her tongue and fiddled with the handle of her pocket-
book.

"Take out the trash, Eileen," said my dad, as though to
appease his sister. I took out the trash. I always just swallowed
my tears, held up a mask of cold stone when I felt bad. I was
glad to have gone for that drive that Sunday. I may have fallen
short of my goal of reaching Boston, but at least I'd avoided

another painful interaction with my aunt. She had flat, silvery hair and a freckled forehead that gave her a sort of boiled and sick look, like a pickled egg. I really didn't like her.

I couldn't tell you the name of the town I'd ended up in, but Moody Street was perfectly pleasant and festive. I meandered up a block of charming storefront displays. Everything was closed, of course. Back then you were hard-pressed to buy a stick of gum on Sundays. On my way back to the car, I passed a narrow alley and saw a teenage couple kissing—"petting" as we called it. I remember the scene clearly. I caught sight of them the moment the girl's tongue slid into the boy's mouth. I was so impressed. The soft pink color of the girl's tongue, the way the clean winter light reflected on its sleek surface, and the contrast in its color and texture to the pure, aquiline face, so beautiful. Sitting in my car, I couldn't shake the image—such erotic force seemed impossible. Of course I'd heard of French kissing and seen the lolling heads of young people necking on the 1-H lookout, but this view of it was as though I'd had X-ray lenses. It struck me just how forward the girl was, how gutsy, how bold to kiss that way, and so of course I thought to myself that I'd never have the guts to be anything like her. The boy was impassive, eyes shut, mouth wide, arms enfolding the girl, the collar of his plaid wool jacket flipped up. It all haunted me and compounded my headache and fatigue into severe anxiety. Sexual excitement nearly always made me feel sick. At home I could have taken a scalding bath, washed vigorously, but I was far from home. So I opened the car door and leaned out and scooped up a fistful of crystalline snow and stuffed it down the front of my trousers and into my underpants. It was very cold and very painful, but I left it there to melt as I drove. I rolled down the windows. How I didn't catch pneumonia is beyond me.

As I did oftentimes when I was disturbed, I headed back up to Randy's. On the drive I thought of his thick arms, his top lip, sensuous yet boyish, the sideways glint of his smile which he tried to hide behind a comic book or some funny magazine. Would he miss me when I was gone? Perhaps he would. "Oh, Eileen," he'd say to the cops when they'd investigate my disappearance. "She left before I ever got the nerve to ask her on a date. I missed out and I'll always regret it." It soothed me to think of us together, perhaps reunited after several years which I'd have spent becoming a real woman, his type—whatever that meant—and we'd embrace each other and cry at the sadness of our lost love and separation. "I was so blind," Randy would say, kissing my fingers, tears coasting down his beautiful cheekbones. I loved a crying man—a weakness which led me into countless affairs with whiners and depressives. I suspected Randy cried rarely, but when he did, it was a thing of great beauty. Did I really drive by his apartment that afternoon, my seat wet with melting snow? Of course I did. I can't say what I was looking for exactly, though I was ever hopeful that he might come out and profess his love, save me, run away with me, solve all my problems. As I idled in front of his place, I was suddenly overcome with nausea. I opened the car door and vomited. The gray, melted ice cream sank into the snowbank, then disappeared.

As soon as I got home that afternoon, I ran upstairs to my mother's room and peeled off my cold, wet pants and underwear. My father, sitting on the toilet across the dim hall, swung the bathroom door open to ask, "Where've you been?"

I pulled on a pair of old woolen tights and went and found a spare bottle of gin I'd hidden in the closet and handed it to my father. He took it and flipped the light on with his free hand. When his newspaper slipped from his knees, I caught sight of the dark patch of pubic hair in his lap. That terrified me. I saw, too, his gun sitting on the edge of the sink. I'd wondered about that gun from time to time. In my darkest moments, I'd imagined easing it out from under my father's sleeping body and pulling the trigger. I'd aim straight through the back of my skull so that I'd slump down over him, my blood and brains oozing all over his cold, flaccid chest. But honestly, even in those darkest moments, the idea of anyone examining my naked corpse was enough to keep me alive. I was that ashamed of my body. It also concerned me that my demise would have no great impact, that I could blow my head off and people would say, "That's all right. Let's get something to eat."

That night I lay on my cot and poked at my belly, counted my ribs with gloved fingers. It was cold up in the attic, and that cot was flimsy. It just barely bore my weight: one hundred pounds with clothes on, if that. If I used too many blankets, the joints of the cot would wiggle, and with every breath the frame would rock and sway like a boat in the tide and I couldn't sleep. I could have found a wrench to tighten up the bolts and screws or whatnot, but like with the car's broken exhaust pipe, I couldn't be bothered to deal with fixing things. I preferred to wallow in the problem, dream of better days. The attic reminded me of where a visiting uncle would sleep, if I'd had one. A good uncle, maybe an army man, inclined to build things, fix things, who never complained of cold or thirst, who would eat the worst cut of beef or chicken full of fat and gristle without a second thought. I imagined his earlobes would be long and flabby and his shoulders small, but his body muscled, eyes wide. Perhaps that good uncle was my real father, I fantasized. I sometimes scanned my mother's wardrobe for evidence of adultery. The discovery of food stains, coffee drippings down the front of a cotton blouse, or lipstick smeared on a yellowed collar was not exactly like hearing a voice from the grave, but I guess I hoped to find something useful. A hint, a greeting, proof that she'd loved me, anything. I don't know. I don't know why I wore her clothes the way I did, for years after she died. I let my dad assume it was some sort of reluctance to part with the dead woman, an old dress like a badge of loyalty, carrying on my mother's spirit, whatever nonsense. But I think I really wore her clothes to mask myself, as though if I walked around in such a costume, nobody would really see me.

I remember sitting up on my cot under a bare lightbulb and surveying the attic. It's a charming picture of misery. There were loose drawers from a dresser stacked full of moth-eaten linens that had belonged to my mother's mother. There were boxes of old books and papers, an old phonograph and several crates of records that I had never tried to play. The sloping ceiling forced me to duck and then crawl toward the window facing the backyard, where not much could be distinguished apart from the white snow and a few bare, black tree branches, everything lit up violet under the dwindling afternoon sky. Somewhere buried down there was Mona, my dead dog. I thought of my mother when she lay sick in bed, her hands in a pile of mis-knitted afghan, complaining to my father at the top of her lungs that were there a God in this world, He was a bastard. "I should be dead, already," she insisted. I dutifully boiled the chicken soup on the stove, day in, day out, and brought her the clear broth in a green salad bowl big enough to catch the spills during the struggle of having to feed the woman spoon by spoon, her arms flailing weakly and haphazardly in resistance.

One day I went out back to hang the laundry and found the dog belly-up in the uncut grass, tall and dried and dead in the bleaching sun. Perhaps God took the wrong soul, I thought in a freak moment of sentimentality, and I cried quietly, back pressed up against the house. I left the wet laundry in the bas-ket, but draped a sopping pillowcase over Mona's body. It took a day for me to muster the courage to go back out there. By then the laundry had congealed and dried, and the sight of the dead dog when I lifted the pillowcase made me gag and spill the con-tents of my stomach—chicken, vermouth—into the dry dirt. It took me several hours to dig a sufficient hole with a trowel, push Mona in with my foot—I couldn't bring myself to touch her with my hands—and cover the body with the brittle earth. A week later, when my father kicked over the dog's dish of stale and smelly kibble, he simply said, "Damn dog," and so I threw the whole thing out, and told no one. A few days later my mother was dead, and I let the tears flow openly at last. It's a romantic story and it may not be accurate at this point since I've gone over it again and again for years whenever I've felt it necessary or useful to cry.

Looking out over the icy backyard that night, I cried again for my dog, sorry that she would have to stay there in X-ville for all of eternity. I considered digging up her bones so I could take her with me. I really considered putting on my ski pants, a heavy wool sweater, snow boots, mittens, the tight knit cap, and going out there with a shovel. I hadn't marked the grave with anything, but I felt that Mona would call to me, that I would intuitively know where to break ground. Of course I didn't even try. I'd have needed some kind of pickax, the kind they use in graveyards. Imagine the labor necessary to bury a whole person without a machine to do the digging. It's not like in the movies. It's not that easy. How did they bury people in the winter in the old days, I wondered. Did they leave the bodies out to freeze until the spring? If they did do that, they must have kept them somewhere safe, in the basement perhaps, to lie in silence in the dark and cold until the thaw.

MONDAY

I remember the shower I took that morning because the hot water ran out while I dillydallied at the mirror inspecting my naked body through the wafting steam. I'm an old lady now. Like it does to everyone, time has blurred my face with lines and sagging jowls and bulging bags under my eyes, and my old body's been rendered nearly sexless and soft and wrinkled and shapeless. So just for laughs, here I am again, my little virginal body at age twenty-four. My shoulders were small and sloped and knobbly. My chest was rigid, a taut drum of bones I thudded with my fist like an ape. My breasts were lemon-size and hard and my nipples were sharp, like thorns. But I was really just all ribs, and so thin that my hips jutted out awkwardly and were often bruised from bumping into things. My guts were still cramped from the ice cream and eggs from the day before. The sluggishness of my bowels was a constant preoccupation. There was a complex science to eating and evacuating, balancing

the rising intensity of my constipated discomfort with the cathar-
sis of my laxative-induced purges. I took such poor care of
myself. I knew I should drink water, eat healthful foods, but I
really didn't like to drink water or eat healthful foods. I found
fruits and vegetables detestable, like eating a bar of soap or a
candle. I also suffered from that unfortunate maladjustment to
puberty—still at twenty-four—that made me ashamed of my
womanliness. There were days on end I ate very little—a handful of nuts or raisins here, a crust of bread there. And for fun,
such as with the chocolates a few nights prior, I sometimes
chewed but spat out candies or cookies, anything that tasted
good but which I feared might put meat on my bones.

Back then, at twenty-four, people already considered me a
spinster. I'd had only one kiss from a boy by then. When I was
sixteen, Peter Woodman, a senior, took me to the high school
prom. I won't say too much about him—I don't want to sound as
though I've carried the memory around with any romantic nostalgia. If there's anything I've learned to detest, it is nostalgia.
And anyway, Randy is the romantic lead in my story, if there is
one. Peter Woodman can't hold a candle to him. My prom dress
was very pretty, though—navy taffeta. I loved navy blue. Whatever I wore in that color reminded me of a uniform, something
that I felt validated me and obscured me at once. We spent most
of our time sitting at a table in the darkened gymnasium, Peter
talking to his friends. His father worked in the police station
and I'm sure Peter only asked me to the prom as a favor his
father owed to mine. We didn't dance, not that I minded. The
evening of the prom ended in Peter's father's pickup truck in

the high school parking lot when I bit the boy's throat to keep him from reaching any farther up my dress. In fact, I think his hand was barely on my knee, I was so guarded. And the kiss was only superficial—a momentary touching of the lips, sort of sweet when I think of it now. I can't remember how I got home that night after tumbling out of the truck, Peter heckling me and rubbing his neck as I watched him drive away. Did my teeth draw blood? I don't know. And who cares anyway? By now he's probably dead. Most people I knew are dead.

That Monday morning in X-ville, I put on my new blue stockings and dressed in my mother's clothes. I locked my father's shoes back in the trunk of the Dodge and drove to work, to Moorehead. I remember conjuring up a new strategy for my getaway. One day soon, when I was good and ready, I'd pile on all the clothes I decided on taking with me: my gray coat, several pairs of wool socks, snow boots, mittens, gloves, hat, scarf, pants, skirt, dress, et cetera, and I'd drive about three hours northwest across state lines to Vermont. I knew I could survive the drive for one hour with the windows up without fainting, and being bundled up would save me the rest of the way with the windows down. New York wasn't that far from X-ville. Two hundred fifty-seven miles south, to be exact. But first I'd lead any search astray by abandoning the Dodge in Rutland, which I'd read about in a book about railroads. In Rutland I'd find some kind of abandoned lot or dead-end street, and then I'd walk to the railway station and take a train down to the city to start my new life. I thought I was so smart. I planned to bring along an empty suitcase to carry the clothes

I'd take off once I got on the train. I'd have some clothes, the money I'd been hoarding in the attic, and nothing else.

But maybe I'd need something to read on my ride to my future, I thought. I could borrow a few of the finer books from the X-ville library, disappear and never return them. This seemed to me a brilliant idea. First, I would get to keep the books as mementos, a bit like when a killer snips a lock of hair from his victim or takes some small object—a pen, a comb, a rosary—as his trophy. Second, I'd give good cause for concern to my father and others who might wonder whether I ever intended to return or under what circumstances I was forced to leave. I pictured detectives poking around the house. "Nothing seems to be out of order, Mr. Dunlop. Maybe she's visiting a friend."

"Oh no, not Eileen. Eileen has no friends," my father would say. "Something's happened. She'd never leave me alone like this."

My hope was that they'd think I was dead in a ditch somewhere, kidnapped, buried in an avalanche, eaten by a bear, what have you. It was important to me that nobody knew I planned to disappear. If my father thought I'd ran away, he would have humiliated me. I could imagine him puffing out his chest and scoffing at my foolishness with Aunt Ruth. They'd called me a spoiled brat, an idiot, an ungrateful rat's ass. Perhaps they did say all that once I really had left X-ville. I'll never know. I wanted my father to despair, cry his eyes out over his poor lost daughter, collapse at the foot of my cot, swathe himself in my smelly blankets just to remember the beautiful stink of my sweat. I wanted him to paw through my belongings like examining bleached bones, inert artifacts of a life he'd never appreciated. If I'd ever had a music box, I'd have liked the song it played to break my father's heart. I'd have liked him to die of sadness at having lost me. "I loved her," I wanted him to say. "And I was wrong to have acted like I didn't." Such were my thoughts on my way to work that morning.

Unbeknownst to me at the time, I would be gone by Christmas morning, and though my memories since then have waxed and waned, I will do my best to narrate the events of my last days in X-ville. I will try to paint a complete picture. Some of my clearest memories may seem wholly irrelevant, but I will include them when I feel they add to the mood. For example, that morning when I got to Moorehead, the boys had been given special holiday sweaters knit by a group of do-gooders at a local church. Since there was a surplus of sweaters, I presume, one landed on my desk wrapped in brown paper. Mrs. Stephens told me it was a Christmas present from the warden. I tore open the package and found a navy blue, expertly knit vest with an orange crucifix across the chest and marked with an "S" for small written in shaky cursive on a scrap of wax paper safety-pinned to the collar. That shade of blue made me wonder. Maybe the warden actually liked me? He could hardly give me a box of chocolates, after all. He wouldn't want to attract the attention of the office ladies, arousing hostile suspicions of favoritism and clandestine love affairs. I pictured embracing the warden in his office, flinging myself at him like a rag doll. Was that what I wanted? My thoughts were like dirty films reeling inside my brain, and I remember them from that morning as well as the dull thudding sound of the drawer when I shut the sweater inside it. I cannot, however, remember the layout of the prison's recreational facilities, or whether the Christmas pageant, as they called it, was held in the gymnasium or the chapel or a small auditorium, which I'm not sure existed at all. I may be thinking of my old high school.

This I remember very well: Around two o'clock, the warden came into our office, followed by a tall redheaded woman and a willowy bald man in a loose, mud-colored suit. My first impression of the woman was that she must be a performer at the special assembly—a singer or an actress with a soft spot for child criminals. My assumption seemed reasonable. Celebrities entertained army troops, after all. Why not young prisoners? Teenage boys were a worthy enough cause. Most of those boys, the ones serving shorter sentences, ended up in Vietnam anyway, I'm sure. In any case, this woman was beautiful and looked vaguely familiar in the way all beautiful people look familiar. So within thirty seconds I'd decided that she must be an idiot, have a brain like a powder puff, be bereft of any depth or darkness, have no interior life whatever. Like Doris Day, this woman must live in a charmed world of fluffy pillows and golden sunshine. So of course I hated her. I'd never come face-to-face with someone so beautiful before in my life.

The man was not interesting to me in the least. He sniffled, rubbed his head with one hand, carried two coats over his other arm—his and the redhead's, I presumed. I couldn't help but stare at the woman. I have a dreamy picture in my memory of how she was dressed that day, in peculiar shades of pink, not unfashionable per se, but not in the fashion of the times and certainly not of X-ville. She wore a long flowing skirt, a sweater set draped around her slim figure, and a stiff-rimmed hat, which I picture now somewhat like a riding helmet, only it was gray and delicate, felt maybe, and held an iridescent feather on one side. Perhaps I've invented the hat. She wore a long gold pendant necklace—that I know for sure. Her shoes were like men's riding boots, only smaller, and with a delicate heel. Her legs were very long and her arms were thin and folded across her narrow rib cage. I was surprised to see a cigarette in her fingers. Many women smoked, of course, more than do now, but it seemed odd for her to smoke just standing there in the office as though she were at a cocktail party, as though she owned the place. And the way she smoked disturbed me. When others smoked, it was something needy and cheap. When this woman inhaled, her face trembled and her eyes fluttered in subtle ecstasy, as though she were tasting a delectable dessert or stepping into a warm bath. She seemed to be in a state of enchantment, perfectly happy. And so she struck me as perverse. Pretentious wasn't a word we used back then. Obnoxious was more like it.

"Listen up," said the warden. He had a wide, red and pitted face with a huge nose and small, inscrutable eyes, but was so well groomed, so clean and militant, I thought of him as handsome. "I present to you our new psychiatrist, Dr. Bradley Morris. He comes highly recommended by Dr. Frye, and I'm sure he'll be an asset to us in keeping our boys in line and on the path to redemption. And this is Miss Rebecca Saint John, our first ever prison director of education, thanks to a generous donation from Uncle Sam. I'm sure she's completely qualified. I understand she's just finished her graduate work at Radcliffe—"

"Harvard," said this Rebecca Saint John, leaning toward him slightly. She tipped her cigarette ash on the floor and blew the smoke at the ceiling, seemed to grin. It was truly bizarre.

"Harvard," the warden continued, titillated, it seemed to me. "I know you will all welcome our new additions with respect and professionalism, and I hope you'll show Miss Saint John around in her first few days as she learns our customs here." He pointed vaguely to the office ladies, me included. It all seemed very strange, such a young, attractive woman appearing out of nowhere, and to do what? Teaching writing and arithmetic seemed like a ridiculous objective. Those Moorehead boys struggled just to walk around, sit down, eat and breathe without beating their heads against the walls. Dr. Morris was there, for all intents and purposes, to drug them into acting right. What could they possibly be taught in their condition? The warden took Miss Saint John's coat from Dr. Morris's arm, handed it to me, and seemed to smile. I could never tell his real feelings toward me, sweater vest or not. His death mask was thick as concrete, I suppose. In any case, it was my job to assign the new woman a locker. So she followed me back to the locker room.

Rebecca Saint John's face that day had no makeup on it that I could detect, and yet she looked impeccable, fresh faced, a natural beauty. Her hair was long and thick, the color of brass, coarse and, I noted gratefully, in need of a hardy brushing. Her skin was sort of golden colored, and her face was round and full with strong cheekbones, a small rosebud mouth, thin eyebrows and unusually blond eyelashes. Her eyes were an odd shade of blue. There was something manufactured about that color. It was a shade of blue like a swimming pool in an ad for a tropical getaway. It was the color of mouthwash, toothpaste, toilet cleaner. My own eyes, I thought, were like shallow lake water, green, murky, full of slime and sand. Needless to say, I felt completely insulted and horrible about myself in the presence of this beautiful woman. Perhaps I should have honored my resentment and kept my distance, but I couldn't help myself. I wanted to be close to her, to get an intimate view of her features, how she breathed, what her face did when her mind was busy thinking. I hoped to be able to spot her superficial imperfections, or at least find flaws in her character which could cancel out the good marks she got in the looks category. You see how silly I was? I wrote out the combination to her locker on a slip of paper and took a whiff of her when I handed it over. She smelled like baby powder. She wore no ring. I wondered if she had a boyfriend.

"Now let me have you stand here and watch me and let's see if I can figure out this lock," she said. She had a haughty, precisely articulated accent, the kind of accent you hear in old movies set in the south of France or fancy Manhattan hotels. Continental? I'd never heard anyone in real life talk like that. It seemed absurd in such a place as Moorehead. Imagine the well-mannered tone of a British noblewoman politely bossing around her maid. I stood with my back against a column of lockers as she spun the dial of the combination lock.

"Thirty-two, twenty-four, thirty-four," she said. "Well, look at that, practically my measurements." She laughed and pulled the locker door open with a clang. My own measurements were even smaller. We both paused, and as though we were each other's synchronized reflections, looked down at our own breasts, then at each other's. Then Rebecca said, "I prefer being sort of flat chested, don't you? Women with big bosoms are always so bashful. That, or else they think their figures are all that matters. Pathetic." I thought of Joanie, her body so conspicuous in its fleshiness, a main attraction. I must have made a face or blushed because then Rebecca asked, "Oh, have I embarrassed you?" Her sincerity seemed genuine to me. We exchanged smiles. "Busts," she said, shrugging and looking down at her small breasts again. "Who cares?" She laughed, winked at me, then turned back to her locker and fiddled with the dial again.

Perhaps only young women of my same conniving and tragic nature will understand that there could be something in such an exchange as mine with Rebecca that day which could unite two people in conspiracy. After years of secrecy and shame, in this one moment with her, all my frustrations were condoned and my body, my very being, was justified. Such solidarity and awe I felt, you'd think I'd never had a friend before. And really, I hadn't. All I'd had were Suzie or Alice or Maribel, figments, of course, imaginary girls I'd used in lies to my father—my own dark ghosts.

"Of course I'm not embarrassed," I told her. To declare this took more courage than I'd needed in years, for it required the brief removal of my mask of ice. "I completely agree with you."

What is that old saying? A friend is someone who helps you hide the body—that was the gist of this new rapport. I sensed it immediately. My life was going to change. In this strange creature, I'd met my match, my kindred spirit, my ally. Already I wanted to extend my hand, slashed and ready to be shaken in a pact of blood, that was how impressionable and lonely I was. I kept my hands in my pockets, however. This marked the beginning of the dark bond which now paves the way for the rest of my story.

"Well good," said Rebecca. "We have better things to do than worry about our figures. Though that's not the popular opinion, wouldn't you say?" She raised her eyebrows at me. She was really remarkably beautiful, so beautiful I had to avert my eyes. I wanted desperately to impress her, to elicit some clear indication from her that she felt as I did—we were two peas in a pod.

"I don't care much about what's popular," I lied. I hadn't ever been so brash before. Oh, I was a rebel.

"Well, look at you," said Rebecca. She crossed her arms. "Rare to meet a young woman with so much gumption. You're a regular Katharine Hepburn." The comparison would have sounded like mockery if made by anyone else. But I wasn't offended. I laughed, blushed. Rebecca laughed too, then shook her head. "I'm kidding," she said. "I'm like that, too. I don't give a rat's ass what people think. But it is good if they think well of you. That has its advantages."

We looked at each other and smiled, nodded sarcastically with widened eyes. Were we serious? It didn't seem to matter. It was like all my secret misery had just then been converted into a powerful currency. I'm sure Rebecca saw right through my bravado, but I didn't know that. I thought I was so smooth.

"See you around," I said. I figured it was best not to come on too strong. We waved to each other and Rebecca flew off back through the office and up the hall like some exotic bird or flower, utterly misplaced in the dim fluorescent light. I walked mechanically, heel-toe, back to my desk, hands clasped behind my back, whistling nothing in particular, my world now transformed.

That afternoon I prepared certain phrases and responses to use on Rebecca. I was terribly concerned that she think well of me, that she understand I was not the provincial dolt I feared I appeared to be. Of course she knew I was a provincial dolt—I was that—but I thought at the time that I'd fooled her with some kind of radical point of view, what with our mutual distaste for large breasts, the cold wisdom of my gaze, my general attitude. I wasn't radical at all. I was simply unhappy. So I sat at my desk and practiced my death mask—face in perfect indifference, no muscles twitching, eyes blank, still, brow furrowed ever so slightly. I had this childish idea that it is best when dealing with a new friend to withhold all opinions until the other puts forth her opinions first. Nowadays perhaps we'd call the attitude blasé. It is a peculiar posture of insecure people. They feel most comfortable denying any perspective whatsoever rather than proclaiming any allegiance or philosophy and risk rejection and judgment. I thought I had to bite my tongue and seem as aloof as possible until Rebecca set the rules of the game, so to speak. So if she were to ask me how I liked my job, I'd have shrugged and said, "It's a paycheck." If she asked me about my past I'd say, "Nothing really worth mentioning." But I would allude to my mother's death as though it were an event cloaked in mystery, as though she'd been slaughtered by the mob in some moonlit scene under a pier. Or maybe I'd killed her—snuffed the life out of her with a pillow and never told a soul until now. I had all kinds of made-up hooks I'd have used to snag her. If Rebecca wanted to know what my interests were, my hobbies, I'd say I read books, and if she wanted to know which, I'd say it was personal. I'd say that to me, reading was like making love, and I didn't kiss and tell. I thought I was very cute. I figured, Rebecca being a teacher or whatever she was, she'd appreciate me as highly literary. Of course I couldn't really discuss literature. It was easier for me to discuss the things that mattered in my own life. "Do you drink gin?" for example. If she wanted to know why I was curious, I'd shrug and say, "There's something about people who like gin, and people who don't." And depending on her answer, I'd categorize gin drinkers either as idiots, or harbingers of great grief, or heroes. I pondered all this, but I knew I'd never have the guts to be so obnoxious. Rebecca was very intimidating to me.

"Yoo-hoo, Eileen. Time to sort the mail," said Mrs. Murray, twiddling her fingers and snapping her gum. My stomach fluttered as I got to work. The clock snored on.

On my way down to the Christmas pageant in the afternoon, which I now seem to recall was in the chapel, I stopped in the

ladies' room to check my face in the mirror and apply more lipstick. I had a habit of wiping my face with the sleeve of my
sweater to smear off the grease which got absorbed in the powder I used. I always had a fine row of pimples along my hairline,
even after the more violent attacks of acne had subsided in my
teenage years. My skin has always been problematic. Even now
my rosacea flares up, and I've had gin blossoms since my late
twenties, although I hardly ever drank gin, as I told you. Perhaps gin blossoms are my cross to bear, some kind of marker,
penance. I like how I look now. But back then, I hated my face,
oh, I was truly tortured by it. I smoothed my hair back and put
on a heavy coat of Irreparable Red, blotted my lips with a paper
towel, checked my teeth. They are small, childlike teeth, still,
and they looked yellow in contrast to the lipstick I wore. I rarely
smiled genuinely enough to forget to hold my lip down over my
teeth. I think I've mentioned how my upper lip had a tendency
to pull up my gums. Nothing came easily to me. Nothing.

When I used the toilet, I discovered that my monthly visitor
had arrived, much to my disgust. In hindsight it's a miracle that
I menstruated at all, considering my wrought nerves and terrible
nutrition. Not that I ever put my rugged fertility to good use.
There was something once, but it went away before it turned
into anything to write home about. And then another time, but
I got rid of it. I can't say I'm not sorry I never had any children,
but there's no use in regrets. That day at Moorehead, instead of
going back to my locker for the proper supplies, I unspooled a
length of paper towel to the floor, folded it up and stuck it in my
underwear. It was dry and rough paper the color of shopping

bags from the grocery store. This I remember since it contrib-
uted heavily to my self-consciousness as I walked down the halls,
remembering suddenly—how had I forgotten?—that the boys,
Randy, James even, might see me and stare directly at my rear
end as I passed by. I might add that I didn't wash my hands after
using the toilet.

Despite the brutal misery of Moorehead, the way I picture
the prison that day is less like a prison and more like a children's
nursery. The halls were decked thanks to the volunteers from
the church who had come in over the weekend to stick up fright-
ening hand-drawn portraits of Jesus and Santa Claus. Christmas
has always been a charade and I refuse to acknowledge it now.
It's too painful. I remember a man I met in my thirties who bent
my ear one night babbling about his happy childhood—presents
under the tree, cocoa, puppies, chestnuts roasting on an open
fire. There's nothing I detest more than men with happy childhoods. Perhaps Dr. Frye thought Christmas was good for the
psyche. He had always encouraged the boys to take part in holiday activities, like singing carols and making one another
Christmas cards. That backfired every time, as the boys in the
prison were humiliated by singing and would get into fights,
calling each other names and laughing and pointing at whoever
dared open his mouth. And whatever cards they received from
one another were always loaded with threats and insults and
pornographic drawings. I knew because the corrections officers
would confiscate them, then show them around to the guards
and other staff, then tell me—simply to humiliate me, I'm sure—
to file them. "Marry fucking XXX-mas." The rest of the year the

boys were generally docile and dull. They were all on pills under Dr. Frye. Perhaps he'd let up on their prescriptions for the holidays. Otherwise they were heavily sedated and on strict diets.

That afternoon I watched as the boys filed into the chapel and sat in the first few rows of seats, slumped and irritable. Randy stood at the foot of the stage, facing them. To fulfill my duties, I sat on the high stool in back and plugged in the old spotlight that swiveled around in a cast-iron frame attached to the rear wall. I steered it so it illuminated the stage, shining a bright circle onto the wrinkled orange curtains. It reminds me now of the opening credits of Bugs Bunny cartoons. That tune plays in my head from time to time as a way of making light of deranged situations. I remember the scenes of that Christmas performance in vivid Technicolor. It was just absurd.

A moment before the lights went down, Rebecca appeared in the doorway carrying a small notebook with a pen stuck through the wire spiral spine. The guards' eyes and mine followed her small, childlike bottom down the aisle. She took a seat off to the side near the front, next to Dr. Morris, where Randy was standing guard. This made me edgy. I would have preferred that the two of them, Rebecca and Randy, never cross paths. Rebecca was too pretty for Randy not to notice her, and despite our new bond, I was still full of envy. It didn't matter at all that I'd been fantasizing my great escape, never again to return to X-ville and certainly not to Moorehead, Randy soon to become what he is now, an expired dream, a ghost, a shadow. "Good-bye, Randy, good-bye," I imagined sobbing on my train to New York.

I remember that a row of boys, each wearing a blue or gray knit vest, erupted in a flurry of curse words and tossed fists as the lights went down. Randy broke from his statuelike posture to dissolve the fight. It was wonderful to watch him at work. He moved so efficiently, so coolly, without judgment, but with swift force. I could barely breathe watching how his muscles strained against the stiff give of his uniform. I suppose I really was in love with him in the worst sense: I cared only for his looks, his body—I barely knew him at all.

When the boys were all back in their seats, the warden walked out onstage. I steered the spotlight up to his face, but let it rest first—accidentally or not—for a moment at his crotch. A few boys laughed. The warden took the microphone and said something like this:

"Merry Christmas, prisoners, staff, and visitors. Every year we hold a special assembly to commemorate this most important of holidays, and every year we remark on just how much of the story of Christmas can be gleaned to uphold our principles, which is a great deal, and we pray to see if and where we are failing and just how the story of a child, not so unlike many of you boys born also to young parents without much money, little hope, could show us the errors of our ways and inspire us to change, be good, and live a life clear of outbursts, dereliction and destruction. So I hope you will all sit back and watch with open minds, questioning in your hearts where you can be improved, and what the teachings of our holy scripture say for us to be. Our dear friends at Mount Olive have helped to direct this year's performance of the Nativity and I want every single boy to now sit on his hands and zip his lips. If I hear one laugh or moan or any wayward comment, it's straight to the cave. And don't test me on that. We also welcome two additions to our prison staff, Dr. Morris, our new sanity professional, as I like to think of you—welcome, welcome. And Miss Saint John, our education expert. She may be easy on the eyes, fellows, but I assure you, she's very clever and will have more to make of your sick minds than I could ever hope to. You will all meet with her in due time. If that is not incentive enough to keep you quiet this afternoon, I don't know what is. And now, without further ado."

It disgusts me now to think how I had an odd sort of crush on the warden. Perhaps I envied his self-possession, I don't know. He did always seem very pleased with himself. Although it barely masked his stupidity, there was a sureness about him I guess I found attractive. I was so easily swayed by the vestiges of power. I remember the warden untangling himself from the microphone cord, then extending his hand to an elderly priest in a wheelchair. In hindsight, the warden was probably a homosexual. He made a point of spanking the younger boys alone in his office, I heard. But that is a whole other story and not mine to tell.

When the orange curtains parted, a spartan set was revealed, made up to look like the interior of a prison cell. A bunk bed, a Bible on a small table. One of the boys, bloated and pale and dressed in the standard inmate uniform, a blue cotton jumpsuit, walked out onto the stage, hands in his pockets. He mumbled under his breath, but I can guess what he was meant to say since it was the same every year: "Oh, what am I to do? Sentenced for

three years to sit indoors among boys of my same creed—plain
bad. So much time to plot what evildoings I'll undertake as soon
as I get out. But in the meantime I suppose I could read a book."

"You can't read!" a voice cracked from the first row as the
blushing actor picked up the Bible. The boys all laughed and
throttled each other in their seats. Randy approached, gestured
casually with one hand raised in a fist and the other holding a
finger to his lips. The play went on.

The boy onstage sat on the bottom bunk bed and opened
the Bible. Two more children crossed the stage toward him,
both dressed in robes, one wearing a wig and, it seemed, a pillow over his abdomen under the robe. From where I was sitting,
I could see Rebecca shifting in her seat. Of course it bothered
me to watch what was happening on stage, that kind of humiliation. But I put up with it. I did not have the courage to care
enough to get upset. Nobody did. The boy dressed as Mary
spoke in a high voice: "Well, I'm pretty tired, can we rest in that
barn over there?" and pointed offstage, fey as a rabbit. The audience laughed. The boy dressed as Joseph set down a sack and
wiped his forehead. "Better than paying for a hotel." Rebecca
looked around, craning her neck as though searching for a particular face in the crowd. I hoped the face she was looking for
was mine. I could just barely make out her expression in the
darkened chapel. I nearly swung the spotlight at her to illumi-
nate her delicately furrowed brow, her mouth pinched adorably
with displeasure. She was so pretty, a miraculous sight in such
an ugly place, it surprised me that others weren't pointing and
staring. How was it that Dr. Morris, Randy, all those boys

carried blithely on, as though she were invisible to them? Was my assessment of her beauty wrong? Had I lost all perspective? Was I seeing things? Was she not the most radiant, most elegant, most charming woman in the world? I wondered. She continued to scan the audience row by row.

The play went on, Joseph and Mary reciting lines sometimes stiffly, sometimes with tongue-in-cheek bravado. More children in multicolored robes appeared, heads bowed in embarrassment or boredom. Their voices were barely audible through the taunts and laughter from the boys in the crowd. One of the players, a younger child, began to cry, chin wobbling, jaw gritted. That was when Rebecca stood up, scowling, and trudged back up the aisle, her pendant bouncing between her small bosoms as she strode. I watched her. Her body was very beautiful, slender as a ballerina and just as tense. She noticed me when she reached the back of the chapel, then waved and shook her head in disbelief, mouthed something I couldn't decipher, and walked out. I remember thinking, "We are united now, us against them." I would adopt her rage, or pretend to at least, if it meant I could be on her side. That's what it felt like.

I t wasn't that I didn't care at all about the boys. It was just that I was young and miserable and had no way of helping them. I felt, in fact, that I was one of them. I was no worse or better. I was only six years older than the oldest of the boys in there. Some of them looked like men already—tall, lanky with beards and mustaches coming in and big, thick hands, low voices. They were mostly white from blue-collar families, but there were quite a few black boys, too. I liked those boys the best. I sensed they understood something the others didn't. They seemed to be more relaxed, to breathe slightly more deeply, to wear perfect death masks while the other boys winced and frowned and spat and chided one another like little children, brats in a schoolyard. I often wondered what they all thought of me when they saw me standing outside the door during visitations, if they even noticed me at all. They rarely looked my way, never once lifted their grainy, warm slow eyes to mine in recognition. I thought perhaps they couldn't identify me from one day to the next, as though my role were played by innumerable similar-looking young women. Or maybe they sat with their mothers during visitation and called me "that bitch," and motioned with their chins when my head was turned and I was thinking of Randy and not listening. Or maybe they said, "She's the only one I don't hate." Or maybe they thought I was crazy. I certainly could have passed for crazy on days when I'd not slept and showed up unkempt and hungover, rolling my eyes at every noise and gnashing my teeth at every flicker of light. In my childish self-centeredness, I fantasized that this was what the black boys talked about with their mothers: how much pain Eileen is in, how Eileen seems to need a friend, how Eileen deserves better. I hoped they saw right through my death mask to my sad and fiery soul, though I doubt they saw me at all.

I wouldn't be the first to admit that working as a young woman in an all-male institution had its perks. This is not to say that my position at Moorehead gave me any sense of my power as a female, nor did it bring me closer to realizing any imagined romantic encounters—none of that nonsense. But working at Moorehead did give me a sneak peek into the male disposition. I could, at times, stand quietly and observe the boys like animals in a zoo—how they moved, breathed, all the nuanced gestures and attitudes that made each of them seem special. It was through studying the comportment of imprisoned youngsters that I developed my understanding of the strange spectrum of male emotions. Shrugging meant "I'll punch you later." Smiling was a promise of undying love and affection or severe hatred, cutthroat fury. Did I derive erotic pleasure from looking at these boys? Only a little, honestly, since I didn't get to observe them on a regular basis, and never in their natural state. I only watched them filing in and out of assembly meetings or the cafeteria, and during their visits with their mothers. I wasn't in a position to observe them at rest in their bunks, at work in the rec room, or playing in the yard, where I imagine they were more at ease, more animated, and expressed more subtlety, more vulnerability, humor, spontaneity. In any case, I liked their fluctuating, miserable faces. The best was when I could see the hard face of a cold-hearted killer breaking through the chubby cheeks and callow softness of youth. That thrilled me.

It may not have been at that particular Christmas assembly performance, but I remember a boy who played Mary ripping out the pillow from under his costume and throwing it on the ground and sitting on it. A wise man mimed a strip tease once. So the boys were charming in a way. Would I miss them once I was gone? Of course I wouldn't, and I didn't miss them, though

I wondered, staring at the backs of their heads in the chapel that day, if I'd remember any of their faces, if I'd be sorry if any of them died. Would I have helped them if I could have? Would I have sacrificed anything for their benefit? The answer was a shame-faced but honest no. I was selfish, solely concerned with my own wants and needs. I remember watching Randy standing there in the dark of the auditorium. I wondered if his nether regions were squashed inside his pants. I imagined he must have kept them to one side to accommodate the way the pants were made. They were tight. I can't bring back the precise image right now, but I regularly studied the arrangement of folds in the groin area that would have suggested which side he preferred. I wasn't completely unfamiliar with the male parts. I don't actually remember seeing any male parts in my father's dirty magazines, now that I think of it, though they were inferred, I guess. My knowledge was limited to anatomical drawings. I'd sat through health class sophomore year of high school, after all. Sweating behind that hot spotlight, I worried that my inexperience with men would make Rebecca think I was childish and pathetic. If she found out I'd never had a boyfriend, she would dismiss me, I feared.

Once the drama onstage had unraveled, the warden reappeared and started a long soliloquy on the nature of sin. I abandoned my post behind the spotlight and left the chapel to stroll down the prison halls, hoping to run into Rebecca. The rec room and offices were empty. The library, which held mostly religious tracts and encyclopedias, the dining hall with its long steel tables strewn with dirty plastic cutlery—all was quiet. The boys' sleeping quarters were in the far back. The small windows there looked out on the rolling, snow-filled dunes. The ocean beyond like a canyon of woe, tumbling and icy all day and night, was so thunderous, I pictured God himself emerging from the water, laughing at us all in spite. It was easy to imagine the depressive thoughts that view must have inspired in those little boys. The windows were at such a height from the floor that one had to either stoop down or kneel to get a good look out there. I listened to the waves rumbling in the empty room for a moment. Bunk beds lined the circumference of the room, which was bell-shaped and had lines painted on the floor in guiding paths that showed where to stand during morning announcements, where to kneel at night to pray, which way to walk to the showers, which way to the cafeteria. The baby-blue laminate squeaked under my feet so loudly on my way out, I thought I'd stepped on a mouse.

I remember scurrying back up to the kitchen and stealing a carton of milk from the vacant cafeteria line. It was a very impressive kitchen, all gray steel, heavy machinery. When the boys were being punished for bad behavior, they were made to do double duty washing pots and pans and forced to sleep in a room that had been the old meat locker behind the kitchen—solitary confinement. They called that room "the cave." A boy sent to the cave would not be allowed out except to use the shower and wash more dishes. He'd eat his meals in there, use a bucket as a toilet. I remember that bucket was of great interest to me. As one might guess, I was easily roused by the grosser habits of the human body—toilet business not least of all. The very fact that other people moved their bowels filled me with awe. Any function of the body that one hid behind closed doors titillated me. I recall one of my early relationships—not a heavy love affair, just a light one—was with a Russian man with a wonderful sense of humor who permitted me to squeeze the pus from his pimples on his back and shoulders. To me, this was the greatest intimacy. Before that, still young and neurotic, just allowing a man to listen to me urinate was utter humiliation, torture, and therefore, I thought, proof of profound love and trust.

There was a boy who'd been in the cave for several weeks. I went around back and found the old meat locker whose original stainless steel door had been replaced by a heavy iron one with a small window, and padlocked. The Polk boy was inside, sitting on his cot, staring at the wall. I recognized him as the Polk boy from the day he'd arrived at Moorehead a few weeks earlier. My father had been following stories about him in the *Post*. During the intake procedure, the boy had been silent and withdrawn. He hadn't struck me at first as particularly attractive or special. He had a stiff posture, I remember, and was thin but had broad shoulders—the awkward confluence of a young boy's ease and a man's imposing heft and brutishness. There were newly tattooed letters on the knuckles of his right hand but I couldn't make them out clearly. I watched as he lifted his gaze as though reading something written on the ceiling. His eyes were light, skin olive, and his hair shorn and brown. He seemed contemplative, wistful, sad. The saddest boys at Moorehead were the runaways locked up for vagrancy or prostitution. How much, I wondered as I watched through the window, would it cost to defile a young boy like this one? He had intelligent eyes, I thought, long elegant limbs, a pensive tilt to his head. I hoped he'd charged a lot, whatever he'd done. Back then I still pictured male prostitutes working in service to wealthy housewives, entertaining them while their husbands were away on business—I was that naive. I watched as the boy bent his neck this way and that, sensually, as though to relax himself. He yawned. I don't think he saw me through the window. To this day, I don't know that he ever even knew my name. I watched as he lay down on the cot, turned on his side, closed his eyes and stretched. For a minute he seemed to be falling asleep. Then his fingers, mindlessly it seemed, fell to his groin area. I held my breath as I watched him cup his genitals under his uniform. His body curled up like a small animal. In my effort to understand the movements of his hand, I pressed my face to the window. My tongue, cold from the milk, met the surface of the glass. I watched for a minute or two, rapt, stunned, mystified until noise from the hall made me jump and scurry back up to the office. I really don't think the boy saw me. I learned later on he was only fourteen. He could have passed for nineteen, twenty. I wasn't immune to him either.

That afternoon, as Mrs. Stephens was putting on her coat to leave for the day, I deigned to ask her what the boy had done to get put into solitary.

"Polk," she said in a huff, double-chinned. She pulled linty woolen mittens over her fat, chapped hands. "Troublemaker," she said. "Nasty boy." It strikes me now that I was relentlessly unforgiving of Mrs. Stephens. Everything she did I interpreted as a personal affront, as a direct attack of some kind. Though I never retaliated, I considered her my enemy. It's true she wasn't warm or even pleasant, but she never really harmed me. She was just endlessly crabby. Once she was gone, and the other office ladies had left for the day, I found the Polk file, the papers slightly yellowed inside the folder. "Crime: patricide." The file was thick with Dr. Frye's notes, mostly dates and times and incomprehensible Latinate scribbles. In a newspaper clipping affixed to the short rap sheet, I read that Leonard "Lee" Polk had slit his father's throat while he was asleep in bed. The boy had no history of violent behavior, the report said, and neighbors had called him a "quiet child, well mannered, nothing special." Something like that. His face in his mug shot was surly, with tight, down-turning lips and unfocused, exhausted eyes. In his file, under "comments," it read "mute since day of crime" in my own messy schoolgirl cursive.

Just then, like birdsong at midnight, a magic, melodic voice rang out from down the dim hallway. It was Rebecca saying good night to James. I tried to collect myself, listening as the ticktock of her heels got louder. After a moment, she stood before me in a long black coat, briefcase in hand. Hours had now passed since the ridiculous Christmas pageant. I tried to smile, fumbling to put Leonard Polk's file back in order, but I lost my grasp on the folder and its contents spilled out, pages flapping onto the dirty linoleum.

"Uh-oh," I said like a fool. Rebecca came behind the office counter to help me pick up the papers. I watched her from behind as she squatted down to reach under Mrs. Stephens's desk. She gathered the fabric of her skirt up so that it wouldn't drag on the floor, revealing her calves—refined, gentle curves, nothing like mine, which were spindly and childish. "My goodness," she said, reading the document in her hands. "Can you imagine killing your own father?" She handed the paper back to me, eying me knowingly, I thought.

"Thank you," I said, blushing.

"It's a story for the ages, of course. Kill your father, sleep with your mother," Rebecca went on. "The male instinct can be terribly predictable." She leaned over my shoulder, squinting at the photograph of the boy. Her hair fell like a curtain between us. She swept it back and strands fluttered against my cheek like feathers. She bit her lip. "Leonard Polk," she read aloud. I could smell cigarettes on her breath, and violet candies.

"He's been in solitary," I told her. "I've never seen him out here at all. No visitors."

"Now that's a shame," said Rebecca. "May I?" She spread her palms open before me. I handed her the folder.

"I was just doing some filing," I told her stupidly, hoping she wouldn't suspect me of snooping.

Rebecca flipped through the papers in the folder. I pretended to look busy, rearranging things on my desk, scanning an old questionnaire. "Name your favorite celebrity. What time do you go to bed at night?"

"I'll just borrow this," Rebecca said, slipping the Polk file into her briefcase. "Fun bedtime reading," she quipped. I sat back down at my desk, anxious and awkward, while she buttoned her coat. "Some show today."

"They do it every year."

"I'd call that cruel and unusual punishment," she replied. She flung a fuzzy mohair shawl over her shoulders, untucked her hair. I felt I had utterly failed to impress her. I resolved to say more, be cooler, more charming, smarter, funnier, more alive the next time we talked. "Well, see you in the morning," she said, and ticktocked down the hall to the blustery evening outside.

On the way home that night, I stocked up on alcohol for my father at Lardner's, then stopped in a drugstore for violet mints and a pack of cigarettes for myself. I rarely smoked, but when something had me riled up I did enjoy a cigarette or two. I tried to put Leonard Polk out of my mind, though the image of him touching himself in the cave had excited me. It was what I'd always hoped to see in all my spying on Randy, just a little glimpse of him being obscene. I shook my head gruffly, as though the image of the boy would get dislodged from my brain, scuttle out my ears, and leave me alone. I wasn't a pedophile—a word I remembered from Latin class years earlier. Browsing the cosmetics aisle, I found a new shade of lipstick—a glossy, blood red: Passionate Lover. I slipped it into my pocket. The sleeves of my coat—it had been my mother's— were long and wide at the cuffs, so I could easily lift almost anything. I've been good at stealing all my life. I still pinch things from the grocery store from time to time—dental floss, a head of garlic, a pack of gum. I don't see the great harm in it. I figure I've given away or lost enough over my lifetime to even out my debts.

That night I did pay for, along with a humiliating package of sanitary napkins, a small compact of pressed powder, the lightest shade they had: Snow Queen. A fashion magazine on the rack at the checkout counter caught my eye, too. The cover showed a bony, melancholy woman pouting in a gray fur hat, looking upward as though at some disapproving statesman. "Isn't it romantic . . ." it said on the cover. The fur, I thought, looked like a house cat. I plunked down the money. The salesgirl handled my package of sanitary napkins as though they were already soiled, pushing it with her fingertips into the paper bag she propped open, cavelike on the counter. She slipped the magazine into its own flat paper bag, which I liked. Back inside the Dodge, I arranged all the brown paper packages on the passenger seat. The bottles of booze, the napkins, the magazine. I took the lipstick from my pocket and applied it liberally over my mouth, blind. When I got home my father said, "Whose rosy ass have you been kissing?" Then he plucked the bottles from under my arm. "Not your color," he sneered, padding back to the kitchen. Like Leonard Polk, I didn't say a word.

TUESDAY

A grown woman is like a coyote—she can get by on very little. Men are more like house cats. Leave them alone for too long and they'll die of sadness. Over the years I've grown to love men for this weakness. I've tried to respect them as people, full of feelings, fluctuating and beautiful from day to day. I have listened, soothed, wiped the tears away. But as a young woman in X-ville, I had no idea that other people—men or women—felt things as deeply as I did. I had no compassion for anyone unless his suffering allowed me to indulge in my own. My development was very stunted in this regard. Did I know that the boys at Moorehead—like prisoners around the world, so it seems—might be being pressured by guards to fight one another for sport at night, that they were made to defecate in their pillowcases, routinely forced to strip by the corrections officers who spat on them, beat them up, tied them down, humiliated and abused them? Rumors surfaced, but their implications didn't register. I barely even noticed that the boys were handcuffed by the guards when they were escorted to and from the visitation room. Why should my heart ache for anyone but myself? If anyone was trapped and suffering and abused, it was me. I was the only one whose pain was real. Mine.

Had that Tuesday at work been a typical Tuesday, I would have spent it idle at my desk, watching the clock, sketching out my escape from X-ville for the hundredth time. If I left the Dodge at a filling station in Rutland—at a gas pump even—and just walked away, my head covered with a scarf, and simply boarded the next train to New York from Rutland station without anyone noticing me, people in X-ville might suspect I'd been kidnapped by some modern-day highwayman, expect to find me headless somewhere across the country, dumped by the side of the road or in some gruesome cheap motel scene. "Poor Eileen," my dad would sniffle. I imagined. I dreamed. But that Tuesday I wasn't thinking of any of those things. Instead, I thought of Rebecca, whose arrival at Moorehead seemed like a sweet promise from God that my situation could improve. I was no longer alone. Finally, here was a friend I could admire and open up to, who could understand me, my plight, and help me rise above it. She was my ticket to a new life. And she was so clever and beautiful, I thought, the embodiment of all my fantasies for myself. I knew I couldn't be her, but I could be with her, and that was enough to thrill me. When she arrived that Tuesday, bustling in from the frigid morning snowdrifts, she whirled off her coat as though in slow motion—this is how I remember it—and shook it like a bullfighter as she strode up the corridor toward me, hair rippling behind her, eyes like daggers shooting down straight through my heart to my guts. She was pure magic. Her coat was a crimson wool swing coat with a gray fur collar. It was the same kind of fur I'd seen on the magazine cover. I stood up nervously when she got closer, expectantly, as though I were her assistant, her secretary, her maidservant. She nodded politely to the old ladies in the office and caught my eye on her way back to the locker room, which is where I followed her.

I had dressed for the occasion. From my mother's wardrobe I'd composed an ensemble I thought made me look more cosmopolitan—navy blue, of course. I even wore an old fake pearl necklace. I'd brushed my hair and applied my lipstick more carefully that morning, dabbing at the edges of my mouth with the pressed powder so it stayed in place. I remember this because, as I've said, I was obsessed with my looks. Ironically, despite my preoccupation, my appearance on most days was slovenly, offensive even. "Disgraceful," said my father. I thought, though, that I looked much better that morning. "Fancy" was probably the word I would have used. In any case, I followed the sound of Rebecca's delicate heels ticktocking across the linoleum floor, and in the locker room she turned to me, saying, "Can you help me open my locker again? I can't seem to do it." She held up her long hands and twiddled her fingers in her skin-tight dove-gray leather gloves. "All thumbs," she said. This helplessness was some kind of flirtation, I think, a manipulation of roles to keep me at her service, though I couldn't have understood that at the time. I was perfectly pleased to spin the dial with finesse, blushing as though my talent for opening a locker was a sign of great virtue.

"But how do you know my combination?" she asked.

The locker opened with a sharp clank. I stepped back with pride.

"All the combinations are the same," I told her. "But don't tell the old ladies. They'd all have strokes."

"You're funny," said Rebecca, wrinkling her nose. She carried her briefcase and a small leather purse from which she transferred her cigarettes into the pocket of her sweater. Her sweater looked so soft—it must have been angora, cashmere—it seemed to float around her like cotton candy. That day, just the second time I'd seen her, she wore all different shades of purple—lavender, violet, mauve. If she'd been any other woman, I would have discounted her as a hussy since her dress was so formfitting, so elegant, completely inappropriate for work in a prison. This wasn't some romantic evening, after all. But Rebecca was no hussy. She was divine. I gazed at the elegant bend in her arm as she hung her coat up in her locker.

"I know it's wrong to wear fur," she said, seeing me stare. "But I can't help myself. Chinchilla." She petted the collar of her coat inside the locker as though it were a cat.

"No, no," I said. "I was just admiring your cigarette case."

"Oh, thanks," she said. "It was a gift. See, it has my initials." She pulled it out from her pocket and showed me. It was a striated silver cigarette case, the size of a pack of cards. I wanted to ask, "A gift from whom?" but held my tongue. She opened it and offered me a cigarette. They were Pall Malls, thick and filterless and the harshest cigarettes I've ever smoked. I was on them for several years later in life, always rather moved by the unexpected beauty of the motto written across their logo—a shield between two lions—*Per aspera ad astra.* Through the thorns to the stars. That described my plight to a tee, I thought back then, though of course it didn't. Rebecca lit my cigarette with a flourish of the wrist. That thrilled me. When she lit her own, she tilted her head like a thoughtful bird, sucking in her cheeks just slightly. I remember all this with precise acuity. I was infatuated with her, clearly. And I felt in a way that just by knowing her, I was graduating out of my misery. I was making some progress.

"I don't usually smoke," I said, choking a bit, though I had a pack of Salems in my purse.

"Nasty habit," Rebecca said, "but that's why I like it. Not very becoming of a lady, though. It turns your teeth yellow. See?" And she leaned in toward me, a finger hooked on her bottom lip, stretching her gums apart to show me the inside of her mouth. "See the discoloration? That's coffee and cigarettes. And red wine." But her teeth were perfect—small, and white as paper. Her gums were pink and glossy, and the skin on her face was miraculously smooth, like a baby's, flawless and radiant and light. You see women like this from time to time—beautiful as children, unscathed, wide-eyed. Her cheeks were full but firm, buoyant. Her lips were pale pink and bow-shaped, but chapped. By that slight imperfection I felt subtly disappointed, and yet redeemed.

"I don't drink coffee," I said, "so I guess I should have perfect teeth. But they're all rotted due to my propensity for sweets." This word, *propensity,* was not in my day-to-day vocabulary back then, and it was awkward to say it, and I worried Rebecca would see through my attempt to sound smart and laugh at me. But what she said next made my heart nearly burst in ecstasy.

"Well, I wouldn't think to look at you!" She smiled wide, putting her hands on her hips. "You're positively tiny! I admire that so much, how petite you are." That was heaven. And then she went on. "I'm thin, too, of course, but tall and thin. Being tall has its advantages, but most men are just too short for me. Have you noticed, or am I imagining, men these days are getting shorter and shorter?" I nodded, rolling my eyes in solidarity although I couldn't possibly answer her question. She put her purse in the locker and shut it. "They're like little boys. Hard to find a real man, or at least a man that looks like one. To tell you the truth," she began—I held my breath—"I've forgotten my locker combination. But I won't trouble you again. You have better things to do, I'm sure. I have it written down in my desk. Now to find my way back to that office they gave me yesterday. I won't ask for help with that either. I should be able to follow my nose. The smell of ancient leather." She paused. "There's that old couch in Bradley's office next door to mine, you know, the fainting couch. How Freudian," she said, widening her eyes sarcastically. "How outdated, I mean."

"Bradley?" I'd forgotten Dr. Frye's replacement, Dr. Bradley Morris, with the bald head. Was he scrawny? Was he a real man by Rebecca's standards? I had no idea. Was she involved with him somehow?

"The new headshrinker," said Rebecca. "To tell you the truth"—there was that phrase again—"I don't think his head's been shrunk down quite enough, if you know what I mean." It took me a moment to compute. Was this a comment on his proportions? I was like a pubescent boy, fumbling for words. Seeing my blank look, Rebecca said, almost apologetically, "Big headed, I mean. But I'm kidding. He seems like a perfectly nice person."

I cursed myself for being so slow, so dense. I wanted to explain that I was intelligent, well-read, that I'd been to college, that I knew who Freud was, that I didn't belong in that prison, that I was exceptional, I was cool, but it seemed petty to defend myself.

"I've never been inside that office," I said instead. "Dr. Frye always kept it locked, and only the boys ever went in there." I didn't have a quick wit like she did. I was graceless, pedestrian and dull. Apart from my size, I couldn't impress Rebecca at all. I should have asked her about herself, her plans at Moorehead, how she got interested in prison work, what her goals were, her dreams and ambitions, but my mind didn't work that way back then. I had no manners. I didn't know how to make friends.

"Come visit any time," she said, nevertheless. "Unless, of course, the door is closed. Which means I'm with one of the boys."

"Thank you," I said. I meant to sound professional. "I'll stop in next time I'm passing by."

"Eileen," she said, pointing her finger at my gut. "Right?"

I blushed deeply, and nodded.

"Call me Rebecca," she said, winking, and ticktocked away.

I could have swooned with embarrassment and exhilaration. She'd remembered my name. That meant a great deal to me. I'd forgotten all about Leonard Polk's file. Earlier that morning I'd hoped Rebecca would give it back in case Mrs. Stephens found it missing and questioned me about it. But what did I care now? I had a real friend—someone who knew me, wanted my company, someone I felt connected to. I would replay that conversation with Rebecca, and every other one I had with her, again and again for years afterward as I came to terms with what would happen in the days ahead. At that moment, I felt happy. Meeting Rebecca was like learning to dance, discovering jazz. It was like falling in love for the first time. I had always been waiting for my future to erupt around me in an avalanche of glory, and now I felt it was really happening. Rebecca was all it took. *Per aspera ad astra.*

I had to set aside my reflections on the brief exchange with Rebecca that morning since it was a day for visitors and I had to work. There was already a gaggle of tearful mothers and small children sitting impatiently on the chairs in the waiting room by the time I got back to my desk. I remember one of the mothers had come to see her twelve-year-old son who had burned down the family house. He was a short, full-cheeked, brown-haired boy with duck feet and the beginnings of a mustache on his upper lip. I paid close attention to those strange hairs growing there. His reminded me of my own upper lip. I used to pluck those hairs routinely with tweezers. All the time I wasted plucking my face at the bathroom mirror, I could have written a book.

I could have learned to speak French. My eyebrows were always thin and weak, so I never had to pluck them. I've heard having weak brows is a sign of indecisiveness. I prefer to think it is the mark of an open heart, an appreciation of possibility. In that fashion magazine with the cat-fur hat, I'd read how some women draw their eyebrows with a pencil to be thick and dark. Ridiculous, I'd thought. Standing outside the visitation room, I tapped the bony points of my hips with the butt of my fist, a habit which assured me, somehow, of my superiority, my great strength.

When the little arsonist was seated across from his mother at the table, he did what all the younger boys did. They crossed their arms and faced the wall, steeled themselves, pouty and squinty, unreachably cool. But once they took one look at their mothers' pained faces, they burst into tears. The arsonist burst into tears. His mother pulled a handkerchief from her pocket and handed it across the table. Randy bolted into the room, holding one firm open palm in front of the boy, blocking the mother's extended hand with the other. "Sorry," he said, monotonously. "That's not allowed."

"You can hug him when you leave," I chimed in, "but you can't give him anything. It's for security, to keep the children safe." I had some practiced speech like that.

Of course, the rule wasn't there to protect children from handkerchiefs. I knew what I'd said just wasn't true. But I was young enough, and had been enslaved enough by my public school education and my father and his Catholicism, and was frightened enough of being punished or questioned or singled out, that I obeyed every rule there was at Moorehead. I followed every procedure. I clocked in and out every day on time. I was a shoplifter, a pervert, you might say, and a liar, of course, but nobody knew that. I would enforce the rules all the more, for didn't that prove that I lived by a high moral code? That I was good? That I couldn't possibly want to hike up my skirt and move my runny bowels all over the linoleum floor? I understood perfectly that the rule that prohibited parents from giving gifts to their children was to keep the boys in a state of desperation. The warden proselytized at every possible occasion. His logic was quite sound, I believed. Only a desperate soul would feel remorse for his sins, and if the remorse was deep enough, the boy would surrender and hence he'd be pliable, finally willing to be transformed, so the warden said. The last people on Earth I'd put in charge of transforming anyone were that warden and Dr. Frye, or Dr. Morris—though I never knew him— or, sorry to say, Rebecca. She may have been the worst of all. But I speak with hindsight. At first, yes, Rebecca was a dream to me, she was magic, she was powerful and everything I wanted to be. So no handkerchiefs. No toys, no comics or magazines or books. Let the children cry. No one was offering me any tenderness, after all. Why should any of those boys have any more or better than I had? I lowered my gaze down to Randy's crotch as he walked back out of the visitation room. He just sucked his teeth and sighed.

"I'm fine," said the little arsonist, wiping his face with the hem of his smock. His mother whimpered. I remember she wore a white scarf, and when the scarf fell away I saw that the skin on her neck was raised and welted in pink and yellow scars from burns. The visitation was over when the clock showed that seven minutes had passed—visits were seven minutes long and I suppose that had some religious significance—at which point I waved to James, who delivered the arsonist back to the rec room or wherever and brought in the next boy. Randy stood around in the doorway while I collected a final signature from the weepy mother on her way out. Her vitriol came through in her penmanship. While the earlier signature was clean, careful, the outgoing signature was violent, jagged, and rushed. It was always like that. Everybody was broken. Everybody suffered. Each of those sad mothers wore some kind of scar—a badge of hurt to attest to the heartbreak that her child, her own flesh and blood, was growing up in prison. I tried my best to ignore all that. I had to if I was going to act normal, maintain my flat composure. When I was very upset, hot and shaking, I had a particular way of controlling myself. I found an empty room and grit my teeth and pinched my nipples while kicking the air like a cancan dancer until I felt foolish and ashamed. That always did the trick.

Something struck me as I watched Randy scratch his elbow, then lean against the door frame of the visitation room: I was no longer in love with him. Looking at him with eyes now glazed over in my new affection for Rebecca, he seemed like a nobody, a face in a crowd, gray and meaningless like an old newspaper clipping of a story I'd read so many times, it no longer impressed me. Love can be like that. It can vanish in an instant. It's happened since, too. A lover has left the warm rapture of my bed to get a glass of water and returned only to find me cold, uninterested, empty, a stranger. Love can reappear, too, but never again unscathed. The second round is inevitably accompanied by doubt, intention, self-disgust. But that is neither here nor there.

When James returned, the boy he was guiding up the hall was, to my great surprise, Leonard Polk. Leonard walked casually, almost jauntily with his hands cuffed behind his back. He was taller than I expected, and loose limbed with that awkward softness young men have before their bodies harden. There was a strange bounce in his step. His face was bright and relaxed, awake and serene in a way no other boy's face had ever seemed, a loose reservedness which I found myself admiring. He looked pleased, impenetrable, and cold as though nothing could ever disturb him, and yet still as innocent as the silent creature I'd seen earlier touching himself absentmindedly on his cot in the cave. I searched for something in his face, anything his mask of contentment might betray, but there was nothing. He was a genius in that sense—a master. His was the best mask I'd ever seen.

James ushered him by the glass wall of the waiting area. When they passed Mrs. Polk on the other side, Leonard smiled. I imagined this boy in his parents' darkened bedroom, standing over his sleeping father with a kitchen knife, moonlight flickering on the blade like lightning as he brought it down hard and fast, tearing across the man's throat. Could this strange, supple creature have done such a thing? Randy took him into the visitation room, set him in the chair, undid his cuffs, and stood in the doorway.

"Mrs. Polk?" I called out.

The woman rose from her seat in the waiting area and came toward me. I remember this first vision of her with excellent clarity, though she was utterly unremarkable. She wore sharply creased black trousers, tight around her swollen thighs. Her sweater looked like an afghan blanket, the different colored squares lined up over her chest and large gut. She was repugnant, I thought, in her fat and dishevelment. She was not an obese woman, but she had quite a paunch and seemed bloated and tired and nervous. She walked stiffly, shifting from side to side with each step as some fat people do, and carried a brown coat over her arm, no purse. As she entered the room I noticed some white pieces of fluff stuck in the back of her frizzy hair, which was pulled tight into a bun. Her lipstick was a cheap and insincere fuchsia. I stared steadily at her face, trying to determine what sort of intelligence was there. Since she was overweight, I assumed she was an idiot—I still tend to judge those types as gluttons, fools—but her eyes were clear blue, sharp, with the same strange twist as her son's. I saw the resemblance in the eyes, the freckles, the pouty lips. She looked nervous handing her coat to Randy as I patted her down. My palm landed with a thud on the small of her back, which was soft and wide. I stifled an odd impulse I had to embrace her, to try to comfort her a little. She seemed so dowdy, so pitiful, like a sow awaiting slaughter.

"All set," I told her. She took her coat back from Randy and sat across the table from Leonard, or Lee, as he was called. Mrs. Polk was shifty-eyed. The boy just smiled. I looked from mother to son. If Rebecca's theory of Oedipus was correct, perhaps I had grossly misjudged what kind of women young men found attractive those days, because Mrs. Polk was nobody I could imagine anyone would kill for. Then again, maybe Lee Polk was out of his mind. It was impossible to tell what he might be thinking. His mask didn't waver. It was not my stony, flat mask of death, nor was it the stiff, cheerful posturing popular among housewives and other sad and deranged women. It was not the cutthroat bad boy mask set to ward off potential threats with the promise of violence and hot rage. Neither was it the lily-sweet bashfulness of men who pretend they're so weak, so sensitive, they would crumble if anyone ever challenged them even a little. Lee's look of calm contentment was an odd mask, peculiar in its falseness as it hardly looked fake at all.

In an effort to keep from crying, it seemed, Mrs. Polk pinched her eyes shut and exhaled. After a moment she folded her hands and placed them on the table, opened her mouth to speak. But then, from down the hall, loud clicking footsteps made us all stop and turn. It was Rebecca. Here she came strutting toward us. She carried her notebook in one hand, a cigarette in the other. Mrs. Polk, Randy and I all froze as she approached, a wobbly silhouette at first, and then a vision in lavender, loose russet hair bouncing around her shoulders. When she got closer, she was serious, quiet, and I saw that her fingers clutched her notebook like the legs of a lizard grappling a rock. There was something tense about her. She tried to smile, her eyes nervous and glittering. She was human and neurotic underneath that beauty, after all. That was comforting. The coincidence of her timing struck me. Had she invited Mrs. Polk? What had Rebecca done with Leonard's file? She nodded to me and Randy and stood between us in the open doorway, holding the note-book close to her body. As she watched mother and son sitting there, she wrote continuously without looking down at the paper, ashing her cigarette absentmindedly at the floor as it burned down to her fingers.

Mrs. Polk kept her nose in the air as she spoke. I don't remember what she said to him, but it wasn't much. Such and such about his cousins, maybe something about money. Noth-ing important. Her son remained silent. At some point Mrs. Polk sighed, frustrated, and stared off at the wall in exaspera-tion. When I tried to peek under Rebecca's hand to read what she'd been writing, it looked like chicken scratch. Since I'd never seen shorthand before, I assumed it was simply nonsense, lines on a paper she'd made so as to appear that she was taking notes. I didn't understand it. Dr. Frye, when he'd come to observe the family visits, had never taken notes. I wondered, of course, why Rebecca was there at all. Dr. Bradley never made a single appearance.

After a minute of silence, the boy staring at his mother's hands on the table between them, Mrs. Polk lifted her face, looked Lee straight in the eyes. Her wrinkles were long and saggy, as though her face had once been bigger, fuller, but had been deflated, leaving deep folds dug like trenches. She began to cry. If I heard what she said, I don't remember it precisely, but I assumed the gist of it was, "How could you do this to me?" her voice plaintive and soft. Then she cleared her throat and grunted aloud. Her hands were small and red and cracked, I saw as she pulled out a tissue. She blew her nose into it, then balled it up like an angry child and stuffed it violently back in her pocket. In that moment, she reminded me of my mother and her quick switches, how one minute she'd be sunshine and singsong and the next she'd be cursing in the basement at the laundry, kicking at the walls. It was that kind of duplicity: talking one way but acting another. Rebecca had stopped scribbling and was leaning on one leg, twisting her opposite heel into the floor, stubbing out her cigarette. Randy looked at that arrant, flirtatious foot out of the corner of his eye, or at least I think he did. Rebecca had her pencil in her mouth, and when I turned to face her, I saw her tongue well up and a bubble of saliva burst as her teeth closed down on the pencil's eraser tip. To see inside her open mouth like that, the mouth of a child, clean, pink, bubbling with youth and beauty, hurt me deeply. I burned with envy. Of course Randy would choose Rebecca over me. She was easy to love. I donned my death mask, bristling underneath with shame. When Lee's seven minutes were up, I knocked on the door frame and Randy motioned to Rebecca to step aside so that Mrs. Polk could exit. But first Mrs. Polk made sure to let a few tears splat on the table, and then said, more to us than to her son, "I blame myself." Lee looked up at the clock, unfazed.

I followed Mrs. Polk back out into the office, but turned to watch as Rebecca stepped into the visitation room and slid the mother's now vacant chair up close to Lee's. She spoke to him, and his grin faded. His head bowed as he listened. It looked like they had an intimate rapport, but when could that have developed? Rebecca had just arrived at Moorehead, and already she was leaning in close toward him, bending her face down below his, her eyebrows raised, eyes sparkling and searching up at his. I guided Mrs. Polk toward the counter, handed her a pen, and watched her sign her name: Rita P. Polk. It wasn't an angry penmanship. It was casual, unconcerned—irrelevant. She didn't look back at her son, just blinked heavily, sighed as though clocking out at work, then swung her coat up around her shoulders and walked back down the hall. I imagined her returning to her home to crochet another terrible sweater, swear and grind her teeth every time she missed a stitch. I felt sorry for her. I knew instinctively that the woman, this widow, had no other children.

Following protocol, I signaled to James to prepare for the next boy's visit. But Rebecca was still talking with Lee. Lee had turned away from her and laid his hands across the table. I walked into the room to tell them to clear out, suddenly full of courage. I saw clearly then the word tattooed on Lee's fingers. It was "LOVE." That disturbed me deeply. I said nothing, but watched as the boy sniffed, and gruffly swept a tear off his cheek with the butt of his hand. Rebecca put her hand on his shoulder. And then she put another hand on his knee below the table. This, in plain sight, and with me standing there, she dared get so close to the boy, touching him like that, leaning over enough that he might simply lift his gaze to peer down the front of her blouse, that he could easily raise his chin to meet his lips with hers. I stared disbelievingly. Did they really not see me? How was it that the boy didn't fidget and squirm? He seemed quite comfortable, really. How could I interrupt them? I stared at the floor. When James returned with the next child, he knocked lightly on the door frame.

"I'm sorry," I managed to say, "but we need the room."

"Of course," said Rebecca. Then she spoke quietly to Lee. "We can talk more in my office. You want a Coke?" Lee nodded. "I'll get you a Coke," she said. As they got up, Randy came in with handcuffs. "Oh no," Rebecca said. "That isn't necessary." And she took Lee by the arm back down the hall, leaving James stunned and blushing until I cleared my throat, pointed at the new boy at his side. I watched Lee's now tepid gait as they walked away. It was so very odd, and it angered me because I couldn't understand what had happened and because Rebecca seemed to care more for this Lee Polk than she did for me.

For the remaining visiting hours, I replayed the scene again and again: Rebecca leaning so close to the boy, her hair spilling across her back and shoulders, so near that surely he could smell the scent of her shampoo, her perfume, her breath, her sweat. And she must have felt him responding to her, the tension in his shoulder building under her hand, chest rising and falling with every breath, the heat coming off of him. But then to put her hand on his knee, I couldn't imagine what that could mean. If I hadn't been there, if they'd been alone, would her hand have begun to knead the boy's thigh, travel up along his inseam, gently cup his private parts? Would he have swept Rebecca's hair away and would his lips have parted as he inhaled the scent of her neck? Would he have kissed her neck, held her face between his almost manly hands, run his fingers, LOVE, over her slender wrists and up her arms to her breasts, kissing her, pulling her toward him, feeling all of her, warm and soft and all there in his arms? Would they have done all that?

I fantasized as best I could, jealous first of Rebecca, then of Lee, and switching back and forth as I considered their roles and how they'd betrayed me, since already I'd decided that Rebecca was mine. She was my consolation prize. She was my ticket out. Her behavior with this boy really threatened all that. Was this what they'd taught Rebecca to do at Harvard—to win these boys over with charm and affection, then educate them? Perhaps this was some new way, I tried to think, some kind of liberated thinking. But the more I considered it, the crazier it seemed. What was she saying to him? How close could they have become in a matter of days? What had Rebecca done or said to earn Lee's trust? I imagined the scene back in Rebecca's office. I wanted to know what was happening. Visitors came and went. I felt sick with abandonment. I was so very dramatic. I figured I ought to leave then and there, to spare myself any more misery. Once again I imagined driving my Dodge off the cliffs and down onto the rocks by the ocean. Wouldn't that be thrilling? Wouldn't that be the way to show them all that I was brave, that I was tired of following their rules? I would rather die than stand around, be among them, drive on their nice streets, or sit in their nice prison—no, not me. I nearly cried standing there. Even Randy, beautiful and smelling of smoke and polished leather, couldn't cheer me.

But then I saw it—the notebook. Rebecca had left it on the ledge of the window behind the table. And so when the last

visitor left, I snatched it and walked down through the corri-
dors toward Rebecca's office, quite pleased that I'd found such
a good excuse to poke my nose in. I hoped that Lee was still in
there with her and I could catch the two of them red-handed.
I don't know what I was expecting to find, but I put my ear to
the door, straining to hear sighs and moans, or whatever people
sounded like when they made love. I'd never heard my parents
make love. If they made love, they did it silently, like bank
robbers, like surgeons. I heard, felt nothing. I knocked on
Rebecca's office door.

"Oh, Eileen," she chirped when she opened it. "Are you all
right?"

I took a step back, feeling like a child, a nuisance. I extended
the notebook toward her. She took it, thanked me, said she
hoped I hadn't read it.

"Of course I didn't," I told her. I couldn't have, anyway—
that chicken scratch was indecipherable.

"I'm only teasing," she laughed. "My book of secrets." She
clutched the notebook to her chest. She had a way of laughing,
head thrown back, jaw cut so smooth and white and hard, as if
it were rimmed in porcelain, eyes first pinched in ecstasy, then
wide and wild—devilish eyes, beautiful eyes—then face lowered, beaming with affection or derision, I couldn't tell. I turned
to leave, but she stopped me by laying a hand on my shoulder.
This sent chills down my spine. Nobody had touched me like
that in years. I forgave her instantly for betraying me with the
boy. I could hear him inside clearing his throat.

"Say," she began. "Would you be up for a drink after work

tonight? I don't know anyone in this darn town, and I would love to treat you to a cocktail, if you're game."

The way she talked was so canned, so scripted, it inspired me to be just as canned. "Say." People didn't really talk like that. "A cocktail." If she seems insincere, she was. She was terribly pretentious, and later, in hindsight, I felt she'd insulted my intelligence by selling me her scripted bunk. "Darn it all." But at the time I felt I was being invited into an elite world of beautiful people. I was flattered. And I was flustered. I had never received such an invitation in my life, so this was as thrilling and terrifying as hearing someone tell me, "I love you." I was full of gratitude. I didn't think of my father, my evening duties, any of that. I just said, "OK."

"OK? I've twisted your arm?" Rebecca joked. She let the door swing open a bit. I could see Lee Polk sitting in a chair in front of her desk, looking through a large book of pictures. When he saw me he held the book up to hide his face.

"Sure," I said. "How about O'Hara's around seven?" I was shocked by how easily the words came out of my mouth. I hoped my death mask had not betrayed me, prayed I sounded cool. O'Hara's was just a dark dive with hard wooden booths, a place working-class locals went. The usual clientele were cops and firefighters and men from the shipyard who stank powerfully of sweat and salt. Two single women alone at a place like O'Hara's would inspire strange looks, or worse. But I was game. I was a peon and I was a child, but I was not a coward. "It's the only bar in town," I added.

"Sounds perfect," Rebecca whispered. She made a playful,

conniving face. "I'll see you there. With bells on! Is that the expression?" She shut the door.

So that was something. You have to remember I was what you'd call a loser, a square, a ding-a-ling. I was a wet blanket. I had never gone out at night. Even in college, the dances were chaperoned, and among the girls in my dorm was the sense that to stray from the flock meant you were a floozy, a prostitute, a sinner, greedy, disgraceful, a threat to civilization, bad. Setting foot in a place like O'Hara's would have been frowned upon. But if Rebecca was doing it, I would do it, too. What did I have to lose? I left work early to give myself time to go home and change. I figured I had to put on a dress, do my makeup, find my mother's perfume. Getting dolled up was completely silly, of course. You can always tell something when a woman is overdressed—either she's an outsider, or she's insane.

I wasn't a stranger at O'Hara's. Sandy, the bartender, was a thick and slow-moving man with deep acne scars and a gold cross, a flirt. I'd been there plenty of times, first as a young girl sent in to fetch my father from an extended after-work beer with his fellow cops while my mother waited in the car, and later as a sober escort when he'd get drunk and refuse to accept a ride home. I remember one autumn evening in particular when I was home from college for the weekend, my mother sent me to the bar to pick up my dad. Driving home along the moonlit streets, he laid his head on my shoulder, told me I was a good girl, that he loved me, that he was sorry he couldn't be better, that he knew I deserved a real father. It moved me at first, but then his hand went to my breast. I beat him off easily. "Quit fussing, Joanie," he said, slumping back in his seat. I never mentioned it to anyone.

Before I left Moorehead that day, I finished the vermouth in my locker, and then I drove to the liquor store for more gin and beer for my father and another bottle of vermouth for me. I'd need a drink before meeting Rebecca at O'Hara's, I was that nervous. At home, I set the bag of booze down next to my father, who was sleeping in his recliner with his face smushed against the cushion, eyebrows raised, forehead clenched, body twisted and clunky under the flannel robe. I ran up into the shower as silently as I could. Let me be clear about this: I was not a lesbian. But I was attracted to Rebecca, yearned for her attention and approval, and I admired her. You could call it a crush. Rebecca might as well have been Marlon Brando, James Dean. Elvis. Marilyn Monroe. In such company, any normal person would want to look right, smell good. I worried what might happen if Rebecca wanted to lean in close to me the way she did with Lee. What if she could smell that I was menstruating, and that I hadn't washed? What if she smelled it clear as day but didn't say anything? How, then, would I know whether or not she'd smelled it, and how ought I act to pretend I didn't know Rebecca smelled it? My poor nether regions. My body's readiness to bear a child seemed classless and vulgar to me, and I felt that if Rebecca had any idea that I was menstruating, I would be humiliated. I would die. These were my thoughts as I scrubbed.

Once I got out of the shower, I put my hair up in a towel and listened for the sound of my father fussing downstairs, hoping

I could sneak out without having to talk to him. The prettiest song I'd ever heard was the silence of the house that night, just the pipes gently clanging, the wind howling outside. I dressed per usual from my mother's closet, choosing what I thought would look nice—a black wool dress with a high neck, a golden broach of leaves in a circle. I brushed my hair, which was still wet, put on my new shade of lipstick, pulled on a fresh pair of stolen stockings, then stood perplexed at my mother's closet full of shoes, which were all one-half size too big. I didn't own any shoes besides my beat-up loafers and my snow boots, so I wore the snow boots. They made me feel oafish and silly, but it was winter, after all. I chose a black cape from my mother's collection of winter coats, grabbed my purse, shut the door softly, and ran out to the car. It was so cold that by the time I was out of the driveway, my hair had frozen in strips. They rattled like dead insects by my ears while I drove with the windows up, holding my breath. I parked under a broken streetlamp across from O'Hara's, reapplied my lipstick in the rearview mirror and skidded over the ice to the bar.

When I opened the door to the dark, warm din, there was Rebecca, legs crossed high on a bar stool, facing a booth full of scruffy young men. They all seemed to be sweating a little, smiling, nervous as kittens and swirling their beers. Each wore the customary heavy wool jacket in blue, gray, or red plaid, and a hat—either a tight-fitting knit cap or the kind with the flaps that come down over the ears—and their faces were red and chapped from windburn and sunburn and cold. The four of them listened as Rebecca went on about something I couldn't hear.

"Oh, Eileen!" she exclaimed, interrupting herself. Her voice sang through the smoke and Christmas carols playing on the jukebox—Perry Como or Frank Sinatra, I couldn't tell the difference. The booth of men fell still, all eyes on Rebecca and none on me as I walked toward her. Nevertheless, I felt important, like a celebrity, even. Rebecca swirled around on her bar stool, ignoring her audience of admirers, and waved to me as though we were good friends coming together again after a dramatic period of separation, as though she were leaning over the rail of some romantic ocean liner, me a sight for sore eyes, so much to talk about. She was drinking a martini, and I studied the way she held the glass, which fingers she used, pointer and pinky raised in the air like at an elegant soiree. She was utterly out of place at O'Hara's. She wore her same outfit from work, but she had tied her hair back into a braid. Her coat lay across the seat of the stool next to her. As I approached her, she turned and pulled the coat off and added it to the pile of fur hat and leather gloves on the seat to her left. "I was saving both these seats," she said, "in case someone tried to sit down, know what I mean? Well, have a seat. What'll you have?"

"I'll have a beer, I guess," I said.

"A beer, how neat," said Rebecca. This was quaint to her, this beer. It was clear that she was from what you'd call an affluent family, so affluent that she seemed to care not at all what anybody made of her. She was motivated by something other than money—personal values, I suppose. But while she had the unmistakable ease and refinement of someone from the upper class, or at least a good deal higher in class than me and the fine patrons of O'Hara's, there was also something earthy about her. Her hair, especially in its red color, its roughness, its wild beauty, kept her from seeming like a snob. Sandy walked toward us, drying his hands with a rag. He slapped it over his shoulder, put his elbow down on the bar, and leaned in toward Rebecca.

"So what's next, sweetheart?" he said, ignoring me. Rebecca barely looked at him. To my surprise, she put her hand over mine. Hers was hot and light.

"Oh, my stars, you're absolutely frozen," she said. "And your hair is wet." She turned to Sandy. "One beer, please, and maybe also a little whiskey to warm up my girl. What say, huh?" She looked at me and smiled. "I'm so glad you made it out." She gave my hand a squeeze and leaned back as though to survey me, a funny look on her face. As I unwrapped my cape, she said something like, "Oh my, you look very glamorous."

I blushed. I was not glamorous. She was being kind, and that embarrassed me. I drank my whiskey. "I thought I'd have a hard time finding the place, but here it is," she sang, pointing out the stuffed hammerhead on the wall. "Isn't it funny? It's sort of sad, actually. Well, not so sad." She was babbling. The men kept standing up and leaning on the bar next to her, but she didn't seem to notice them. Somebody played "Mr. Lonely" on the jukebox, the Bobby Vinton song. I always hated that song. I drank my beer in small quick sips as Rebecca complained about the cold, the icy roads, the New England winters. I was grateful just to sit there and be with her and listen to her talk.

After a minute or two, her eyes darted around my face. "You feel all right?"

"Oh yeah, I'm fine," I said. Rebecca looked at me expectantly, so I thought of anything I could tell her. "There's something wrong with my car," is all I came up with in the moment. "So I have to drive with the windows down or else it fills with smoke."

"That sounds positively awful. Have another whiskey. I insist." She motioned to Sandy, gestured at our empty glasses. "Can't your husband get that fixed for you?"

"Oh, I'm not married," I told her, embarrassed that Sandy could hear me. But of course I wasn't married. She was teasing me.

"I don't want to assume. Some people are funny about bachelorettes." She spoke carefully. "Personally, I don't see what the big deal is. I'm single myself." She tickled the stem of her glass with her nails. "I'm just not interested in marriage."

"Don't tell that to those guys," I said, impressed by my own wit. I'd been keeping an eye on the men in the booth as they mumbled secretively to one another, seeming to be weighing their options, planning something. They all looked familiar—they could have been friends of Joanie's—but I didn't know their names.

"You're funny, you know that?" Rebecca went on. "I've always been single. And when I have a guy around me, it's just for fun, and it's brief. I don't stay long anywhere, with anything. It's sort of my modus vivendi, or my pathology—depending on who I'm talking to." She paused, looked at me. "Who *am* I talking to? Who am I babbling at?" she widened her eyes comically.

"Eileen," I answered innocently, then blushed as I realized she'd only been making a joke of my reticence.

I was glad Rebecca wasn't married or just out to find a husband. That's what girls did back then—hunted for husbands. I wonder if she ever did get married. I like imagining her with a short, nebbish sort of husband—a Jew most likely—because I think that's what she'd need, someone intelligent and serious and neurotic, unimpressed by her gregariousness and sparkling repartee. Someone controlling. Sandy set new drinks down in front of me.

"This is all on my tab," Rebecca said, circling her finger at my glasses.

"It's on theirs," said Sandy, nodding toward the table of men.

"Oh, God, no," said Rebecca. "That won't do. Here, as a retainer." She slid a twenty-dollar bill across the counter. Sandy let it sit there and made her another martini, probably the second martini he'd made in his life. I remember these scenes very clearly, and I recount them because I think it says something of how Rebecca appealed to me as a young woman, how she managed to gain my trust. First she solicited my envy, then she worked to extinguish it. By completely dismissing the men at the bar, and then men in general, she put to rest my earlier suspicions about her relationship with Lee Polk, and tempered my fear that she might steal Randy away from me. She sipped her drink, poked at the twenty-dollar bill she'd put down on the bar. "Men and their money." She knew just what to say. "But enough about me," she said. "Tell me about you. How long have you worked at Moorehead?"

"Three, four years?" I could barely count. My past seemed to flatten down into nothing in Rebecca's presence. "It was only going to be temporary, while I moved back here for a bit when my mother was sick," I explained. "And then she died and I just stayed on at the prison. And time's just flown by," I said, escalating my voice to sound chipper, funny.

"Oh no. Oh dear," Rebecca shook her head. "That sounds absolutely awful. Prison is no place for time to fly. Jeez Louise. And your mother dying. You must be eager to get out of here. Are you?"

"I'm happy here," I lied, sipping my beer.

"You know, I'm an orphan, too," said Rebecca. I didn't bother to correct her, tell her my father was still alive. "My parents both died when I was young. Drowned," she said. "My uncle raised me out west, where the sun shines. I'll never understand how you all do it up here winter after winter. Positively creepy, all the darkness, and so cold. It just about drives me mad." She talked about the ocean, how she loved the beach. Growing up she'd play for hours in the sun and sand, and so on. And then she spoke about her move to Cambridge, how she and her girlfriends rowed boats on the Charles. She praised the foliage, the history, mocked the intellectuals—"the stiffs"—said she was in a "strange love affair with New England." She never mentioned her studies at Harvard. She said nothing about her professional life at all. "Things feel very real out here, don't they? There's simply no fantasy. And no sentimentality. That's what fascinates me. There is history and pride, but very little imagination here."

I just listened. I had my whiskey and beer and Rebecca, and I hardly cared to disagree with her assessment of the place, my homeland. I just nodded. But of course she was dead wrong. We New Englanders are uptight for sure, but we have strong minds. We use our imaginations effectively. We don't waste our brains on magical notions or useless frills, but we do have the ability to fantasize. I could name countless thinkers and writers and artists as examples. And there was me, after all. *I* was there. But I didn't say much. I just sat there dumb, twisting my foot to the music. After a while she said, "I'm sorry. I've had too much to drink. I tend to talk too much when I drink."

"That's all right," I said, shrugging.

"Better than talking too little," she said, winking at me. "Only teasing." She swiveled on her bar stool, jostling my legs before I had a chance to feel offended. "The real silent one is that Leonard Polk. You saw him today?"

I nodded. The coincidence of Rebecca's new interest in Lee Polk with his mother's sudden appearance at Moorehead still struck me as odd, but I didn't feel it was my place to ask questions. I was just a secretary, after all.

"What did you make of that scene with his mother?" Rebecca asked. "Strange," she squinted at me, "didn't you think so?"

I shrugged. I suppose I still felt ashamed that I'd spied on the boy in the cave. Even just remembering the look of him through that little window made my heart beat faster—the hands moving under his uniform, his eyes hooded and sleepy. It excited me even then. The shame of arousal, the arousal of shame. "I don't know," I began. "Maybe he stopped talking because he had nothing nice to say. You know what they say to children—if you can't think of anything nice to say, say nothing."

"They say that to children?" Rebecca's face grimaced in disgust. "Well, I wondered whether Lee might have something to hide, or whether he'd taken his vow of silence to protest his incarceration. Or was it just to torture his mother, be the thorn in her side since he hadn't had the chance to slit her throat, too? I read his whole file, you know."

"I guess that makes sense," I said. "There's nothing worse than when someone won't talk to you. Drives me crazy, at least." I didn't tell her how my father would go silent for days, ignoring me, eyes glazed over as though I were invisible, saying nothing no matter how much I begged him to answer me. "What have I done wrong? Please tell me." Rebecca didn't press me for details.

"But did she seem angry to you, Mrs. Polk?" she asked.

"She seemed upset. They're always upset, those mothers," I told her. I wasn't sure what Rebecca was getting at.

"Perhaps his silence is for her benefit. His silence could be charitable, know what I mean?" She cocked her head thoughtfully, searched my face for a response. I hadn't followed her reasoning, but I nodded, tried to smile. "Secrets and lies?" she said, dipping her finger into her drink and sucking it. "I tell you, doll," she said. I blushed. "Some families are so sick, so twisted, the only way out is for someone to die."

"Boys will be boys," is all I could think to say. Rebecca just laughed.

"The warden said the same thing this afternoon when I

asked him about Leonard." This surprised me. She finished her martini, then swung around on her bar stool, again facing the table of men. Lighting a cigarette, her posture now became angular and seductive. She blew the smoke in a tall plume up at the low ceiling. "I asked him," she began, voice modulated into a higher register, eyes squinting at the men who seemed to stiffen, wipe their mouths and look alive, "what Leonard had done to get so many days in the cave, as you all call it. And he said what you said, Eileen." She put her hand on my knee and then just left it there, as though it had found its rightful place on my leg. "Boys will be boys. I bet it was for something of a sexual nature. Something deviant. They don't like to tell us gals such things. Leonard has the look. You know what I mean?" she asked.

I was shocked, of course. But I knew exactly what she meant. I had seen "the look" through that little window the day before. "I know," I told her.

"I thought you might," she said, winked, and squeezed my thigh.

"What'd you say your name was?" one of the men hollered, interrupting our private moment. Rebecca lifted her hand, placed it against her chest, looked wide-eyed.

"My name?" she asked, uncrossing and recrossing her legs. The men stirred in their seats, expectant as young dogs. "I'm Eileen," she said. "And this is my friend." Her hand found mine, still ice-cold and limp in my lap. "Do you all know my friend here?"

"And what's your name, sweetheart?" one of them asked me.

I can't tell you how fun it was sitting there with Rebecca, a table full of men at our disposal. At least that's how it seemed.

"Tell these boys your name, doll," prompted Rebecca. When I looked at her, she winked. "My friend is feeling shy tonight," she said. "Don't be shy, Rebecca. These boys won't bite."

"Unless you ask us to," the first man replied. "Jerry here's got some missing teeth, though. Show 'em, Jerry." Jerry, the man nearest to me, smiled, peeling up his top lip to show a comical gap. "Go easy, Jerry," his friend said, patting him on the shoulder.

"How'd that come about, Jerry?" Rebecca asked. Sandy set more drinks for us on the bar. I drank mine fast. I had a moderate tolerance for alcohol, but an extreme thirst for it once I got started. I was probably already drunk by that point. "Did you get in a fight with your wife?" Rebecca teased.

The men laughed. "That's it. You guessed right. His old lady has an arm like Joe Frazier."

"Oh dear," Rebecca shook her head, turned to pick up her martini, winked at me surreptitiously. "To Jerry," she said, raising her glass. The rest toasted and cheered and for the silent moment while everyone gulped from their drinks, I looked around, astonished at my new place in the world. There I was, a lady, celebrated and adored.

"Tell me, gentlemen," Rebecca went on. "Do any of you know how to fix a broken exhaust pipe? You all look pretty handy."

"Your car got problems?" Jerry asked, lisping like a twelve-year-old.

"Not my car," Rebecca answered. "Belongs to my friend here. Tell them."

I shook my head, hid behind my glass of beer.

"What'd you say your name was, honey?" one of the men asked.

"Rebecca," I answered. Rebecca laughed.

"Feel like dancing, Rebecca?" she asked me.

As if by magic, the jukebox kicked back on. I set down my glass. I can't say where I suddenly found the courage to dance. I never danced. I was drunk, of course, but even still, it astounds me how easily Rebecca pulled me off of my stool. I followed her to the little space by the jukebox, took her hands in mine, and let her lead me around, giggling and stopping every few seconds, covering my face in embarrassment and glee as we swayed and shimmied. We danced for what felt like an hour, first to quick, happy dance tunes, laughing, and then we waltzed around to slow love songs, sardonically to start, but eventually we were lulled into the heady, sweeping pulse of the music. I stared disbelievingly into Rebecca's serene, wistful face, her eyes closed, her hands on my shoulders like an angel and a devil debating the logic of longing. Rebecca and I moved together in a little circle as we danced, and I held her around her waist, with only my wrists pressed lightly against her body. I kept my hands stiff and stuck them out at an angle so that they wouldn't touch her. The men in their booth were at first mesmerized and entertained, but then they grew tired. None of them tried to dance with us. By the time the music quit, my head was spinning. Rebecca and I went and sat down at our drinks again. Still entranced and nervous, I shot back the whiskey and finished the beer. "I've had plenty," Rebecca said, and pushed her martini away. I drank that, too. It was gin.

Sandy came over, counted out Rebecca's change.

"How's Dad?" he asked me.

"Is this your brother?" Rebecca asked, shocked.

"No, he just knows my father," I explained.

"Small towns," Rebecca said, grinning.

I never trusted Sandy. He seemed terribly nosy. He's not an important figure here, but for the record, Sandy Brogan was his name and I disliked him. He said something like, "Don't know if it's a good thing I ain't seen him, or it means something else."

"It means something else," I said, and put my cape back on, pulled the hood over my head. I was feeling very brazen. "Can I have one of your cigarettes?" Sandy shook his pack out toward me and I pulled one out. He lit it for me.

"Quite a gal," said Rebecca.

"This one's a good kid," Sandy affirmed, nodding. He was an idiot.

I smoked awkwardly, holding my cigarette like a nine-year-old would, hand stiff, fingers outstretched, watching the burning tip, going cross-eyed as I brought it to my lips. I coughed, blushed and laughed with Rebecca, who took my arm. Together we left the bar, ignoring the men as we walked out.

Out on the street, Rebecca turned to me. The dark, icy night sparkled behind her, the snow and stars a galaxy of hope and wonder with her at its center. She was so alive and lovely. "Thank you, Eileen," she said, looking at me oddly. "You know, you remind me of a Dutch painting," she said, staring into my eyes. "You have a strange face. Uncommon. Plain, but fascinating. It has a beautiful turbulence hidden in it. I love it. I bet you have brilliant dreams. I bet you dream of other worlds." She threw her head back and laughed that evil laugh, then smiled sweetly. "Maybe you'll dream of me and my morning remorse, which you can count on. I shouldn't drink, but I do. C'est la vie." I watched her get into her car—a dark two-door, is all I recall—and drive away.

But I didn't want to go home yet. The night was young and I was beloved. I was someone important at last. So I went back into O'Hara's, passed the same booth of men who were drunk, laughing, slapping the table, spilling their beers. I took the seat Rebecca had sat on, feeling just a hint of the warmth she'd left behind. Sandy slid an ashtray toward me, slapped a cocktail napkin beside my curled hand on the bar, red from the cold. "Whiskey," I said, and stubbed out the cigarette.

The next memory I have is of waking up in the morning slumped over the steering wheel of the car, which I'd parked half inside a bank of snow in front of my house. A frozen pool of vomit sat next to me on the seat. My panty hose were full of runs. In the rearview mirror I looked like a madwoman—hair sticking out in all directions, lipstick smeared down my chin. I blew on my frozen hands, turned off the headlights. When I reached for the keys, they were missing from the ignition. I'd lost my cape, the trunk of the car was open, and my purse was gone.

WEDNESDAY

The house was locked. I could see my father asleep in his chair in the kitchen through the windows, the refrigerator door wide open. He sometimes left it that way when the heat from the stove and the oven made him sweat. And on my father's feet, shoes. With the exception of Sundays, when he was closely chaperoned by his sister to church and back, if my father had shoes on, it meant there would be trouble. He wasn't a violent threat, but when he got out he did things the warden would have called morally offensive—falling asleep on somebody's front lawn, folding up postcards at the drugstore, knocking over a gum-ball machine. His more aggressive indiscretions included pissing in the sandbox at the children's playground, yelling at cars on Main Street, throwing rocks at dogs. Each time he got out, the police would find him, pick him up and bring him home. How I cringed at the sound of that doorbell when an X-ville cop stood outside on the front porch with my father, drunk and tugging at his chin, eyes crossed. The officer would take his cap off when I answered the door, speak in hushed tones while my father busted into the house in search of booze. And if he chose instead to stay and take part in the conversation, there were handshakes and pats on the shoulder, the respectful pretense of love and loyalty. "Routine check, sir," the cop would say. If a cop tried to express even the slightest concern, my father would take the guy aside and launch into a rant about the hoodlums, the mob, the strange noises in the house. He'd complain of ill health, heart trouble, back pain, and how I, his daughter, was neglectful, how I was abusing him, how I was after all his money. "Will somebody please tell her to give me back my shoes? She has no right!" And as soon as he turned to me, hands trembling and creeping up toward my neck, the cop would nod, turn and close the door and leave. None of them had the guts not to play into his delusions—ghouls and gangsters, ghosts and the mob. They would have let him get away with murder, I imagined. "America's finest," the prison guards of the civilized world, those police. I will tell you frankly that to this day there is nothing I dread more than a cop knocking at my door.

That morning I rang and rang the doorbell, but my father wouldn't budge. I figured the keys were in the pocket of his robe or, worse, around his neck, wearing them the way I used to, a noose at the ready if I'd ever thought of it. I could have tried to walk to work that day, stick my thumb out, that's true. Nobody would have looked twice at my outfit at the office. Nobody cared.

I went around the back of the house and tried to open the

cellar door. Bending over and tugging at it had me burping up and gagging. It was not a pleasant morning. Nothing is more disturbing than waking up to the taste of vomit. With bare hands I cracked through the glazed layer of ice over the high snow and filled my mouth with it. It hurt my head. Maybe that was when the previous night came back to me: Rebecca, Sandy, leaving the bar and going back in. I recall sitting down in a booth, the sparks of matches, wobbling over manly fists with my Salems, the itchy wool of my dress or a man's rough sweater rubbing against my neck, then falling down and laughing. "Rebecca," someone had said, and I responded, "Yes, doll." I'd been Rebecca for a night. I'd been someone else completely.

A night of heavy drinking would kill me now. I don't know how I managed it back then, though I'm sure my shame and embarrassment were far worse than the hangover. I shook off my fractured recollections and tried to gain access to the house. The cellar door was locked, of course. I considered busting through a back window with the heel of my boot, but I didn't think I could reach up high enough to get my arm through and undo the lock on the inside of the back door. I pictured severing my arm on the broken glass, blood spewing across the snow. Surely my father wouldn't stay mad at me if I was bleeding to death in the backyard. The image of blood-stained snow turned my stomach and I bent down to retch but all that came up was yellow bile. My head throbbed remembering the frozen pile of vomit waiting for me in the car. I wiped my mouth with the sleeve of my dress.

When I went back around the front of the house and rang

the bell again, I saw that my father was missing from the chair. He was hiding from me. "Dad?" I called out. "Dad!" I couldn't raise my voice too high or the neighbors would hear. And given that the day was starting, mothers sending their kids off to school, men leaving in their cars for work, they would soon see the old Dodge smushed into the bank of snow. The car was fine, but clearly the person who'd parked it was out of her mind.

Already we, the Dunlops, were regarded as something of a case in the neighborhood. Even my father's reputation as a cop—an upstanding citizen, a man of service to his country—couldn't make up for the fact that in recent years our lawn was never mowed, our hedges never trimmed. A neighbor would do that once or twice a summer, to keep up appearances, I'm sure, but it was passed off as a gesture of appreciation for the old man's good work and sympathy for me, the skinny girl with no mother and little hope for a husband. We were the only house on the block without Christmas lights strung in our bushes, no fancy tree twinkling through the living room windows, no wreath on the door. I'd buy treats for Halloween, but no kids ever rang our doorbell. I ended up eating all the candy myself, chewing it up and spitting it all out in the attic. I didn't like any of our neighbors any more than my father did—not the Lutherans, none of them, no matter their gifts or favors. They were goody-goodies, I thought, and I felt they judged me for being young and sloppy, and for driving a car that filled the whole block with smoke when I started it. But I didn't want to earn any more of their scorn. I didn't want to give anyone more fodder for gossip. I had to get the car into the driveway before it aroused suspicion. This was my thinking. And I had to clean the seat full of vomit before my father saw it.

But, of course, he'd seen it already. I suppose he'd been waiting up for me the night before and came out and yanked the keys out of the ignition after I'd passed out. It occurred to me all at once: He kept me from carbon monoxide poisoning that night. He may have saved my life. Who knows whether the engine had been running when he came out and yanked out the keys. It's possible. The windows were up when I came to. Perhaps he simply wanted his shoes from the trunk, and that's why he took the keys. Still, I like to think that somehow his instincts as a father—his desire to protect me, to keep me alive—kicked in that night, overrode his madness, his selfishness. I prefer to tell myself that story than to believe in luck or coincidences. That line of magical thinking always leads to too fine an edge. In any case, I was grateful to be alive, which was nice. At first I was all the more frightened at what my father would have to say, what he might want in return for saving my life. But then I thought of Rebecca. With her around, I didn't need to beg for my father's mercy. He could yell and cry, but he couldn't hurt me. I was loved after all, I thought.

Again I tried to knock on the front door, but my father still ignored me. I climbed over the wrought-iron handrail that went up the brick steps and jumped down behind the front bushes and looked through the living room windows. They hadn't been washed in years. I rubbed a spot through the frost, but there was still a thick layer of dust on the inside. I could barely see in. I caught then a weird vision of my father—pale, naked from the waist up, thin and frail but full of tension, jolting slowly past the living room windows with a bottle in his hand. He seemed to have grown small breasts. And when he turned, I thought I saw long purple bruises up and down his back. How he stayed alive for as long as he did is sheer proof of his stubbornness. I pounded my fist on the thick glass, but he just waved his hand and kept on walking. I ended up sneaking in through a dirty living room window. It was, strangely, unlocked.

I was an adult, I knew that. I had no curfew. There were no official house rules. There were only my father's arbitrary rages, and once he was in one he would only relax if I agreed to whatever odd, humiliating punishment he came up with. He'd bar me from the kitchen, order me to walk to Lardner's and back in the rain. The worst crime I could commit in his eyes was to do anything for my own pleasure, anything outside of my daughterly duties. Evidence of a will of my own was seen as the ultimate betrayal. I was his nurse, his aide, his concierge. All he really required, however, was gin. The house was rarely dry—as I've said, I was a good girl—but somehow everything I did, my very existence, rubbed him the wrong way. Even my *National Geographic* magazines gave him cause to bewail my unruliness. "Communist," he'd call me, flicking at the pages. I knew he was furious that morning. But I wasn't scared. I stood on the carpet in the foyer, snow sliding off my boots. "Hey," I called out to him. "Have you seen the keys?"

He emerged from the closet with a golf club, thudded up the steps, and sat on the upstairs landing. When he was truly enraged, he got quiet—the calm before the storm. I knew he would never try to kill me. He wasn't really capable of that. But he seemed sober that morning, and when he was sober, he was especially mean. I don't recall exactly what we said to each other while he sat up there, tapping the golf club along the rungs of the banister, but I remember I held my hands over my face, in case he threw the golf club down.

"Dad," I asked again, "can I have the keys?"

He picked up a book from where they were piled along the hallway walls and threw it down at me. Then he went into my mother's bedroom and took a pillow off the bed and threw that down, too.

"Make yourself comfortable," he said, setting himself on the top step again. He rapped the golf club against the rungs of the banister like a prison guard with a baton against iron bars. "You're not going anywhere till you read that book. From cover to cover," he said. "I want to hear every word." It was a copy of *Oliver Twist*. I picked it up, turned to the opening page, cleared my throat, but stopped there. A week earlier I would have acquiesced and read a few pages until he got thirsty. That day, though, I just put the book down. I recall looking up at him, still shielding my face with my hands. Through my fingers, to my regret, I caught sight of his gray scrotum peeking out one side of his billowy, yellowed shorts.

"You see the car keys?" I asked. "I'll be late to work."

His whole body seemed to blush with rage. The shoes he had on were his worn black oxfords.

"Out all night, nearly crashed the car, sleeping in your own sick, and now you're worried about getting to work on time."

His voice was eerily measured, grave. "I can hardly look at you, I'm so ashamed. Oliver Twist would be grateful for this home, this nice house. But you, Eileen, you seem to think you can just come and go as you please." His voice cracked.

"I went out with a girl from work," I told him. It was a mistake to disclose this, but I suppose I was proud and wanted to rub it in his face.

"A girl from work? Do you think I was born yesterday?"

I refused to defend myself. In the past I'd have begged his forgiveness, done anything to appease him. "I'm sorry!" I would have cried, falling to my knees. I'd gotten good at being dramatic; he was only ever satisfied by complete self-abasement. That morning, however, I wasn't going to stoop to his level.

"Well," he said, "who is he? I at least want to meet the boy before you get knocked up and sell your soul to Satan."

"Please, can I have the keys? I'll be late."

"You aren't going anywhere dressed like that. Now really, Eileen. How dare you? That's the dress your mother wore to my father's funeral. You have no respect," he said, "for me, for your mother, for anyone, and least of all for yourself." He let go of the golf club, startling himself with the racket it made as it tumbled down the stairs. Then he started shaking. He sat on his hands, bowed his head. "Trash, Eileen, just trash," he whined. I thought he might start to cry.

"I'll go get you a bottle," I said.

"What's his name, Eileen? Give me the boy's name."

"Lee," I answered, almost without thinking.

"Lee? Just Lee?" He winced, wiggled his head back and forth mocking me.

"Leonard."

He ground his teeth, jaw pulsing, and rubbed his palms together.

"Now you know," I said, dropping my hands from my face as though my lie itself could shield me from my father's wrath. "Keys?"

"Keys are in my robe," he said. "Come back quick and change. I don't want anyone to see you in that getup. They'll think I'm dead."

I found my father's robe thrown in the empty fireplace. I got the keys, unearthed my purse from a pile of junk by the front door, put on a coat, and went back out to the car. The vomit was already melting, the edge of the puddle coinciding with the strap of the seat belt. It was awful. The smell transferred to everything I wore and lingered on my coat long after I'd abandoned the Dodge and disappeared a few days later. I had no intention of going to the liquor store, which would have been closed anyway at that early hour. But I had to extricate the front of the car from the snowbank. That took some effort. My father may have saved my life that night, but he clearly didn't care much for my well-being. He wasn't capable of much, I knew that. The one time I'd dared to ask him not to pick on me, he burst out laughing, then feigned a heart attack the next morning. When the ambulance arrived, he was sitting on the sofa smoking a cigarette. He said he felt fine. "She's on the rag or something," he told the paramedics. They all shook hands.

Once I got the car out of the snowbank, I drove back to O'Hara's. If I'd had my wits, I could have taken off then and there. I could have just sped off into the morning, a free woman. Who could stop me? But I couldn't leave yet. I couldn't leave Rebecca. I parked in front of the bar and went inside.

It was dark as ever in there, just thin daggers of light needling through the chipping black paint on the window over the door. The smell of stale beer made my stomach churn. Sandy stood behind the bar drinking a glass of water.

"Can I borrow a bottle of gin?" I asked him.

"You're back," he said. His smile perturbed me. He looked like a man who'd fondle children. He was a real creep.

"My dad needs a drink," I said.

"You girls drank all the gin I got last night," Sandy chuckled. "Would your dad believe that, huh?"

"You have anything else I can borrow?"

"I've got gin, dear," he said, fatherly. He walked behind the bar, ducked and disappeared for a moment, came back up with a bottle of Gordon's. "And consider it a Christmas gift. To your dad, not you. You deserve much better," he said. "Have a drink with me first, though," he said, plunking down two shot glasses, breaking open the bottle with a violent twist, a crack like bones breaking as he twisted the cap. "One drink with me and the rest is yours." He nudged the glass toward me. I swallowed it quickly. The soapy, burning taste at least seemed to cut through the taste of bile in my mouth. "Good girl," Sandy called me.

When he handed me the bottle, he lifted his other hand to caress my face. I jerked myself away.

"Tell your dad this is from me, OK?"

"I'll tell him," I said. "Thanks."

That was the last time I saw him. In the years since, I've wondered what memories of Sandy I may have buried from that previous night, perhaps of his thick, beer stained hands grappling me, maybe his mouth on me somewhere, a sour tongue probing my throat, disgusting. Who knows? Sandy, wherever you are buried, I hope you've stayed out of trouble. But if you haven't, I'm sure you paid for it somehow. Everyone does, eventually.

*B*ack home, my father appeared to be sleeping when I set the bottle down on the kitchen table, but before I could leave he bolted up out of his recliner. His hand darted out and gripped my wrist.

"Leonard, you said? Leonard what?" he asked.

"Polk," I answered, stupidly.

"Polk," he repeated. I could see his rusty gears turning. He shook his head. "Do I know him?"

"I doubt it," I answered, wresting free of his weak grasp and flitting up the stairs. I was relieved to hear him crack open the gin. My guess is he washed away any memory of this exchange immediately. He never mentioned the Polk name again, though my hope is that it vexed him as a clue he'd failed to follow when I disappeared. "I should have known she was in trouble," I've imagined him saying.

From under the bathroom sink I grabbed a bunch of rags and went back out to the car and slid the vomit off the passenger seat and into the snow. It was remarkable how easy it was to remove the frozen puddle in one piece, but it left a stain. I sprinkled dishwashing powder on it and covered it with a towel. I'm sure I was gagging and retching the whole time, though what I really remember is rushing up into the shower afterward. I scrubbed myself vigorously down there again—a mess had been brewing all night—and washed the vomit I found dried in my hair. My hands were swollen and tight as I fumbled with the towel, still damp from the night before. Those navy stockings were by then tattered, looked like ghosts where they lay dashed out across the bathroom tile. I dressed quickly, combed my wet hair, grabbed my coat and purse and ran back down to the car.

I suppose the details of my behavior that morning are unnecessary, but I like to remember myself in action. I'm old now. I don't move vigorously or frenetically anymore. Now I'm graceful. I move with measured and elegant precision, but I am slow. I'm like a beautiful tortoise. I don't waste my energy. Life is precious to me now. In any case, when I went back out to the car, there was a police cruiser blocking the driveway. I was aghast. The cop's name was Buck Brown. I remember him because we'd gone to grade school together. He was big and dopey and talked with a lisp, eyes still full of sleep, white spittle at the corners of his mouth, the kind of man to act dumber than he is, to deceive you into lowering your expectations. I really dislike men who do that. He corrected his cap and stuck his hands in his pockets.

"Miss," he began, lisping. "May I have a word?" The police were always very formal. After how many years of knowing me, they never called me by my name. Never trust anyone who holds so strictly to decorum. "It's about your father," Buck began. Of course it was.

"I'm listening, Buck," I said impatiently. I tried to smile, but I was too tired. And there seemed to be no point in trying to appease him. Before Rebecca, I'd always been too ashamed and nervous to ever act as cranky as I felt. "What do you want?"

"It's about the gun" was his answer.

For a moment I imagined my father inside, perhaps down in the basement, bleeding from a bullet wound he'd inflicted when I didn't return fast enough with his gin. Maybe he'd left the phone off the hook in the kitchen, line open to the police station, "I'm ending it!" his last words. But of course I'd just seen him alive and well enough to torment me a moment before.

"What about the gun?" I asked.

"We came by last night but you were out," he said, looking at me accusingly. I really despised him, everyone. After a pause, he explained. "Yesterday afternoon we received several calls from neighbors, and from the school principal, that Father Dunlop," he halted, "that Mister Dunlop was sitting at that window," he gestured toward the living room window, "pointing his gun out at children walking home from school."

"He's inside," I said. "Go talk to him yourself." Or maybe I wasn't quite so forceful. Maybe I said, "Oh dear," or "Dear Lord," or "I'm sorry." It's hard to imagine that this girl, so false, so irritable, so used, was me. This was Eileen.

"Ma'am," he said. I could have spat in his face for calling me that. "I've talked with your father," he said, "and he's agreed to relinquish his property to your care, as long as you promise not to use it on him. His words."

I really didn't understand the fuss. I didn't think he kept the gun loaded. He was too afraid to, I assumed. He still cleaned it regularly, that I knew.

"Ma'am," he said, and pointed at the house. "I must put it on your person."

"What does that mean?"

"Orders are to give the gun to you immediately. Children will be walking to school any minute." I'd never wanted to go to the prison so badly. "It won't take a moment," Buck said, and walked with me along the front walk and up the steps.

Inside, I called out to my father. "Dad, there's someone here to see you."

"I know what this is about," he said, tottering out from the kitchen in his robe now streaked with soot stains from the fireplace. He was smiling that drunken grin I'd come to recognize as an expression of compliance—mouth pulled flat, eyes nearly closed, just squinty enough to make him look the slightest bit delighted. He opened the front hall closet, shuffled around and pulled out the gun. "Here," he said. "It's all yours."

"Thank you, sir," said Buck. The ceremony of all this was both comical and maddening. "I trust Miss Dunlop will take excellent care of the weapon."

"As she does with all things, as you can see," said my father, motioning with the gun in a circle around the dilapidated house. Buck took a step back in alarm. I pictured one of those icicles hanging above him cracking off at that moment and diving straight into his skull. My father handed the gun to Buck, who placed it gently into my flat open palms.

I'd never handled my father's gun before, or any gun for that matter. It was a heavy thing, far heavier than I'd expected, and ice-cold. Holding it frightened me at first. I couldn't have told you at the time what kind of a gun it was, but I remember the look of it clearly. "Dunlop" was etched into the wooden handle. I've since looked in books about guns and have identified it as a Smith & Wesson Model 10. It had a four-inch barrel and weighed nearly two pounds. I kept it for a few weeks once I ran away, then I threw it off the Brooklyn Bridge.

"That should do it," Buck said. He waddled back down to his cop car.

My father shuffled away, mumbling to himself, then said clearly, "Your lucky day, Eileen." He was right. I put the gun in my purse. I didn't know what else to do. I expected my father to put up a fight to get it back, but all I heard was a glass clink in the kitchen, then the recliner squelch under his weight. It's not quite right to say that this ordeal with the gun disturbed me since I'd been numbed down for years by its presence in the house. Still, it was odd to hold it now. I locked the front door gently, mindful of the icicles, and left. In all his dysfunction, my father, while I'd been scrubbing the vomit in my car, I suppose, had left his shoes for me out on the porch. Perhaps it was to remind me that I had a job to do, that I was, above all, his caretaker, his minder, his prison guard.

As I drove to work, I considered what advantages that gun might afford me. It was the gun my father had carried around all his years on the police force. While I was growing up it even seemed to have its own place at the dinner table—Dad at the head, Mom across from him, Joanie and I on one side, the gun on the other. Then, in the years since his retirement, he concealed it in his holster against his bare abdomen while he clunked around the house. At a red light, I carefully removed the gun from my purse, thinking I would shove it into my glove compartment. But when I saw that frozen mouse in there, I decided against it. That little critter stayed in there to the bitter end. It doesn't signify much of anything, but I do remember its little face—long snout, mouth agape, tiny teeth, soft white ears. That was probably the last time I saw it. I kept the gun on my lap as I drove. It did something to me, as I expect it would do to anyone: It calmed me down. It soothed me. Perhaps it was just my hangover which made me lackadaisical, but when I pulled into the Moorehead parking lot that morning, instead of locking my purse in the trunk with the gun inside it, I carried it with me into the prison and let it sit out in the open on my desk. The ugly brown leather stirred my heart with fear and excitement every time I reached out to touch it.

I suppose it was a typical morning at Moorehead, but every footstep I heard, and every time the door opened to let in a blast of wind, I would first cringe—the headache of my hangover like a blow to the brain—then look up, devil-eyed and excited to see Rebecca walk in, but she didn't appear. I was eager to be with her again, to reaffirm what I had felt the previous evening. I could smell my excitement leaping up from my body like the pungent shock of burning sulfur when a match is struck. How could I leave X-ville now that Rebecca was in it with me? Maybe she would come with me when I disappeared, I wondered. She'd said she couldn't spend too long in one place, didn't she? We would have fun together. I fantasized how I'd change my appearance once I got to New York, the clothes I'd wear, how I'd cut my hair, color it if need be, or wear a long wig, a false pair of glasses. I could change my name if I wanted, I thought. "Rebecca" was as good a name as any. There was time, I told myself, to sort out the future. The future could wait, I thought. At some point that morning I went to the ladies room to apply my lipstick. That's when Rebecca squealed the door open and shimmied up beside me, aligning her face with mine in the mirror.

"Well hello, old gal," she said to my reflection. She was playful. She was funny.

"Good morning," I said. I made my mind up on the spot to sound confident, good-humored, like I was just fine and dandy.

"Aren't I cute in my holiday colors?" she asked, twirling. She wore a red wool skirt suit and a green scarf around her neck. "Dizzy," she said, holding her head melodramatically.

"Adorable," I said and nodded.

"I'm afraid I don't give a damn about Christ," she said, or something crass like that. "Kids like Christmas though, I think." She strutted into the bathroom stall and continued to talk while she urinated. I listened and watched my face turn red in the mirror. I wiped my lipstick off. That new shade wasn't any good on me—far too bright. My father had been right about it. It made me look like a child playing around with her mother's makeup. "I was wondering what you're up to Christmas Eve," Rebecca went on, "seeing as we have time off." She flushed the toilet and came out, slip exposed, hiking up her stockings. Her thighs were as thin as a twelve-year-old's, and just as taut. "Would you be up for a drink tomorrow at my place? I think it'd be nice. That is, unless you have plans."

"I don't have plans," I told her. I hadn't celebrated Christmas in years.

Rebecca pulled up her sleeve and took a pen from her breast pocket. "We'll do it like this. Write down your phone number. This way I won't lose it, unless I take a shower, which I won't," she said. "Barring a visit to the doctor, or from a gentleman caller," she laughed, "I barely shower. It's too cold up here anyway. Don't tell." She lifted her arms and comically craned her neck back and forth between her armpits, then held a finger to her lips as though to hush me.

"Me too," I said. "I like to stew in my own filth sometimes. Like a little secret under my clothes." We were the same, she and I, I thought. Rebecca understood that. There was no reason to hide anything from her. She accepted me—liked me, even— just as I was. She handed me the pen and stuck her arm out for me to write on. I gripped the pale, narrow wrist and wrote my digits up her forearm on skin so clean and soft and firm I felt I was defiling something as pristine as a newborn baby. My own hands under the fluorescent lights were red and burnt from the cold and rough and swollen. I tucked them into the cuffs of my sweater.

"I'm leaving early today," she said. "I'll call you tomorrow. We'll have fun."

I pictured a lavish table spread with gourmet dishes, a tuxedoed butler pouring wine into crystal goblets. That was my fantasy.

By noon I was grateful to have to drive out to the nearest grocery store to buy my lunch. It meant I could hold the gun again, let the Dodge coast, feel the wind in my hair. My hunger that day was like no hunger I'd ever felt. I purchased a carton of milk and a box of cheese crackers. I ate them voraciously sitting in my car in the Moorehead parking lot—stink of vomit still strong—then gulped the milk like a football player. Nothing had ever tasted so delicious. The gun, a hard weight in my lap, seemed to have something to do with my appetite. At any moment I could have pointed it at someone and demanded his wallet, his coat, that he do something to please me, sing a song or dance or tell me I was beautiful and perfect. I could have made Randy kiss my feet. The Beach Boys came on the radio. I didn't understand rock 'n' roll back then—most rock songs made me want to slit my wrists, made me feel there was a wonderful party happening somewhere, and I was missing it—but I may have jiggled a little in my seat that day. I felt happy. I hardly felt like myself.

Out in the parking lot, I ground my heels into the rocky salt, took in the view of the whole of the children's prison. It was an old, gray stone building which, from afar, reminded me of a rich person's summer home. The carved stone details, the rolling sand dunes beyond the fenced gravel, might have looked beautiful under different circumstances. The place felt like it was meant to be restful, peaceful, to inspire contemplation, something like that. As I understood from the odd display case of historical drawings, maps and photographs in the front corridor, the place had been built more than a hundred years earlier, first as a temperance boardinghouse for seamen. Then it was expanded and converted to a military hospital. The sea breeze was refreshing, after all, good for the nerves. At some point it was used as a boarding school, I think, when that part of the state was prosperous, full of smart, wealthy people who preferred quiet lives outside the big city. Once there was a monument to Emerson out front, a circular drive, a fountain with an English garden, as I recall. Later the place turned into an orphanage, then a rehabilitation hospital for ailing veterans, then a school for boys, and finally, twenty-something years before I got there, it became the boys' prison. If I'd been born a boy, I probably would have ended up there.

Leaning out the open window of my car, ears bright red from the cold, I powdered my nose in the side-view mirror and watched a corrections officer escort a young man out of the back of his cruiser and into the prison. I was especially excited when a new inmate arrived, which was only about once a week. There would be paperwork for me to process. There would be fingerprinting. There would be photographs to take.

The office ladies gave me the stink eye when I walked in late from lunch that day. My mood and health feeling much improved, I whirled my coat off onto my chair, used my teeth to pull off my useless gloves, fingered the sleep out of the corners of my eyes and rubbed my hands together. Mrs. Stephens chatted with the corrections officer while the new boy fidgeted with his handcuffs. He was a pudgy blond teenager with an upturned nose, large, fleshy hands, but small, girllike shoulders. I remember him. He squeezed his eyes shut in an effort not to cry, which touched me. He sat across from me, handcuffed and sedated. I asked his name and wrote it down, took his height, his weight, noted his eye color, checked for facial scars, handed him the starched blue uniform. I felt like a nurse, dry and caring and untortured. I talked to him quietly, took his picture. I remember the look on his face in the viewfinder, the strange passive mix of resignation and rage, the tender sadness. Like when I'd peek at that dead mouse in my glove box, the boy's picture bolstered me. "Glad I'm not you" was my sentiment. All the while the corrections officer stood behind the boy with crossed arms, waiting to witness his signature. Two guards milled around in case the boy tried to make a run for it or attack me, though none of them ever did. He couldn't have been older than fourteen, as I recall. My heart went out to him, I guess, because I was in a good mood and he was rather short and plump for his age, and from his sorrow I gathered that, like me, he was an odd child, deeply pained by the hard world around him, tender, distrustful. When I put his file away in the cabinet I read his charge: infanticide by drowning.

When I was conducting these little intake exams, I felt

normal, just a regular person going about her day. I enjoyed having a set of clean instructions, following protocol. It gave me a sense of purpose, an easiness. It was a brief vacation from the loud, rabid inner circuitry of my mind. I'm sure people found and still find me odd. I've changed considerably over the last fifty years, of course, but I can make some people very uncomfortable. Now it's for entirely different reasons. These days I'm afraid I am too outspoken, too loving. I'm a sap, too passionate, too effusive, too much. Back then I was just an odd young woman. An awkward youngster. Angst wasn't quite so mainstream back then. My old deadpan stare would terrify me if I saw it in the mirror today. Looking back I'd say I was barely civilized. There was a reason I worked at the prison, after all. I wasn't exactly a pleasant person. I thought I would have preferred to be a teller in a bank, but no bank would have taken me. For the best, I suppose. I doubt it would have been long before I stole from the till. Prison was a safe place for me to work.

Visiting hours came and went. It delighted me to see the ugly brown leather purse now hanging by its worn strap from the back of my desk chair. If I or anyone jostled it, the gun inside the purse would clank against the chair's hollow metal backing. What would Rebecca think, I wondered, if she knew I was thus armed? I had the vague notion that bearing arms was in poor taste. Unless you were terribly wealthy, hunting was for the brutish lower class, uncivilized country folk, primitive types, people who were dumb and callous and ugly. Violence was just another function of the body, no less unusual than sweating or vomiting. It sat on the same shelf as sexual inter-course. The two got mixed up quite often, it seemed.

For the rest of the day, I did my duties mechanically. I tried to fixate again on Randy, as usual glancing over at him as he sat on his stool, but my fascination fell flat. Like a favorite song you've heard so many times it begins to annoy you, or like when you scratch an itch so hard it begins to bleed, Randy's face now seemed common, his lips childishly plump, almost feminine, his hair silly and pretentious. There was nothing mesmerizing about his crotch, nor did his arms seem at all special—the magic of his muscles had vanished. I even felt a bit sick when I imagined him coming toward me in the dark, his breath smelling of sausage, burnt coffee, cigarettes. The heart is a moody, greedy thing, I suppose. He really was special, though. I wish I'd just told Randy I loved him when I had the chance, before Rebecca came along. He had captivated me. It's rare to meet someone who can do that to you. Randy, wherever you may be, I saw you, and you were beautiful. I loved you.

I left Moorehead for the last time that afternoon, though I couldn't have predicted that. I left my desk a mess. The vermouth and chocolates sat in my locker, a library book in my drawer. I don't recall my last moments in that prison, and I occasionally wondered what became of my belongings, or what the office ladies had to say about me when I didn't show up for work after the holidays. Mrs. Stephens was probably put back in charge of visitation, Mrs. Murray intake. I doubt much fuss was made. If Rebecca went back there, maybe she tried to cover for me. "She's visiting family," she might have lied. I don't care. I haven't lost any sleep thinking about what I left behind at Moorehead.

I was exhausted on the drive home that evening, and already suffering from the powerful wrenching pain that usually accompanied my period on the third day. I was too tired to stop by Lardner's on my way home that night. If my father needed something, that was his problem. It wouldn't kill him to drink a glass of milk, spend a single night sober, I thought. Or perhaps it *would* kill him. Either way, I didn't care. I suppose it was at that moment, with the weight of the gun in my purse on my lap, turning into the dark and icy driveway between the tall walls of piled up snow, that I thought of trying to put him out of his misery. I could have shot him, but that would have been messy and might get me in trouble. My mother's pills were a better idea, but there were only a few left in the bottle. She had taken them to alleviate the pain of dying, as the doctor had prescribed. She said, however, that she took them to protect her daughter, poor me, from having to hear her moan and yelp and gripe and complain all day. I took one, too, from time to time as I waited for her to finally "kick the bucket." This was how I described what had happened when I called Joanie on the phone the morning after she died. I'd spent the night before in the blackness those good pills provided, then woke up to a cold dead body in the bed beside me, my mother's angry corpse.

The gun was heavy in my purse on my shoulder as I walked up the front steps that night. I let myself in through the front door, careful under the dripping daggers of ice. Even through the dimness, it was apparent that the foyer had been cleared of old newspapers and bottles, even swept. The cool shape of a white circular tablecloth on the kitchen table told me that someone had been cleaning. Perhaps the station had sent over a rookie after word got around that my esteemed father had been living in a pigsty. Or maybe my father had cleaned up on his own—boiled a strong pot of coffee, got industrious, sober for a day. He had undertaken projects to improve the home in the past—building a shelf to organize the basement, insulating the attic—projects he always abandoned as soon as the coffee got cold and he figured he deserved a beer. None of his pledges to get off the bottle lasted more than an afternoon. When I left, there were still bright pink rolls of insulation stuffed in the slanted corners of the attic. I'd stared at them for years every night as I fell asleep.

My father's coat was hanging on the hook by the front door. When I turned the light on in the kitchen, I found his chair empty. I pulled out two slices of bread from the refrigerator, slathered some mayonnaise on one, slapped the two pieces together, and let each bite melt on my tongue. That was my dinner. It took me years to learn how to feed myself properly, or rather it took years to develop the desire to feed myself properly. Back there in X-ville, I desperately hoped I could avoid ever having to resemble a grown woman. I didn't see that any good could come of that.

When I went upstairs, I saw there was a light on in my mother's bedroom, the door closed. Through it I heard the loud, irregular breathing of my sleeping father. My mother's old pills were in a drawer of the bedside table, but I dared not go in there and risk waking him. A half-empty bottle of gin lay at the top of the stairs. I took it up to the attic with me. The previous summer, my father had fallen down the attic stairs one morning on his way up to wake me, yelling that there were mobsters in the cellar planning to kill us. I was barely awake when I heard him trip and thunder down the steps, splinters cracking like lightning until his body hit the landing with a low thud. I had to get dressed and help him limp to the car. I drove him to the emergency room, where they pumped him full of liquids, measured his liver, and a doctor told me the bad news, which was that if he stopped drinking he might die, and if he continued, it would surely kill him. "It's quite a quandary," the doctor told me, looking down at my bruised knees. "Eat a can of spinach, young lady," he said. I went home. I did the laundry. I took a bath. The house without my father in it felt as though it belonged to strangers. All my belongings were there, but the rooms all felt so empty, unfamiliar. It irked me. Eventually my father was sent home with a cane and a bandage on his ankle, a stitch on his chin. He wore his wound proudly, cleaning it meticulously at first, then excessively, with rubbing alcohol, of which he demanded more and more. I liked the smell of it, too, and when my father wasn't looking, I took a sip of it and nearly choked.

That night I took the gin and my purse to the attic, changed into pajamas, and slipped the gun under my pillow. Doing that felt like a prayer, or like when my first tooth fell out as a child and I placed it there before I went to sleep. I recall waking up to

two shiny nickels under my pillow once. What shocked me was
not the transformation from tooth to silver, but the idea that I
had slept through the disturbance of my mother or father sneaking in during the night, that I had been unconscious, completely
unaware, vulnerable. I remember my question that morning—
what else had they done to me in my sleep? I've often wondered
about everything I may have slept through, what arguments,
what secrets. When I think back on my childhood, not much
appears but the house itself, the furniture and its arrangements,
the change of seasons in the backyard. There are no faces on
people, only their shadows slipping out of sight as they leave the
room. What I remember most about my mother is the slight
weight of her in the bed the morning she died, her cold hands
when I held them, perhaps for the first time since I'd been a
child, the give of her shoulder when I leaned into it and cried.

I drank for a while that night, remembering. Then I put
down the bottle, pulled out my reading materials. I must confess that amidst my stack of *National Geographic*s were hidden
several issues of my father's pornographic magazines. I pulled
one of them out and leafed blithely through its pages until I fell
asleep.

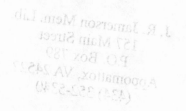

CHRISTMAS EVE

My mother never packed lunches for me to take to school when I was growing up. I'd sit and stare down at my knees while the other children ate their sandwiches, my stomach empty and rumbling. As soon as I'd get home in the afternoon, I filled my belly with bread and butter, all that I could find to eat in my mother's messy kitchen. When I was a child, Dunlop dinners around the kitchen table were hardly nourishing. Mealtimes were brief and uncomfortable. My parents only ever fought in front of Joanie and me, as though they'd needed our audience to discuss their private matters. Our mother would whine and our father would groan, throw his fork across the table, eye his Smith & Wesson, which lay next to his plate. If Joanie or I fussed, Mom would whip a rag at the floor to make a popping sound, sudden and loud, like lightning, like a firecracker. I don't remember what they were always arguing about. I'd just chew my food fast and bring my plate to the sink and run up the stairs. Furthermore, the meals my mother cooked were awful. I didn't eat good food until my second husband. He explained that steak was not a leathery flap of sinew burned in a frying pan, but a thick, fragrant, lovely thing, the best of which could be eaten with a dull spoon. I gained ten pounds, I think, the first month we were together. Back in X-ville, Dunlop dinners had been, at best, dry chicken, mashed potatoes from a box, canned beans, limp bacon. Christmas was little different. A store-bought sponge cake was all I remember enjoying year to year. The Dunlops were never big eaters.

But the booze always flowed freely over the holidays. Of course it did. Imagine the festivities: Mom getting the cocktail shaker down—"Let's do this properly!"—to make drinks she called Diplomats and Stormy Weathers. Those old drinks had great names. Maggie Mays, Old Fashioneds. She made hers and Dad had me make his, Blue Blazers and highballs, with the good stuff he'd get every Christmas from his so-called friends on the force. We had a little book with different recipes. I took sips no doubt, chewed up half the bottle of maraschino cherries on my way back and forth to the kitchen, where I mixed Lee Burns, Mamie Taylors, Manhattans. Whiskey Milk Punch was my favorite since it tasted like a milkshake. I remember another one, the Morning Glory, had me cracking eggs like some kind of short order cook. Those are fun memories: records playing, fire roaring, me, offstage and dutiful, slurping the foam off a cocktail in the kitchen and still expecting something good for Christmas—a microscope, a set of paints—and Joanie entertaining in the living room, twisting her limbs in time to Elvis.

Christmas was one of the few times a year my parents had guests over. My aunt Ruth, my only aunt, took little interest in Joanie and me as children—something I've never understood or forgiven—and drank only gin martinis. There was gin running through the Dunlop bloodline for generations, I'm sure. Perhaps Aunt Ruth just got down to her destiny sooner than my father did. Those martinis never seemed to do her much good. She was always frowning, skin so waxy, her face so flat it almost looked wet, shiny as a puddle. Bitterly is the best way to describe the manner in which she displayed her affections. For Christmas she'd bring over something like a canned ham or a jar of peanuts, cheap scotch for Dad, maybe some chocolates for my mother. She was childless and bossy and the only one to insist we pray before we ate. My mother, drunk already, would roll her eyes, pinch me under the table, make me laugh. Mom wasn't so bad, it seemed, at Christmas. My hopes were always high as I got into bed, drunk and full of sponge cake. Inevitably, Christmas mornings Dad would give Joanie and me each a dollar bill, wadded up and stuffed with lint from the pants pocket of his uniform. A few times our mother gave us new socks or pencils. That was all.

My father and I had silently agreed to do away with Christmas when my mother died. Only one year I did give him a gift—something cruel in its uselessness, given his predicament— a tie. Joanie would send a card if she thought of it. She'd have Christmas parties of her own, I knew, but she never invited me. I don't hold it against her. I wasn't much fun.

When I woke up on that fateful Christmas Eve, the last one of my life in X-ville, I had six hundred forty-seven dollars stashed in my jewelry box. That was quite a sum of money at the time. My life's savings. And I had a gun. Pulling it out from under my pillow, I really felt quite cool. Its strange provenance did not elude me. My father had used it first as a prop of power in the line of duty, and then as a threat to the invisible criminals only he could see. Those phantasms, he claimed, understood he would shoot to kill. One begins to think in terms of grandiose self-conceit when there's a gun in one's hand, that is true. I shall use the gun to clear my path to freedom, I thought that morning, aiming at invisible obstacles. I'm embarrassed remembering how easily that thing filled me with confidence and seemed to open up a world of possibility. I thought about showing it to Rebecca that evening. Perhaps I would suggest we go out to the woods and shoot at trees. Or we could go out to the frozen lake and stand and shoot at the moon. Or to the beach, lie on our backs, make angels in the snow, shoot at the stars. Such were my romantic ideas for the evening with my new best friend.

Lying there on my cot, I agonized over what to wear. I imagined Rebecca would be dressed comfortably—no elaborate gown or expensive jewelry, it was her house after all—but beautifully, perhaps in a thick cashmere sweater and fitted trousers, like Jackie Kennedy on a ski vacation. As for Rebecca's house, I pictured dark rolling Oriental carpets, sumptuous couches with velvet pillows, a bearskin rug. Or maybe it was more modern and austere, dark wood floors, cold glass coffee table, burgundy drapes, fresh-cut roses. I was excited. I dozed, mentally taking stock of the garments in my mother's wardrobe and piecing together what I would wear that evening. I knew every item of clothing inside out. Nothing fit me right, as I've said, so I often wore layers of sweaters or long underwear just to fill things out. Lying there, I had a bad habit of drumming my fists on my stomach and pinching the negligible amount of fat on my thighs. I sincerely believed that if there were less of me, I would have fewer problems. Perhaps it was for this reason that I wore my mother's clothes—to be vigilant in my mission never to reach even her minor proportions. As I've said, her life, the life of a woman, seemed utterly detestable to me. There was nothing I wanted less back then than to be somebody's mother, some-body's wife. Of course, I'd already become just that for my father by the tender age of twenty-four.

"Eileen!" my father yelled, stomping up the attic stairs some-time later that morning. "The store's open already. Come on, get down!" When I opened the door, he was dressed, had his hands on his hips. "Isn't it Christmas Eve?" he asked.

"No, Dad," I lied. "You missed Christmas. Christmas was yesterday."

"Smart ass," he said. "I'll spare you my hell if you get down now, quick."

"All right," I said. "But who's driving?"

"You're driving. Now get in the car and let's go. I'm coming with you."

It was rare that my father dared to make an appearance outside the house like a normal person, but he was adamant about it that morning. Perhaps he sensed somehow that I was going to abandon him. More likely he was afraid of shops closing over the holidays and didn't trust me to buy him enough booze to get him through. He never explained his choice to move from the kitchen chair to the bed upstairs. It might have been a strategic move. Without his gun, he was defenseless against the hoodlums and was better off hiding. My mother's deathbed was just as good a place as any to die, he may have thought. Not that he had surrendered, that was clear. He seemed just as on guard as ever. "Hurry now!" he yelled, busting open the front door to the bright, sparkling morning. "Before they sell out. It's Christmas Eve. Wine for wolves. Get out there. You got the keys? Lock up. People are crazy this time of year. Crime spikes. It's a proven fact, Eileen. Jesus Christ." I went and got his shoes, threw them up on the porch. He kept talking. "Everybody out, probably leaving their doors wide open. Stupid. Idiots. Don't they know this town is full of thieves?" He slid into the shoes and shuffled out to the car, wincing in the sunlight like a man crawling out of a cave, arms held feebly above his head, shielding his eyes. On the passenger seat beside me he lifted his feet one by one, had me lean over and tie his shoelaces.

The roads on the drive to the liquor store glittered with fresh snow once again. The streetlamps were wrapped in ribbon and holly, store window displays were festive, pretty. Along the sidewalks people hustled, dressed up in hats and plaid wool coats and boots and mittens. The hems of women's skirts skimmed the shelves of snow along the sidewalks. People balanced stacks of brightly colored packages in their arms, piling them in the trunks of their cars. There was almost music in the air. Children built snowmen in their front lawns, played in the yard of the public library. I would miss that old library. I couldn't realize at the time how those books had saved me. I rolled my window down.

"It's cold," said my father. I hadn't ever told him about the exhaust problem.

"The air in here is stale," I said. In fact it still smelled of vomit in there, but my father couldn't detect it. The gin reeking through his skin and on his breath obliterated all other smells around him, I assumed.

"Stale? Who cares about stale?" He reached over my lap, brushing my thighs, then stuck an elbow haphazardly between my knees as he rolled the window back up. I just looked ahead calmly. He had no respect for my comfort or privacy. When I was younger and just beginning to develop, he sometimes sat at the kitchen table at night drinking with my mother and called me over to assess my progress, to pinch and measure.

"Not so good, Eileen," he would say. "You've got to try harder."

"Come on now," Mom said, laughing. "Don't be cruel." And then once she said instead, "She's too old for you to touch now, Charlie," and clucked her tongue.

It could have been much worse, of course. Other girls got rubbed and grabbed and violated. I just got poked and ridiculed. Still, it hurt and angered me, and made me lash out later in life when I felt I was being measured and judged. A man I lived with for a time suggested I secretly wished I'd been big breasted, that I felt bad because I'd disappointed my father with my "small rack. Every girl wants daddy's hands on her tits," that man had said. What an idiot. He was just a mediocre musician from a wealthy family. I put up with him for a while because I thought maybe he was pointing to some dark truth about myself, and I suppose he was. I was a fool to be with a man like him. I was a fool about men in general. I learned the long way about love, tried every house on the block before I got it right. Now, finally, I live alone.

"Where in hell are you going?" my father hissed, going stiff and sliding down across his seat as I turned a corner. He wasn't quite right in the head, as I've said. He was scared of his own shadow. I think that's clear by now. "This is not the way. There are bad people here, and goddammit, Eileen, I didn't bring my gun."

"We can throw snowballs," I laughed. The gun was in my purse, of course. My father seemed to prefer to believe he'd just misplaced it. I didn't care. Nothing could disrupt my good mood. Finally, with Rebecca to celebrate it, I would have a Christmas I could enjoy. My father could strip me nude and pelt me with shards of glass, for all I cared. Nothing was going to get to me that day. Soon I'd be at Rebecca's house where I'd be treated like a queen.

"Get me out of here," he whined as he pulled the collar of his coat up over his head. Stopped at a light, he gestured with his thumb over his shoulder. "Hoodlums," he whispered, eyes cloudy with fear. I just chuckled, coasted through the city streets, past the cemetery, past the police station, then back around, looping through the elementary school parking lot. I guess I was trying to torture him. "Tell me what you see," he said. "Are they following us? Did they see me? Act natural. Don't speak. Just drive. And roll down the windows, yeah, that's a good idea. That way if they shoot at us the glass won't shatter."

I rolled down my window gladly. I enjoyed my father's madness that day. He was a comic figure, slapstick almost. When we got to Lardner's he spoke in hushed tones to Mr. Lewis behind the counter, ordered up a case of gin and pulled a few bags of potato chips off the shelf. I bought a bottle of wine for my evening at Rebecca's. Dad didn't ask questions. On the ride home he lay across the backseat, shaking and sweating. And when I pulled into our driveway he crawled out of the car, swam through the snow to the front porch, begging for me to "come faster, open the door, let me in. It's not safe out here." I calmly carried the box of booze up the front walk to the porch, but he was impatient, scrambled through the living room window, chiding me for leaving it unlocked—"Are you crazy?" When he opened the door from the inside, he ripped the top off the box of gin and pulled out two bottles, slung one under each armpit. "I've raised a fool," he said. I watched him scuttle inside, kick off his shoes. "Two days old!" he yelled, and cleared his throat, settling into his easy chair with the newspaper he'd found frozen on the porch. I was too concerned with my own plans to bother to lock his shoes back up in the trunk right away.

Upstairs, I found my mother's pills and put them in my purse but didn't take any. I wanted to save them. If I had to spend Christmas Day at home with my father after he got back from Mass, I wanted to spend it in deep twilight sleep. I went back to my cot and returned to my fantasies of my evening at Rebecca's. I imagined her saying things like, "I've never met anybody like you before." And also, "I've never felt this close to someone before. We have so much in common. You're perfect." And I pictured hours of rapt conversation, delicious wine, a warm fire, Rebecca saying, "You're my best friend. I love you," and kissing my hand the way you'd kiss the hand of an oracle or a priest. I pulled my hand out from under me, red and cramped, and kissed it reverently. "I love you, too," I said to it, and laughed at my own silliness, pulling the covers over my head. I waited for Rebecca's phone call. Somehow I slept. I don't remember those dreams, the last dreams I'd ever have in that house. I wish I could. I hope they were good ones.

I do remember my father's wailing later that afternoon from the foot of the attic stairs.

"What's wrong, Dad?" I yelled, bolting out of bed.

"The phone rang," he said. "Some woman looking for you. Maybe a lady cop, I don't know."

"What did you tell her?"

I stomped my foot waiting for his reply.

"Nothing," he threw up his arms. "I know nothing and said nothing. Mum from me." I flew down the stairs, found the phone in the kitchen dangling off the hook, receiver thudding against the wooden cabinet.

"Well, hello, Christmas angel" is how Rebecca answered when I picked it up.

It's important to keep in mind, given what I'm about to relay, which is everything I remember from that evening, that I had truly never had a real friend before. Growing up I'd only had Joanie, who disliked me, and a girlfriend or two here and there in grade school, usually the other class reject. I remember a girl with braces on her legs in junior high, and an obese girl in high school who barely spoke. There was an Oriental girl whose parents owned the one Chinese restaurant in X-ville, but even she discarded me when she made the cheerleading squad. Those were not real friends. Believing that a friend is someone who loves you, and that love is the willingness to do anything, sacrifice anything for the other's happiness, left me with an impossible ideal, until Rebecca. I held the phone close to my heart, caught my breath. I could have squealed with delight. If you've been in love, you know this kind of exquisite anticipation, this ecstasy. I was on the brink of something, and I could feel it. I suppose I was in love with Rebecca. She awoke in my heart some long-sleeping dragon. I've never felt that fire burning like that again. That day was without a doubt the most exciting day of my life.

She told me to come over whenever I felt like it. She said she would be home, "relaxing. We'll just sit and chat here," she said. "Nothing fancy. It'll be fun. There are some records we can play and maybe dance again, if all goes well." I remember her kind, measured voice, her words all very clearly. I scribbled her address down—it was not a street name I recognized. I hung up the phone, nearly swooning, and stood there for a minute, blinded with glee.

"None of your business," I mumbled at my father when he tapped on the kitchen table to startle me out of my trance.

"Pass me some chips!" he yelled back. He seemed to have forgotten the story of my night out with Leonard Polk. I assumed the lie had been flushed away in last night's gin.

I ran upstairs to get ready. My face in the mirror looked less monstrous than usual. If Rebecca wanted to look at it, maybe it wasn't so bad, I thought. It's amazing what the mind will do when the heart is throbbing. I selected a gray linen suit from my mother's closet, something I thought Rebecca would approve of. Nothing flashy. I must have looked like a dowdy grandmother in that suit, but at the time it felt right—subdued, mature, thoughtful. In retrospect I see that it was what a sidekick would wear, a uniform of service, a blank page. I put on a white nylon slip, a fresh pair of the navy panty hose, my snow boots, my mother's camel coat. I remember these articles of clothing perfectly since they were what I was wearing and all I ended up taking with me of my mother's wardrobe when I left X-ville, after all. Despite my grand plans, I left with just those clothes on my back and a purse full of money, and the gun, of course. I brushed my hair in the mirror. My greasy lipstick seemed suddenly pretentious, cheap, idiotic. I decided to go without makeup. After all, Rebecca didn't wear any. And I suppose my desire to be close with Rebecca, to be understood and accepted by her, allayed my fear of being seen without my mask of cosmetics and indifference.

I remember going and getting the map of X-ville from the car and galloping like a clumsy deer back inside through the glistening mounds of snow. I was full of energy. When I looked out across the yard, carefully shutting the front door, church bells chimed through the bare trees, and I thought how beautiful the light sky was at that moment, tinged orange and blue as the sun set. I was happy. I really was, I thought. I quickly figured out my route to Rebecca's house, which seemed to be on the wrong side of the tracks, as they say—that barely registered as odd at the time—and then I folded up the map and put it in my coat pocket. I still have that map. It's at home, pinned up on the back of my closet door. Faded and stiff now, I carried it around for years and I've cried over it many times. It's the map of my childhood, my sadness, my Eden, my hell and home. When I look at it now, my heart swells with gratitude, then shrinks with disgust.

Before I left for Rebecca's, I drank some vermouth to calm myself, pulled on my mother's black leather gloves and fox fur hat—her only fur—and said good-bye to my father, who was leaning over the sink, peeling a boiled egg.

"Where do you think you're going?" he asked benignly, slurring.

"Christmas party," I answered. I grabbed the wine.

He paused, and looked genuinely perplexed for a moment, then said mockingly, "Just as long as you'll be home in time for dinner." He chuckled and plunked the entire egg into his mouth, wiped his hands on his shirt. The last time we'd eaten a real dinner together was years before my mother's death, perhaps for someone's birthday—chicken burnt to a crisp in the pan, a soggy pot of macaroni. That one boiled egg and a bag of potato chips was all my father would eat all day. Did I feel bad leaving him that evening? I didn't. I figured I'd be home that night to bear the brunt of his misery, hear all his complaints, maybe have a drink with him in the morning before he left for church and I took my mother's last few pills, which I estimated would put me to sleep for the better part of the day. It should have been sad to leave my father alone on Christmas, but if ever my father felt he was at risk for being pitied, he attacked me with an insult aimed precisely at my self-esteem.

"You're pale as a ghost, Eileen," he said, reclining back down in his chair. "You could scare small children out of their socks."

I just laughed at him. In that moment, nothing could hurt me.

I skipped out down the shoveled path and into the black and sparkling wet street. I was on my way to meet my destiny.

*N*othing could have added to the pleasure of my anticipation on that drive through X-ville on my way to Rebecca's house that evening—not the calm roads or the softly falling snow, not the homes full of happy little families, not the gay blinking lights strung up on every Christmas tree. Besides my car's stink of exhaust and vomit, the air from outside smelled of roasting ham and cookies, but I had no use for that holiday cheer. I had Rebecca now. Life was wonderful. My little world of exhaust and vomit was somehow wonderful. I watched out the open window as I passed guests arriving at one house, a child carrying a pie in a glass pan, parents bearing gifts of wine wrapped in red cellophane and ribbon. They looked happy, but I wouldn't envy anyone that Christmas, a holiday best suited to those who thrive on self-pity and resentment. That's what all that eggnog and wine is for, after all. The wine I'd bought for Rebecca sat beside me on the seat, still in the measly brown paper bag from the liquor store. I should have decorated it somehow, I thought. I really ought to have found some wrapping paper, some ribbon. It suddenly seemed disgraceful, insulting really, to show up with such a rough gift. Rebecca deserved better, didn't she? I thought to knock on someone's door or rifle through a garbage can for scraps of candy-striped or holly-patterned prints, but I would never do that. Still, the paper bag was less than ideal.

As though God were listening, when I passed Bayer Street, a long spotlight came on and fell on a nativity scene set up on the snow at the foot of a small hill. I watched an elderly woman swing open the heavy arched door of Saint Mary's at the top and disappear inside. It was the church my father attended every Sunday. I pulled over to take a closer look at the scene, unsure of what was motivating my curiosity. The nativity was simple, just dolls stuck in the snow in front of a piece of brown wooden fencing not more than two feet high. Mary knelt beside Joseph. They were both clothed in burgundy robes tied with twine. There was something wrapped in gold cloth in Mary's arms. I got out of the car. I was inspired.

The nativity figures were made of painted wood and were actually quite beautiful, I thought. I'd loved dolls as a child, but when I turned six my mother collected them and threw them away. The figure of Mary had a wide grin on its face. When I approached it and stood on the cleared sidewalk, I saw that the mouth had been defaced. Someone had painted over it with what looked like bright red lipstick. Black marker crisscrossed within the lips turned her smile into a jack-o'-lantern smirk. It made me laugh. From inside the church I could hear them singing hymns, a piano jangling brightly above the soft and warbling voices. A child cried. I walked closer to the scene, marking my footsteps in the snow. The cloth wrapped around something meant to be the Baby Jesus was a thick, mustard-colored synthetic material, and it was affixed to Mary's extended wooden arms with masking tape. I removed my gloves and fingered the tape. It was gummy from moisture, but the fabric was soft and satiny. The church music stopped. I listened as the pastor began to pray the liturgy. The sound of it filled me with dread, but that didn't stop me from peeling the masking tape off Mary's arms and yanking at the golden cloth. Underneath was an empty canister of motor oil. I was pleased. In the car, I wrapped the wine in Jesus' blanket. It felt appropriate. I consulted the map and drove on.

Certain images come back to me now. For instance, the cemetery covered in snow, an iridescent blue light cast across its surface, the irregular pattern made by the tops of rounded grave-stones peeking up out of the icy crust, and the long, shrinking shadows of trees. The sun having just set, the roads grew darker as I drove across town, streetlamps yellow and hazy, some just flickering. The homes got smaller and closer together. They were not the grand brick colonials of my own neighborhood, but the washed-out wooden trailer-size homes of the less well-to-do— the poor, to be blunt. Their homes were more like cabins, really, a shantytown style of cheap housing built on the coast. I passed a corner store whose windows were plastered in outdated ads for cigarettes and hand-drawn signs proclaiming the cost of bread, beer, eggs.

When I got to Rebecca's street, I found only a few lights on in the sad, narrow houses. That area was nearer to the ocean, windier than my neighborhood, and the houses seemed to be crouched down, huddling close to the ground, hiding. There were chain-link fences around each yard, few cars in the driveways. I counted the house numbers. I couldn't think why Rebecca would want to live in a neighborhood like that. Surely the prison was paying her well enough to get an apartment someplace nice. She appeared to be a woman of means—her clothes were fashionable and looked expensive. But even if she dressed in rags, it would have been clear that Rebecca was not a poor woman. You can see wealth in people no matter what they're wearing. It's in the cut of their chins, a certain gloss to the skin, a drag and pause to their responsiveness. When poor people hear a loud noise, they whip their heads around. Wealthy people finish their sentences, then just glance back. Rebecca was wealthy, and I knew it. That she lived in X-ville at all seemed strange. I'd expected she would have preferred to live somewhere more central, Boston or Cambridge, where there were intelligent and sophisticated young people, and art, things to do. Perhaps she hated the long commute. Anyway, what did I know? Perhaps Rebecca wasn't a snob, and I was wrong to expect her to want to live so comfortably. Rolling down her block, I told myself the street did indeed have a dark charm to it. And I figured it took courage and a big heart for a rich woman like Rebecca to live amongst people who worked in factories and gas stations and on fishing boats, or not at all. I imagined the neighborhood was the place my father had done his best work, beating up teenagers, busting into houses full of drunken yelling, a room full of crying children, men with long hair, and fleshy, wrinkly women with rotted teeth and tattoos, wearing only underwear.

And then I found Rebecca's house, a dark brown two-story home with white trim and a decrepit plant frozen at the top of the front steps. It was slightly less pathetic than the other houses on the block, at least. There were lights on in every window, music on inside loud enough that I could hear it from out in the car. I parked, rolled up my window, primped in the rearview mirror, and got out with my wine. Here my memory breaks down like a film in slow motion. I unlatched the gate and stepped into the yard. My black snow boots found a narrow path hastily cleared of snow, still icy. I walked carefully, not wanting to slip and fall and break the wine or look foolish. I was nervous. It had been a long time since I'd gone any place I wanted to be. Up the steps I saw a shadow move behind yellow curtains. I held the screen with my hip and knocked on the painted plywood door, which swung open as soon as I touched it.

"You made it!"

There she was. My Rebecca. She held in her arms a dirty

white cat which clawed at her loose hair, then looked at me and hissed. "Never mind her, him," she said. "It's upset because its owner has been a little hysterical all day."

"Hi," I said, awkwardly. "Merry Christmas."

"You know I nearly forgot it was Christmas? Come on in," she said.

Rebecca dropped the cat with a heavy thud on the worn wood floor and it slunk away, hissing some more. She seemed agitated, too, Rebecca did, from the get-go. I felt like I might be intruding. I looked for a place to put down my things. The front hall had narrow, chipping maroon walls. An ugly metal railing led up the carpeted staircase which was particularly dirty, stray strands of the rug hanging off where the cat had pawed it.

"I brought wine," I said, unfurling the golden fabric from the bottle and turning the label so Rebecca could read it.

"Well, aren't you a peach," she said. She had an odd way about her. She seemed tense and fake, but I liked what she was saying. "That was so thoughtful." She pulled a cigarette from the pocket of her stained, white terrycloth bathrobe, which she wore over her clothes like a housecoat. I found that bizarre. Perhaps I'd arrived too early? "Don't mind me," she said. "I didn't want to get my clothes dirty." She gestured down at her robe. "Want one?" she asked, lighting her cigarette and handing me the pack. I took one, fumbling with my gloves and the wine and my purse. Rebecca lit it for me, her hand shaking as she gripped the lighter, eyes focused on the trembling flame when I looked up at her. The smell in the air was of cat piss and fresh cigarette smoke and old sweat. It reminded me of my father's armchair. It was cold in that house, too. I kept my coat on.

"I'm sorry the place is such a mess," she said. "I've barely made a dent in cleaning it, but here," she motioned toward the kitchen. "Let's sit down and open that wine."

We passed by what looked like the living room—a wooden coffee table piled high with junk and unopened mail, a TV playing static, a pile of laundry spilled out across the couch. The walls were bare but for several lighter square spots in the dun-colored wallpaper where it was clear there'd been pictures hanging. The record player had on something ridiculous. Rachmaninoff or even *Die Walküre* come to mind, but it was more likely Pat Boone, corny love songs. The effect, nevertheless, was strangely morbid, foreboding. A telephone hung by the kitchen doorway, through which I could see one chair at a small enamel table, a sink full of dirty dishes, an opened package of sliced bread fanned across the yellowed linoleum counter. A clock whirred high on the wall over a calendar opened to May of 1962, a photo of a marine saluting, a chiseled chin. A trash can was set by the kitchen table, ready to catch the overflow of pea-nut shells piled up alongside empty cans of Schlitz. It seemed not unlike my own home. My senses were sharp, but the chaos of the place was buzzing with something I couldn't immediately identify. Rebecca fidgeted with her hair. She seemed different. She seemed terribly uneasy. I felt I'd walked into a scene from a movie in which someone was going mad, the air heavy with sus-pense. I tried my best to look natural, smile, to read Rebecca's stilted cues.

"Here, sit down," she said, ashing her cigarette on the tile floor. "Let me get rid of this." She gracefully swept the peanut shells and the beer cans into the trash can, patted the seat of the tin chair with a yellow cushion. "Sit."

Since I'd walked in the door, Rebecca hadn't looked me in the eye. I felt around on my face to make sure there wasn't something unappetizing on it—a sudden blemish or a crust of sleep, a booger hanging from my nose. But there was nothing. I sat down. We were quiet and awkward, shy for a moment, Rebecca assessing the newly cleared table, flicking her cigarette nervously, me folding my gloves, unbuttoning and rebuttoning my coat. Finally I nodded toward the bottle of wine.

"I hope it's a kind you like," I began.

"Well, that's just swell," said Rebecca, turning confusedly toward the kitchen cupboards. "I probably don't need much, so you drink up. Now let's see where the corkscrew is hiding." She opened a cabinet to reveal shelves of spices and a few cans of food, another of plates and saucers. She pulled out a rattling drawer then slammed it. "There must be one somewhere in all this mess, huh?" She tried another drawer and rifled through spoons and forks. Another drawer was completely empty. "Well, no luck. Hand me the bottle, we'll do it this way."

Rebecca's rings clanked against the glass as she walked to the sink and hovered, hesitated, then grasped the bottle from the bottom and bashed the neck of it against the ledge of the counter. It made a loud cracking sound. "Almost." She banged it again, and the neck broke off and fell, wine spilling across the dirty tile floor. "That'll have to do," she said, throwing a rag onto the red puddle and mopping it with her feet in those tall, leather boots. "I saw that done once without spilling. Maybe he used a hammer. I don't know."

"He?" I would have liked to have asked. "Very inventive" was all I could think to say. I smiled, but inside I was disturbed by the dark unruliness of the house and Rebecca's disregard for decorum, to put it lightly. She paced back and forth for a moment, licking her fingers. Something was on her mind, but I didn't dare ask what. At last she looked me in the eyes and frowned.

"I'm a crummy hostess," she sighed.

"Don't be silly," I told her. "You should see where I live." The ceiling light was a mere bare bulb hanging from a wire. Through the kitchen window I spied a car covered in snow, and another behind it, Rebecca's two-door, with just a dusting of white. It was all very odd. Was this her boyfriend's house? I wondered. Had she shacked up with a local? It was possible, I guessed. Was I disappointed? Surely. I'd expected bone china, mahogany, beveled mirrors, damask, soft pillows, velvet, comfort and decadence, things from magazines. This was a poor person's house. And more so, a poor person in a bad state. We've all seen homes like this, dingy and depressed, no life anywhere, no color, like a grainy black and white television screen. I've lived in countless such places throughout my adulthood, places I wouldn't set foot in today. It's remarkable what people become blind to when they're in such darkness. The only comfort I found in that house was that all in all it was in even worse shape than mine.

I will say this about houses. Those perfect, neat colonials I'd passed earlier that evening on my way through X-ville are the death masks of normal people. Nobody is really so orderly, so perfect. To have a house like that says more about what's wrong with you than any decrepit dump. Those people with perfect houses are simply obsessed with death. A house that is so well maintained, furnished with good-looking furniture of high quality, decorated tastefully, everything in its place, becomes a living tomb. People truly engaged in life have messy houses. I knew this implicitly at age twenty-four. Of course at twenty-four I was also obsessed with death. I had tried to distract myself from my terror not through housekeeping, like the housewives of X-ville, but through my bizarre eating, compulsive habits, tireless ambivalence, Randy and so forth. I hadn't realized this until sitting at Rebecca's kitchen table, watching her crack open a peanut, lick her fingers: I would die one day, but not yet. There I was.

A silly truism comes back to me, "If you loved me, you'd be blind to my flaws." I've tried that line on many men in my life, and the response usually has been, "Then I guess I don't love you." Makes me laugh each time I remember it. I gave Rebecca the benefit of the doubt, tried to justify her grunginess the way I justified my own. The grime on her kitchen table meant she couldn't be bothered to clean. Well, neither could I. And that made sense to me. Surely Rebecca could afford to pay someone to clean for her, and she just hadn't gotten around to hiring anyone yet. She was new in town, after all. I thought she was wonderful. Her nervousness, her scraggly hair, her chapped lips, these quirks only made her more beautiful. I watched her turn and start opening and closing various cupboards and closets. Her bathrobe fell open around her shoulders like a fur stole. There was nothing that woman couldn't get away with.

"Aha," she exclaimed, setting down two cups. They were cheap coffee mugs like you'd find at a diner, chipped and stained brown on the inside. She poured the wine awkwardly from the broken bottle. "You like the music?" she asked, her long finger poking up into the air. She was jumpy. It's possible she had taken something before I arrived, it occurred to me at the time. So many women took pills back then to keep their figures. It made them nervous, creepy. I don't suppose Rebecca was above that. When I think back on her upright posture, her long wild hair, her strange monochromatic outfits, she seems incredibly vain.

"Sure," I said, lifting my eyes as though the music could be seen floating in the air. "I love it."

Rebecca pushed a bowl full of peanut shells toward me on the table. "You can use that as an ash tray," she said. "Just be careful with the wine. There might be some broken glass in there."

"Thanks," I said, and peered into the dark liquid. It smelled much like the vomit from my car.

"Mmm," Rebecca purred, tasting it. "This is just wonderful. I hope you haven't spent too much on it. Cheers." She approached me at the table and held out her mug. "To Jesus Christ, happy birthday." We clinked. She laughed, seemed to relax a bit. "How has your Christmas Eve been so far, Miss Eileen?"

"Pretty good," I answered. "I spent the morning with my father." I hoped to sound well adjusted.

"Your father?" she said. "I didn't know you had family here. Does he live in the area?"

"Not too far," I answered. I could have told her the truth—that I'd been his willing slave until she came along, that he was a crazy drunk, and that I hated him so much I wished him dead sometimes—but the air was already heavy with woe. "He lives within walking distance from my place," I told her. "That's been nice since he's retired. He gets lonely a lot."

"That's lovely," Rebecca said. "That you spend time with him, not that he's lonely, I mean," she laughed.

I attempted a self-conscious chuckle, which fell flat. "Do you live here alone?" I asked, happy to switch the focus onto her.

"Oh sure," she said, to my great relief. "I simply can't have roommates. I like my own space. And I like to make a lot of noise. I can play my music as loud as I want."

"Me too," I lied. "I can't stand roommates. In college I—"

"People are how they are and they do what they do, don't they?" Rebecca interrupted me, leaning against the counter. She didn't seem to be interested in a response. She stared intensely down at her wine, her lips already stained, her face a bit flushed. I really wondered about that bathrobe she wore. It was old and worn and discolored, hardly something a person would wear in the presence of company. Was I not worthy of anything better? "I don't believe we do things we don't want to do," she said oddly, her voice now grave and restrained. "Not unless there's a gun pointed at our heads. And even then, one has a choice. Still, nobody wants to admit they want to be bad, do bad things. People just love shame. This whole country's hooked on it if you ask me. Let me ask you, Eileen," she turned to me. I put down my mug—already nearly empty—and looked up at her, my eyes bright with expectation. "Are the boys in our prison bad people?" she asked.

This was not the question I'd hoped to hear. I tried to mask my disappointment with a thoughtful lift of my eyebrows, as though seriously considering her question about the boys. "I think a lot of them just had bad luck to begin with. Rotten luck, most of all," I replied.

"I think you're right." She put down her mug, dropped her cigarette butt into it. She crossed her arms and looked me bluntly in the eyes. "But tell me, Miss Eileen, have you ever wanted to be truly bad, do something you knew was wrong?"

"Not really," I lied. I don't know why I denied this. I sensed Rebecca could see through my dishonesty, so I tensed and hid behind the mug, gulping the last of my wine. I wanted to be understood and respected, you might say, yet I still felt that I might be punished if I expressed my real feelings. I had no idea how trivial my shameful thoughts and feelings really were. "May I use your bathroom, please?" I asked.

Rebecca pointed toward the ceiling. "There's one upstairs."

I took my purse with me as I plodded up the dirty, carpeted steps, holding the iron rail for balance. I was soothed by the weight of the gun on my shoulder. I just wanted to hold it in my hands for a moment, to get my bearings. As I climbed, I lamented my cowardice. How could I ever be happy, I asked myself, if I didn't allow Rebecca to know me deep down inside? It was silly of me, of course, to take this all so seriously. Still, I kicked myself for being so uptight. Rebecca had invited me into her home, allowed me to see her in her natural state, however slovenly and nervous. That was friendship. I didn't want to disappoint her. But if I had to reveal my true self that evening, if we were to bond in any deep way, I would need more alcohol, I thought.

The bathroom door at the top of the stairs was wide open. It smelled bad inside. It was a pink tiled bathroom, old metal fixtures rusted orange at the seams, a plastic shower curtain rumpled and browned with mold. The knob on the door rattled and wouldn't stay closed, the bath faucet dripped, and the tub itself was ringed green and stank of mildew. The sink, too, was greenish, and on the ledge sat a red, chewed-up toothbrush, a tube of discount toothpaste rolled up tight and crusted. A tube of lipstick was perched under the greasy mirror. I opened it—bright pink, nearly finished. Flesh-colored stockings hung from the shower curtain rod. A bar of soap bore tiny curled hairs dried to its chalky surface. These must be Rebecca's pubic hairs, I thought to myself. I took it and rubbed it on my face, splashed away the suds, and felt a little better. I dried my hands on a rag, then took the gun out. The smooth feel of the wood and metal soothed me. I pointed it at my reflection in the mirror. I held it against my face, cool and hard. I could smell my father on the gun, not the acrid madness of gin he exuded then, but the warm, homey smoke of whiskey from when I was a child and didn't know better than to look up to him. I put it back in my purse and fixed my hair in the mirror.

Before I went back down to the kitchen, I quietly stepped around the banister and peered into the lit-up rooms upstairs. One was a bedroom: green and pink floral bedspread, a cheap desk lamp on a drab dresser, ugly gold earrings on a pale blue saucer, an empty can of beer. A mirror hung on the closet door. I wanted to see Rebecca's wardrobe inside, but didn't dare snoop that far. If in fact she was a slob and her elegance and refinement were a sham, maybe there was hope for me after all. Maybe I could be a sham, and appear elegant and refined, too. The next bedroom meant little to me at the time: a small wooden desk, a twin bed stripped to the mattress, a fan on the bedside table next to a small stuffed bear, a map of America on the wall. None of it made much sense, but I reasoned that Rebecca must have rented the house furnished and never cleaned. I looked in the mirror. A drawn and haggard face looked back at me. I looked like an old lady, a corpse, a zombie. I looked slightly less deadly when I tried to smile. It seemed preposterous that this beautiful woman wanted me around. As I walked back down the stairs, I put on a mask like Leonard Polk's—contented, confident, perfectly at ease.

When I sat back down at the kitchen table, Rebecca was busy looking through the cabinets again. "Aha!" she exclaimed, turning around with a corkscrew. "Too late, I'm sorry. Please, have more wine." She poured out the last of it. "Thank you for bringing it," she said again.

"I guess it's a kind of housewarming party, too, isn't it? Since you've just moved here?" I tried to sound chipper.

"I love that. A housewarming, yes. Thank you," Rebecca answered. "That's very appropriate. The house needs some warming. Drafty old place." She pulled up the collar of her robe and opened her mouth as though to say more, but stopped herself, folded her arms across her chest.

"How long have you lived here?" I asked. "If you don't mind my asking."

"I got to town just a few weeks ago," she replied, adjusting her robe. "I must say I was expecting the cold, but nothing like this. This is pretty brutal cold you have here. Worse than Cambridge. But the snow is pretty. Don't you think?"

The conversation went on like that, perfunctorily. The magic was gone. It was as if we'd broken the ice but the frigid waters had made us slow and phony with hypothermia. I'd missed my chance, I reckoned, to be her real friend. Rebecca had opened the door to me and I'd shut it in her face. I was boring. I had nothing to contribute. I tried, pathetically now, to make up for my flatness with self-pity. "I don't get out much," I told her. "There isn't much to do here in winter. Or in any season."

"Do you ice-skate?" Rebecca asked with false enthusiasm, I sensed.

I shook my head no, smiled, then corrected myself. "But I'd go if you wanted to."

"Oh, that's all right," said Rebecca. It was terribly uncomfortable. The chair was so stiff, the house was so cold. Still, I sipped my wine, nodding and grinning as best I could. I knew what I was hiding—my disappointment, my foiled fantasies, my longing. What Rebecca was hiding, and why, was utterly mysterious to me. She talked at length about how sunburnt she'd gotten over the summer, how her hands cramped while driving, her favorite painters—all abstract expressionists, as I recall. We agreed to take a trip to Boston together in the spring, to the art museums, but she seemed to have retreated to some far-off place in her mind, leaving just the surface of herself to be with me. Perhaps all I deserved was to look at her from afar, I thought. Who was I to think that a woman like Rebecca—beautiful, independent, professional—could ever really care to get to know me? And what did I have to say for myself, anyway? I was a nobody, a nerd. I should be grateful she's doing all the talking. "Do you swim? Do you ski? Where did you buy that fur hat?" I got the feeling she was just humoring me, pitying me, even making fun of me and my dull life, trying to put me at ease with her asinine questions.

Finally I said, "I should be going." There would be other nights, I told myself. Real friendship isn't forged in one evening, anyway. And better to leave on a note of dullness than of discord. I got up out of my chair and began to pull my gloves back on. That was when Rebecca got up from the stool she was sitting on.

"Eileen," she said, coming toward me, her voice suddenly low and stern and sober. "Before you go, I need your help with something." I thought she might ask me to take out the garbage or help her lift a piece of heavy furniture, but she merely said, "Stay. Talk with me a little while longer."

She looked worried. Maybe she's sick, I thought, or expecting a visit from a jealous lover. I would stay, of course. I was desperate for more wine. And I was hungry. As though she'd read my mind, Rebecca got up and opened the old refrigerator. She pulled out a hunk of cheese, a bottle of pickled onions, some ham.

"I'll make us sandwiches," she said. "I really am a bad hostess, I know." I watched her wash two plates, pat them dry with the edge of her bathrobe. "We'll feel better if we eat something."

"I feel fine," I said defensively. It just came out of me, and rang out in that cold kitchen as cutting, rude and untrue. I began to excuse myself, babbling a bit, but Rebecca interrupted me.

"You know as well as I do that there's a bit of tension in the air," she said. "You feel it and I feel it. It's there, so why deny it?" She shook her head, shrugged her shoulders, gave a half smile, then turned her back to me and piled up the sliced bread on the counter.

I let out a high neurotic giggle. I couldn't tell if Rebecca was angry or entertained. "I'm sorry," I mumbled. But she ignored me. Laying aside the awkwardness hanging between us, she turned back to the subject of Moorehead as she worked at the counter. I watched as with unsteady hands she composed our sandwiches. I picked at my chapped lips, fingered the gun inside my purse, listened as she talked. She seemed to relax a bit, her voice now wafting down into its lower registers. With her back turned, she paused now and then, punctuating the air with her knife as she spoke.

"They've hired me to develop some sort of blanket curriculum for the boys, a daily plan for the lot of them, as though they're all the same age and at the same level. As if we could just repeat lessons over and over again. It's a ridiculous idea on its own. I'm not some nineteenth-century farm schoolteacher. And these boys can learn. Most of them are already literate. Of course there will have to be testing, trial and error on my part, to know what works, and then the big questions—what are the goals, what's the point? I'm not here to teach them how to repair car engines, after all. They need to learn literature, history, philosophy, the hard sciences. That's what I think. It's a job big enough for a dozen people. Robert doesn't understand that the boys have minds, that they're even conscious. To him they're just cattle."

"Robert?" I asked. "You mean the warden?"

"The warden," she shook her head. "All he does is punish boys for jerking off." I had a good idea of what that meant. "You knew that, didn't you?" Rebecca turned slightly, showing me the seriousness of her profile. "That guy is really something. His ridiculous Christian rhetoric is completely inappropriate. Then I find out that Leonard Polk got stuck in the cave for 'inappropriate touching.'" She shook her head. "If I were those boys I'd be touching myself all the time. It's about the only fun that can be had in a place like Moorehead, don't you think?" She turned to me then, nose crinkled, eyes shining, suddenly full of sprightly and conniving joy.

"Oh, of course," I said, twisting my hands around in the air to indicate that I was flexible, open-minded, that I had no qualms.

"I swear," Rebecca went on. "I just don't understand what the big deal is." She shook her head. I tried to imagine Rebecca touching herself, what sort of touching she did and how it was different from my sort, as it seemed—given what I knew about her—that she had no shame. I wondered what sort of ecstasy there was to be had without shame to incite it. I couldn't imagine. I was a bit stunned sitting there then, and was grateful that she kept rattling on. She told me how happy she was to be working at the prison, how relieved she was to have finished her degree. She said she was sure she could have a great effect, and how much she cared for the boys already. "Like they're my own brothers" is a phrase I recall clearly. She handed me a plate, plunked a sandwich on it. We sat and ate in silence.

"As you've probably figured out by now, Eileen," she said after a while, "I live a little differently from most people."

"Oh, not at all," I insisted. "Your house is really nice."

"Please, don't be so polite," she said. "I don't mean the house." She looked at me as she stood, munching an onion. "I mean I have my own ideas. I'm not like those women you work with." That was obvious. "Or like your teachers at school, or your mother." She slid her plate back into the sink. "I can tell you have your own ideas, too. Maybe you and I even share some of the same ideas."

Now I felt she was testing me—was I a follower like "most people," or was I "different" like her. I could barely eat the sandwich she'd given me. The bread was stale, the ham was gummy. Still, like a good girl, I chewed and nodded.

"I've realized some things over the years," she said, licking her fingers. "I don't believe in good and bad." She offered me a cigarette. I took it, grateful for an excuse to put down the sandwich. "Those boys at Moorehead, they don't belong there. I don't care what they've done. No child deserves that kind of punishment."

I'd barely drunk two cups of wine, and since it was not in my nature to argue when I wasn't drunk, what I said next surprised me. Perhaps it was the spirit of my father moving in me, because I really didn't care much about the issue. "But those boys are all criminals. They need to be punished somehow," I said. Rebecca was silent. I finished the wine. A few moments passed in which my head grew heavy and spun with regret. It seemed clear that I had offended her. I felt sick to my stomach.

"I should go," I said. "You must be tired." By then, I believe, I'd been in that house less than an hour. My skin felt greasy and hot. The air in the room seemed to be spinning with dust and smoke and the smell of rotting food. I put out my cigarette. Rebecca looked deep in thought—I assumed her thoughts revolved around me, my lack of vision or compassion. What a square I was. What a pig. I worried I might vomit. It seemed imperative that I go home immediately. But Rebecca had other ideas.

"May I confide in you?" she asked, her voice suddenly soft, but urgent. She squatted down toward me, leaning one arm on the table.

Nobody had ever confided in me before. I looked at her squarely in the face, held my breath. She really was beautiful. Suddenly clear-eyed and still and vulnerable, like a scared child in the forest. She held my hand absentmindedly, her fingers cool and soft against my rough skin. I tried to relax, to show that I was open, accepting, available. But I felt my death mask creep up again. I nodded with my eyes closed, thinking that would be a somber and reliable gesture of fidelity. If she had tried to kiss me then, I think I would have gone along.

"It's about Lee Polk," she said.

I really thought that I would vomit at that moment. I began to stand, reaching for my purse, hoping she'd lose her nerve before she could tell me that they'd kissed, or worse. She gripped my hand again, though, and I sat back down.

How relieved I was when she said not, "I'm in love with him," but rather, "He spoke to me." Still there was a kind of perverse look of pride and pleasure on her face. I was reminded of Joanie's self-satisfaction when she'd told me, so many years ago at that point, "He likes to taste me." Rebecca squeezed my fingers, swallowed hard. "He told me everything. What happened and what he did and how he ended up in Moorehead. Look at this." She pulled an old photograph from her robe pocket. It was a photo of the crime scene. Lee Polk's father lay on the blood-darkened carpet, wrapped partly in a tangled sheet, a disheveled bed beside him.

"That's the father," Rebecca went on. "People always think it's Oedipal. Kill the father, marry the mother. That's what I'd assumed."

"Gross," I said. I looked at the photo again. The man's eyes were partly open, as though he were surreptitiously glancing downward, shifty. His arms were held over his head, fingers

jammed and piled up against the bedside table. I'd seen pictures of dead people before in various books and magazines,
mostly important figures lying in mausoleums or photos from
wars—soldiers slumped on the battlefield, starved corpses.
Then of course there was Jesus dead on the cross everywhere
I looked. There had been a few such crime scene photos in
the files of other inmates at Moorehead, but none of them
had captured the essence of death quite like that photo of
Mr. Polk. Not even my own mother's dead body struck me as
powerfully. She'd just faded away, really, a little bit every day
until there was nothing left. Life had been ripped out of Mr.
Polk, however. The death was there, alive in the photo. I twisted
my hand away from Rebecca and got up and flung myself
toward the sink, vomiting that terrible sandwich, all that wine.

"I'm sorry," I said.

Rebecca came up behind me and rubbed my back. "Don't
be sorry," she replied. She handed me a cold, wet and mil-
dewed dishrag. "The picture *should* make you sick." I turned
on the faucet, rinsed my vomit off the plates. "Don't bother,"
Rebecca said.

"I'm sorry," I repeated. I don't know how sorry I really was.
Getting sick like that had excited me. I can't think of any other
time just looking at something has made me vomit. I wanted to
look at the photo again. There was something in it that I couldn't
fully make out. Between the crumpled bedsheets, the thinly
striped sleeping shirt, the black stain puddled on the rug, Mr.
Polk, face sagging and limp, had something to say. Another kind
of life lay behind the blank expression captured in that photo.

I wished I could get inside of it, examine the throat where it was gashed, touch the blood, investigate the wound as though a secret were embedded there, but the throat wasn't visible in the photo. What did those eyes know? What was the last thing Mr. Polk saw? Lee, the knife, the darkness, his wife, his own spirit rising up out of his body? I liked the look of those still, sneaky eyes. Mr. Polk, I knew, held a secret I'd been wanting to understand. He knew death, I suppose. Maybe it was that simple.

"Where did you get that?" I asked Rebecca.

"Lee's file," she said. "Scary, huh?"

I sat back down in the chair, sobered, calm. "Not really," I lied, purposelessly.

"Lee snuck into his parents' bedroom with a kitchen knife and hacked through his father's throat. His mother claims she went into shock. She didn't phone the police right away. She said she woke up and found her husband dead, assumed there'd been a break-in. How do you sleep through something like that, I wonder? Can you imagine? They found the knife in the kitchen sink, and Lee in his bed, holding his teddy bear."

Rebecca's expression hardened as she spoke. I looked closely at her face, at the delicate lines around her eyes, her translucent skin, fresh and rosy. In one moment she looked like a mature woman, in the next, a little girl. My eyes seemed to be playing tricks on me, as though I were peering into a fun house mirror, as if it were all a dream. She tapped my hands to get my attention. "But Lee isn't responsible for this," Rebecca went on. "That's what he explained to me yesterday. The whole ordeal. It's too much for a child to keep to himself." She turned away as though overcome with emotion, but when she faced me again she was calm, steady, even grinning. "It's terrible, this photo, yes. It's disturbing. When I saw it, and then met Lee, I just couldn't put two and two together. A smart, shy boy like that doing something like this. It didn't add up. I asked him if he'd really done it, killed his father." She tapped her finger on the photo, over the dead man's face. "He said that yes, he had done it. Or really he just nodded. I asked him why, but he just shrugged. He didn't open up to me right away, you know. I had to ask the right question. At first I was just stabbing in the dark. Did his dad beat his mom? Did his mom have him kill his dad for the insurance payout? What was it? I just had a sense there was something rotten happening in the family. It's written all over the mother's face, anyhow. You saw her. I knew something was going on. That's why I called her and told her to come in. I told her, 'I think your son would like to speak with you.' You saw them together. The poor boy could hardly look her in the eye. And so afterward I just asked him point-blank. 'What did your father do to you? Did he touch you?' And he spoke. He spilled it all in a matter of minutes. That man, Mr. Polk, was raping him, his own son. Nobody had ever bothered to ask Lee before. Nobody wanted to know."

At this point Rebecca was wild-eyed with enthusiasm, you'd say, nearly salivating, her hands having moved up my wrists and forearms to hold me by the shoulders. I was riveted by the pink of her mouth and gums, the black grit of wine in the chapped corners of her lips. I'd heard of stories like the one she was telling. I had a vague idea of what it all meant. "It doesn't take a degree in psychology to get down to the truth," she went on boastfully. She let go of my shoulders. "And it doesn't take a prison sentence to set things right. The wardens and shrinks of this world are crazier than most killers, I swear. People will tell you the truth, if you really want to hear it. Think about it, Eileen," she said, squeezing my hands again. "What would drive someone to kill his own father?" She looked up at me imploringly, her eyes darting back and forth between mine. "What?" she demanded.

I had spent years debating a similar question. "Killing him," I answered, "would have to be the only way out."

"The only recourse, yes," Rebecca nodded.

We stared again at the photo, her head next to mine, so close that our cheeks touched. She leaned over my shoulder, put her arm around me. The wind shook the house, a spray of snow vibrating the drafty kitchen windows. I closed my eyes. This was as close to another person as I'd been in years. I could feel Rebecca's breath on my hand, hot and quick and steady.

"You have to wonder," she continued, "why the mother didn't *do* something."

I looked up at her. Her strange, shifting expression, strained in the harsh light, eyebrows raised, eyes wide, mouth open in delight or expectation, I couldn't tell. She seemed excited, agitated, ecstatic and full of wonder. I twitched. "My mother's dead," I said defensively. Rebecca wasn't irked by the non sequitur. I held my breath.

"Mothers are very difficult," Rebecca replied. She stood suddenly and gazed down at me as she spoke. "Most women hate one another. It's only natural, all of us competing, mothers and daughters especially. Not that I hate you, of course. I don't see you as competition. I see you as my ally, a partner in crime, as they say. You're special," she said, softening. I could have cried hearing those words. I blinked hard, though my eyes were dry. She reaffirmed her statement by squeezing my hand again, and squatted back down to meet me at eye level. "That mother," she went on, "Mrs. Polk, you remember her, don't you?"

"She was fat," I said, nodding.

"Quiet," Rebecca whispered all of a sudden. She got up, put a finger in the air to hush me. The wind rattled, but otherwise the house was silent. The music had stopped without my noticing it. I held my breath. "Lee's mother," she went on, punctuating the words by clattering her fingernails on the table, "is the real mystery. There's no lovely way to say this, Eileen. It broke my heart to hear the boy tell his story. But as you and I know, it's so important to let the truth out. Lee told me that each evening after dinner, his mother would take him upstairs to give him an enema before bedtime. Then she just sat around watching *The Honeymooners* or painting her nails or sleeping or whatnot until they were done. Why didn't she stop him? The answer is quite plainly that she didn't want to. She must have been benefiting from it all somehow. I just don't understand how."

I was disgusted, of course. But I was also skeptical. "It's really awful," I said, shaking my head back and forth. "Gross," I said again. I watched Rebecca ease back from the table, lean against the counter. She crossed her arms and gazed up at the ceiling. I was suddenly cold and lonely with her so far away. I yearned to get up and go to her, snuggle inside her bathrobe, curl up in her arms like a child.

"You really have to imagine it, Eileen," she went on. "You're just a kid sitting at the kitchen table." She took me through the entire nightly routine at the Polk house as she imagined it, describing in depth how an enema works, the size of the child's anatomy, how the nether regions get torn during the sex act, and then the psychology of the father—how he must have suffered all his life with a desire he couldn't satisfy. "The father's motivation is rather obvious," she said. "He had some wires crossed. For him, doing that with his son, that must have been love. As awful as that sounds, love is like that sometimes. It will make you rape your own son. It's not something we think we'd ever do, but Mr. Polk must have known no other way." I thought of my own father, and my mother for that matter, how little affection they gave me but for a pinch and a poke now and then when I was growing up. Perhaps I was lucky after all. It's very hard to measure out, in hindsight, who had it worse than whom.

"But the mother—Rita is her name—I just don't understand her motivations." Rebecca was intent on getting to a point. I really could not have cared less about the Polks—I had Rebecca now. We were partners in crime. She'd said those very words. I would have cut my palm open with the kitchen knife and made a pact in blood then and there to be friends, sisters, forever and ever. But I sat and listened attentively, feigning interest the best way I knew how, nodding and furrowing my brow and batting my lashes and all.

"I don't get the feeling that the father was threatening her,"

Rebecca continued. "She doesn't come across to me that way."
I knew what she meant, actually. When Mrs. Polk had visited
earlier that week, she hadn't come off as a victim. She held her
head high, seemed more angry than sorrowful, had an air of
judgment in the way she gazed at us—me, Randy, Rebecca,
Leonard. And she didn't seem like the type of woman who
would try very hard to please others. She was fat. She wore ugly
clothing. "I believe something crucial must be resolved with
that woman," Rebecca continued, "before Lee can really move
on. And like I said, I don't believe in punishment, but I do
believe in retribution. Lee's father raped him. He did a bad
thing, so he got killed. Lee killed his father, so he's in prison.
The mother is guilty of her own crime, and she hasn't suffered
any consequence. And Eileen?" She leaned forward, grabbed
me by the calf. "You can't tell anyone about this, you promise?"
I nodded. Rebecca's hand on my leg was enough for me to promise her the world. I still couldn't understand her earnestness,
her grave intensity about the Polks. What did it matter? Why
did she care? When she stuck out her slender pinky finger,
I hooked mine around it. We shook. This gesture felt so heartfelt, so pure, and yet so perverse, my eyes filled with tears.

"This isn't my house, Eileen," Rebecca said then. "It's the
Polk house. I have Rita Polk tied up downstairs."

I should say that as a rather sheltered young person in
X-ville, I had little experience of direct conflicts between
people. My parents' dinnertime fights when I was growing up

were all for nothing, just gripes covering the surface of whatever deeper grievances they each carried around, I'm sure. Nothing ever came to blows, though in my last years with him my father would occasionally wrap his flat hands around my pencil-thin throat and threaten that he could squeeze the life out of me any time he felt like it. It didn't hurt. His hands on my neck were, in fact, a kind of balm—it was all the affection I received back then. I recall that when I was twelve, a girl a few towns over went missing and they found her naked body washed up on the rocks at the beach in X-ville. "Don't take rides from strangers," and "scream if someone tries to grab you," our teachers said to warn us, but their alarm never scared me. On the contrary, being kidnapped was something of a secret wish of mine. At least then I'd know that I mattered to someone, that I was of value. Violence made much more sense to me than any strained conversation. If there had been more fighting in my family growing up in X-ville, things might have turned out differently. I might have stayed.

I must sound terribly self-pitying, complaining that my father didn't love me enough to hit me. But so what? I'm old now. My bones have thinned, my hair has grayed, my breathing has become slow and shallow, my appetite meager. I've had more than my fair share of scrapes and bruises, and I have lived long enough that self-pity is no longer a pathetic habit of the psyche, but like a cold wet cloth on my forehead bringing down the fever of fear about my inevitable mortal demise. Poor me, yes, poor me. When I was young I didn't care at all for my physical well-being. All young people believe they are invincible, that they know well enough not to heed any silly warnings. It was this kind of brave stupidity that led me out of X-ville. If I'd known just how dangerous a place I was escaping to, I may never have left. New York City was no place for a young woman all alone back then, especially a young woman like I was—gullible, helpless, full of rage and guilt and worry. If someone had told me the number of times I'd get groped and grabbed on the subway, how often my heart would be broken, doors slammed in my face, my spirit smashed, I may have stayed home with my father.

Back in X-ville, I'd read tales of violence in the prison files— awful business. Assault, destruction, betrayal, as long as it didn't concern me, it didn't bother me. Those stories were like articles in *National Geographic*. Their details only fostered my own twisted imaginings and fantasies, but never made me scared for my safety. I was naive and I was callous. I didn't care about the welfare of others. I only cared about getting what I wanted. So when Rebecca's revelation hit me, I wasn't as horrified as you'd expect. I was insulted, however. Suddenly it became obvious to me that her friendship was not motivated purely out of admiration and affection, as I'd have preferred to think. Rebecca had forged a rapport, it was clear, as part of a strategy. She assumed I'd be useful to her, and I suppose in the end I was.

"I'm so sorry," I stammered, trying to hide my disappointment. "I'm really not feeling well." I could have told her she was crazy, that I wanted nothing to do with her, that she ought to be committed, but I was so hurt, so dismayed by her scheme to seduce me into being some sort of accomplice that I failed to muster any cutting words or phrases. "Good luck" might have been enough, I suppose. Anyway, I wasn't going to reveal my brokenheartedness to her—I felt humiliated enough already. I'd been such a fool. Of course Rebecca didn't really like me. I was pathetic, ugly, weak, weird. Why would someone like her want someone like me as a friend? "I should really get going," I said, and got up and headed for the door. In the hallway, however, Rebecca grabbed my arm.

"Please," she said. "Don't run off so quick. I'm in something of a little pinch." I could tell from looking at her that she was scared. I thought of breaking free, driving home to tell my father, calling the cops. But with Rebecca looking at me like that, as though I could save her, saying, "Please, I really need you, Eileen. Be a friend," I began to cave. She pulled a cigarette out for me, lit it with trembling hands. "You're the only one I trust," she said. That was all it took to reel me back in. She respected me after all, I chose to believe. She wanted me on her side. Tears filled her eyes and slid down her cheeks. She mopped them up with the cuff of her robe, exhaled, shuddered, looked up at me imploringly.

"OK," I said. Nobody had ever cried to me before. "I'll help you."

"Thank you, Eileen," she said, smiling through her tears. She blew her nose on her sleeve. "I'm sorry," she said. "I'm a mess." It pleased me to see her scared and vulnerable like that. She took another slice of bread from the counter, picked at it mindlessly for a moment. "I don't know how I got into this. But now that we're in it, we have to finish what we started."

I sat down, straightened my back against the chair, crossed

my legs like a lady, folded my hands in my lap. "We could call the police and just explain what happened," I said softly. "It was an accident, we could say." I knew full well this suggestion was ludicrous. I just wanted to reap all the desperation I could out of her. I deserved at least that much in return for my loyalty, I thought.

"And say what?" Rebecca replied. "That I accidentally tied her up? They'd take me to jail," she cried.

"My father was a cop," I told her. Rebecca looked down at me, wide-eyed. "Of course I won't tell him, but I'm saying, if we said Mrs. Polk threatened you . . ."

"The last thing we need is for the police to get involved. Mr. Polk was a cop, you know. If the police actually cared about justice, I wouldn't have had to come here in the first place. I can't go to jail, Eileen. People won't understand the good I'm trying to do." She flapped the piece of bread around and threw it into the sink, lit herself a cigarette. She peered into the broken wine bottle. It was empty. "I could use a drink," she said.

"No drinks," I said, satisfied that she was desperate enough not to judge me. "We need to keep our wits about us. We have a confession to extract." I tried to sound industrious. I stubbed my cigarette out and clasped my hands. "We have a job to do." Rebecca smiled weakly. "Tell me what happened," I said. "Tell me everything." It tickled me to see her squirm. Her hands flew to her hair, pulling and twirling as she paced the kitchen floor.

"It started yesterday afternoon. I invited myself into Mrs. Polk's home," she said. She steadied her voice so as to seem unruffled, collected, believable, as though rehearsing what she'd tell a judge or jury. "I confronted her about her and her husband's actions, repeating what Lee told me about the enemas, the sexual abuse, all that." She jangled her hand as though to gesture upstairs, where the routine rape occurred. I had just barely comprehended the abuse as she'd described it—what body part had gone where, what the enemas were for. What it all meant was as yet unclear. I was naive and I was perverted and I knew what homosexuality was in theory, but I was inexperienced and couldn't picture sexual intercourse well enough to understand it in this twisted form—the rape of a young boy.

"What exactly did his dad do to him?" I asked. Rebecca stopped pacing and looked at me as though I were an idiot. "Just to be clear," I added.

"Sodomy," she said. "Anal penetration. Is that clear enough?"

I nodded, though this seemed implausible. "Go on." I cleared my throat. "I'm listening."

"Mrs. Polk denied everything, of course," Rebecca continued. "She called her husband a saint, said she'd never even heard the word 'enema' before I'd said it. 'Wouldn't know the first thing it was for.' But I kept asking, 'Why didn't you take Leonard and run away? Why would you allow this to continue? How could you be complicit in such torture?' And she just wouldn't answer. I told her to think it over. I left my number. But I knew she wouldn't call. I couldn't sleep at all last night. It was just eating me alive how that woman had lied to my face. So I came back this morning. She had nothing new to say, of course. Clammed up even more. Called *me* crazy. I threatened to report what she'd done. And I fought with her because what I had to say made her angry. I tried telling her I was there on Lee's behalf, and that I wanted to help her, too. But she wouldn't listen. She was mad. She attacked me. See?" Rebecca opened her robe and lifted her blouse to show me faint scratch marks across her chest, nothing grave, nothing that would leave a mark. Her torso was so narrow and pure, white skin seeming to glow from the inside, ribs like the ivory keys of a piano, abdomen stiff in its fine musculature. Her brassiere was black satin with delicate lace across her small bust. "I had to detain her," Rebecca said, shaking her head. "There was no other option. She was threatening to call the police. What would I tell them?"

"You did the right thing," I said. I steeled my eyes and let my face go slack, hoping to convey to Rebecca that I was fearless, calm and tempered with disdain for the terrible crime against the child, and would work vigilantly to see this thing through to the end, although I had no idea what that would mean. Rebecca's exasperation eased up a bit. She pulled her hair back.

"I didn't really hurt her," she said. "She's not in any pain. She was yelling for a long time, so I turned the music up. But now she's quiet. I figured eventually she'd tell the truth, accept her part of the blame, and then we could set things right. But she's not confessing to anything. She refuses to talk at all. I can't keep her tied up much longer and have her stay down there in the cold. I'm not a criminal. She deserves far worse, but I'm no villain. Do you know what I mean?"

I cannot say for sure why Rebecca had to drag me into her scheme. Did she really think I could help her? Or was I just there to witness her brilliant project, absolve her of her guilt?

I've debated with myself time and again the earnestness of her compassion. Just what was her motivation for getting involved in the Polk family drama? Did she honestly think she had the power to atone for someone else's sins, that she could exact justice with her wit, her superior thinking? People born of privilege are sometimes thus confused. But now she was frightened. Mrs. Polk was perhaps more evil than Rebecca had counted on.

"Leave her down there for a few more hours," I suggested. "That will punish her. She'll talk."

"But she hasn't said a word," Rebecca cried. She threw herself against the counter again, crossed her arms. "The damn woman won't confess. She's simply incorrigible. She's as mute as her son was."

"Get her drunk," I proposed. "People always say things they don't mean to when they're drunk."

"That's beside the point." Rebecca exhaled. "Anyhow the liquor stores are closed by now. What we need is a signed confession. Something she can't deny later. But she isn't scared enough to admit to anything. It's not as though I'm going to beat her up." She looked at me pointedly. "Have you ever beaten anybody up?" she asked, struggling haltingly to pronounce the words.

"No," I replied, "though I've imagined it."

"Of course not, of course." She paced again, kneading a new slice of bread between her fingers into small balls. My stomach churned. "We need to think. Think hard." A few moments passed. Then the solution came to me, so simple and easy I almost laughed. I turned to my purse where it hung behind me off the back of my chair and carefully pulled the gun out and set it on the table.

"It's my dad's," I said, my face uncontrollably giddy, though I tried to hold my mouth closed. I tried not to smile.

"Oh dear," Rebecca murmured, eyes wide, robe falling off her shoulders. She let it drag behind her like a queen as she approached the table. "Is that real?" Her eyes were glassy, awe-struck.

"It's real," I said. She put her hand out to touch it, but I picked it up, held it tight in my right hand. "Better you don't handle it," I said. "It might be loaded," I told her, though I assumed it wasn't. How could it be? My father wasn't that crazy, I thought.

"It's incredible," said Rebecca. But then she asked, "Why do you have that? Why would you bring it here with you?"

What could I have said? What would she have believed? I told her the truth. "My dad is sick," I said, tapping my temple with my finger, "and I worry what he might do if I left him alone with the gun."

Rebecca nodded gravely. "I see. Your father's keeper. Saving him from himself."

"Saving others," I corrected her. I didn't want Rebecca to see me as a martyr. I wanted to be a hero.

"Quite a gal," Rebecca said, giving me that shifty-eyed, con-spiratorial look I'd seen at O'Hara's a few nights earlier. "We make a good team," she said. I could imagine the two of us as some kind of lawless duo: Rebecca with her arrogance and her moral vision, and me with my deadpan glare and my gun. I put it back down on the table. She seemed eager to hold it. "Let's go downstairs," she said, lifting her robe from the floor. She wrinkled her nose and tied the belt of the robe tight around her waist. "It's filthy down there," she said. But I stalled. If there really was a woman tied up downstairs, my time alone with Rebecca was running out.

"What if Lee was lying?" I asked. "What if he made it all up? He's had years to think up a good reason to kill his dad, blame his mom. Mrs. Polk could be innocent. Don't you think?"

"Eileen." Rebecca looked down at me sternly, folded her hands across her heart. "If you saw this boy's tears, heard the story in his own words, felt him shake and cry, you wouldn't doubt him for a second. Look," she said, sliding the photo of Mr. Polk up next to the gun. "This man deserved far worse than he got. Don't you see that?"

I looked again at the photo, those secretive, side-cast eyes. The dead body was so strange, so unsettling, I had to believe he got what he deserved. To believe otherwise would have been too much. Back then I believed whatever I could to avoid the terrifying reality of things. Such is youth. "OK," I nodded. "So you think the gun will work?"

"Memory is a fickle thing," Rebecca answered. She was calmer then, her anxieties seemingly subdued. "Mrs. Polk is in deep denial. She's kept her secret so well, probably never told a soul, she may have a hard time even just remembering what the truth actually is. People pity her, you know. People assume she's just sad and lonesome. Nobody wants to challenge a woman in that state. Nobody even wants to be around someone like her, such a victim. We assume she's pathetic, just miserable. But no

one's ever asked her the right questions. I'm the first to care."
Rebecca pulled her hair back, braided it skillfully with quick
fingers. She was so pretty, even in the harsh kitchen light, even
with her eyes red and puffy. "She hadn't visited Lee once since
he'd been at Moorehead," she said. "Not until I called her, after
I read his file." She seemed to drift off for a moment, thinking
and staring at the cellar door. "Eileen," she said finally, turning
and pounding lightly on the table with her fist. "If Mrs. Polk
believes her life is at stake, she'll have no reason to deny anything. She'll be free to confess. We can set her free this way,
whether she thinks she wants that or not. She'll thank us later.
This is a good thing we're doing. You'll see. Here." Rebecca
pulled my scarf from around my neck. "We'll cover your face. It
will be scarier for her this way, and she won't know who you are.
She won't be able to recognize you from Moorehead. If she
does, it might confuse things." She tied my scarf around my
head, then pulled it down over my face so that only my eyes
were showing. My body tingled from her touch as she swept the
hair out of my eyes. She giggled. "You look fine," she said. "Now
hold up the gun. Show me how you'll hold it." I did as I was
told, holding the gun with both hands, extending my arms out
straight, lowering my face. "That's very good, Eileen." Rebecca
smiled, put her hands on her hips and clucked her tongue.
"Quite a gal," she said again.

I watched her go to the cellar door, slide the chain off the
lock, and pull it open to a dark and steep staircase. She reached
around the air and tugged on a dirty string. The light went on.
She turned, breathy and smiling, and gripped my shoulder.

"Come on," she said. I picked up my purse with my free hand and followed her down the stairs.

*R*ita? It's just me," Rebecca called out. Her voice was cautious, kind, the voice of a nurse or teacher, I thought. It surprised me. The scarf over my mouth made my face sweaty and tickled my nose, but I could see fine. The stairs were so steep, took so long to descend, it felt as though we were walking into the bottom of an old ship or tomb. The light from the bare bulb swung around, throwing sharp black shadows that stretched and contracted across the plain dirt floor. I walked carefully, step by step, not wanting to fall and embarrass myself. A new calm came over me down there. The basement's dark, cool dampness arrested my racing anxieties, softened the loud thudding of my heart. I thought of Joanie's busted-up hardcover Nancy Drew mysteries. *The Cellar of Secrets.* Of course I'd been grossly miscast in my role as Eileen the conspirator, Eileen the gun-wielding accomplice, but once underground, I was becalmed. That basement was somehow my domain. At the bottom of the stairs, I dug my heels resolutely into the dirt. "Be cool," Rebecca said to me. But I was cool. The gun in my hand was level and steady. When I turned the corner, I saw Mrs. Polk. There she was on the floor, legs akimbo, with her back against the wall. She had on dirty white bobby socks, a yellowed nightgown with lace at the throat. Her hair was loose and frizzy, face wet with tears. I have that picture set deep in my mind. She looked like a fat, old Cinderella, pale eyes darting back and forth innocently from Rebecca's face to mine. Rebecca had tied the woman's wrists together with the belt of her housecoat and strung them up to a pipe in the ceiling. There was little else to get tied to down there—an old rusty reel lawn mower, a broken wooden chair, a pile of wood pieces that looked like dismantled furniture—a dining table or a crib, perhaps.

"Don't shoot," the woman cried, uselessly trying to cover her face with her bound hands. "Please," she begged. "Don't kill me." It seemed ridiculous at the time. Of course I wasn't going to shoot her, I thought. I was glad my face was covered. It kept me from consoling Mrs. Polk with an assuring smirk or smile. Still, I kept the gun raised, pointed in her direction.

"She very well may shoot you," said Rebecca softly, coaxingly, "unless you tell us the truth."

"Which truth?" the woman cried. "I don't know what you want. Please." She peered up at me, as though I had an answer. I remained quiet. Even down there, pointing the gun at the poor woman, the situation had a curious element of make-believe. I may as well have been playing a party game, seven minutes in heaven, grappling around in the dark, doing things I'd never do in the light of day. I'd never played any of those make-out games, but I imagined that once you came out of the closet, you acted as though nothing had changed. No damage had been done. Everything seemed to go back to normal. Under the surface, however, either your popularity and prestige rose, or if you didn't perform well, your reputation suffered. The stakes down there in the basement were still only as high as Rebecca's esteem for me, my own happiness. Yet I had faith that her plan would work: Mrs. Polk would feel so relieved when she admitted what she and her husband had done to their son that she'd actually thank Rebecca for extracting the long-buried truth, saving her from her haunted world of secrets and lies. She could reunite with her son on new terms. She could live again. And Rebecca and I would be best friends forever as a result. Everything would be beautiful.

"Please," said Mrs. Polk. "What do you want from me?"

"An explanation." Rebecca puffed her chest out, put her hands on her hips. "We know it wasn't easy for you, Rita, married to a man who likes little boys. We understand that you've been suffering alone in this house with your guilty conscience. It's obvious you're having a hard time. Just tell us why you helped your husband do what he did—why you gave Lee the enemas. Why didn't you tell anybody what was going on? Tell us. Get it off your chest."

"I don't know what you're talking about," Mrs. Polk asserted, averting her eyes. "I'd never do anything to hurt Lee. He's my son. My flesh and blood. I'm his mother for Christ's sake."

"Eileen," Rebecca said. I started at my name. "Do something."

Holding the gun out, I approached Mrs. Polk. She let out an odd warbling scream, then yelled out again and again for help. A dog started barking somewhere aboveground and the sound echoed around the cellar between the woman's cries. Rebecca covered her ears with her hands.

"Quiet," I said. But Mrs. Polk's screeching was too loud for her to hear me. "Screaming won't help you," I yelled, amplifying my voice in a way I'd never had to before. "Shut up!" She stopped screaming and looked at me, sucking in quick short breaths, her mouth sputtering with saliva. I took a step closer, the gun aimed straight at her face. I tried to think of what my father would say and do in my situation. "Don't think I won't pull the trigger," I began. "Who would miss you? You could rot here forever. We could bury you right here," I stamped my foot on the hard dirt floor, "and nobody would come digging because nobody cares if you live or die." I can only say that given my home and professional life, I'd had years to learn how to speak in a way that made a person feel she had no option but to obey. In fact, I was uniquely prepared and qualified by experience to wrench the disgusting truth from this woman, I thought. I looked at Rebecca. She seemed to be deeply impressed by my performance. She took a step back, her mouth slightly open, and fluttered her hand as though to tell me to keep going. It was exciting. I adjusted the scarf over my nose and bent down to Mrs. Polk. Her face was wet with tears, red as a roasting pig.

"Death would be a blessing for someone like you," I continued. "Admit it. You've got too much pride to own up to what you did to your son. You'd rather die than confess that you've done anything wrong. Pathetic," I said, kicking at her feet. "Little piggy," I added. My voice bounced off the walls with a strange quick echo. Mrs. Polk turned away, her face tense with fear, eyes pinched shut but cracking open to glance at the gun every now and then as I spoke. She whimpered. "You want to die?" I rushed toward her suddenly, bringing the gun just an inch from her face. I looked up at Rebecca. She stood in the swirling shadows, wide-eyed and smiling. "Admit it!" I screamed at Mrs. Polk, my voice louder than it had ever been. I felt so buoyed by my convincing display of rage, I actually began to feel enraged. My heart pounded. The basement seemed to go black but for Mrs. Polk's blubbery body vibrating on the floor. As though I were drunk, I came at her violently again. I squatted down and tried to hit her with the gun across the top of her skull, but I barely grazed her. The butt of my fist just mussed her hair. Still, the gesture had her panting and crying even harder.

Rebecca stepped up. "I can't protect you unless you confess," she said. "Eileen has killed before," she added.

"That's right," I said. It was a ridiculous scene, two girls making things up as they went along. If I had to do it again, I would have calmly pressed the barrel of the gun to the woman's heart and let Rebecca do all the talking. I wouldn't have lost my temper the way I did. Looking back, it still embarrasses me. But however silly I looked waving it around, the gun was having its effect on Mrs. Polk. Her face had lost its arrogant pout and when she opened her eyes, they were terrified and ready. "Tell us what happened in this house," I said viciously. I put the gun to her temple.

"Please, don't hurt me," she whimpered, shaking.

"I won't have to hurt you if you talk," I agreed. But still, she just howled and sobbed. My arm got tired after a few minutes and I lowered the gun. Each time Mrs. Polk opened her eyes, I would raise it again. Finally she lifted her chin, grit her teeth.

"All right," she said. "You win."

"Are you ready to talk?" I asked her, my voice raised unnecessarily.

"Oh good," said Rebecca, clasping her hands. "Thank God."

I backed away from Mrs. Polk and sat down on the cold dirt floor, pulled my knees up toward my chest inside the warmth of my coat. The steam of my breath made my face wet beneath the scarf. I watched the woman catch her breath, collect herself. The gun had warmed in my hand. "We're waiting," I taunted her. She nodded. I wondered how well my father had known the Polks when he was still a cop, if Mr. Polk and he had shared chitchat over coffee, complained about their wives, their children. I don't remember ever meeting Mr. Polk but if I did, he made no impression on me. I guess that is how those sick people get by. They look like nobodies, but behind closed doors they turn into monsters. Sitting there, I imagined that if Mrs. Polk were to go and confess everything to the police, they'd simply dismiss her as a woman with a sick imagination. The ball and chain concocting some unbelievable story to make her old man look bad. Trashy. That would have been my father's explanation, I'm sure.

"I'll be right back," whispered Rebecca.

Startled, I raised the gun again. "Where are you going?" I asked, watching her cross the cellar floor. Mrs. Polk wheezed and sniffled, looked around, confused.

"To get something to write on," Rebecca answered, hushed. "You'll give us a signed confession," she said louder, to Mrs. Polk. "And we'll agree, you and I, that we won't ever go to the police about any of this. We'll put it in writing," she said. Turning, she gestured for me to point the gun at Mrs. Polk, which I did. Then she flitted up the steep cellar stairs, closing the door to the kitchen behind her. I could hear her footsteps through the house, fainter as she walked up to the second floor. I propped the gun on my knees, looked at Mrs. Polk.

"I really don't care what you did," I told her. "Just confess and she'll let you go, and you'll never see us again." I figured the struggle was over. Mrs. Polk had surrendered. I expected Rebecca to come back and untie her, rub the woman's back while she scribbled and sobbed, begged God to forgive her. I aimed the gun in her direction, expecting more fearful shrieks. But she just looked at me, frowning.

"I tell you things, and then what?" she asked. "What am I supposed to do?"

"I don't know," I said honestly. "Run away?" She cried some more, quietly, her face slick with snot.

"There's nowhere to run to," she said. "I don't have any money. I don't have anyplace else to go."

I shrugged. I thought of my stash of cash in the attic back home. Would I give my money to Mrs. Polk, forfeit my own escape to set her free and keep the authorities out of our hair—Rebecca's and mine? The thought crossed my mind. Upstairs I heard Rebecca clanking around, floorboards creaking. I yearned for her to return, to heap praise on me, to thank me from the bottom of her heart, tell me I was her hero, an angel, a saint. Then we could take off together. In New York, people were kissing under mistletoe, dancing and pouring champagne and falling in love. And where was I? I was alone in a basement with a woman tied to a pipe. I didn't want to watch Mrs. Polk cry anymore. I had played my part well, I thought. I stood up, dusted the dirt off my backside and gestured with the gun up at the ceiling. "She just wants to help," I said. I could go to jail, I realized, if something went wrong. Still, I wasn't afraid. I put the gun back down.

"She's right, you know," Mrs. Polk began. "That lady. Your friend?" Her voice was high and monotonous and clicked with phlegm as she spoke. "My boy wasn't lying about his father. Mitch, my husband, he had bad habits. You know, strange tastes. I thought some men were just like that. I never got used to it, but you have to understand. I couldn't just leave. You take an oath when you get married to honor and obey your husband. That's what I did. Where was I supposed to go?" Her eyes glittered in the weak light. She swallowed, looked up at the ceiling and cleared her throat. Where was Rebecca? "At first I thought Mitch was just checking on him in his sleep, like a good father would," Mrs. Polk went on. "Like he just wanted to be sure his son was safe and sound in bed. We all do that. But he'd spend a while. Bit by bit, longer each time, I guess. I don't know how often. Sometimes I'd feel him getting out of bed. Sometimes I'd just feel him when he'd come back, and he'd kiss me or hold me, and you know. We hadn't really been together since Lee'd been born. I'd lost interest. We'd lost interest. But suddenly Mitch wanted to be with me again. I was flattered. But I started getting these infections down there. Oh God," she sighed, "in my private parts. The doctors said I had to wash more. I figured it was my fault. And then I wondered if Mitch had brought something home from a trip he took one summer to visit his brother in Toronto, or so he said. The clap? I don't know what I was thinking. But I kept getting these infections. Then one night I got up in the middle of the night and went and looked and I saw Mitch in Lee's bed. At first I had no clue what they were doing, and I just went back to bed. It didn't dawn on me right away, I swear to you. You don't expect your husband's going to do a thing like that. It's a hard thing to believe. But as time went on, I came to accept it. It couldn't have hurt that much, I said to myself. Couldn't be that bad, I thought. And Lee never said anything, so I figured it was OK. Maybe I'd been confused all along about men, I thought. Maybe all men do this with their sons. You start thinking that. It could be true. What did I know? And Lee seemed fine. Quiet kid, good kid, decent grades, sweet boy. Barely said a word, played nice with the neighbors, nothing out of order. So I got used to it. And then I figured, if he was clean, it would be better for all of us. Maybe I wouldn't get those infections. They hurt, you know, when Mitch and I were together. Lee wasn't a big eater anyway, and I got to know what foods ran through him which ways," she said, "to make the enemas easier. It sounds funny, I know. I knew what I was doing wasn't quite right. But Lee was such a sweet kid, brave, you know, he didn't question it. He always just wanted to make everybody happy. He'd say, 'I just don't want anybody to be mad at me.' Made me all kinds of pretty cards at school for Christmas and Valentine's. Good boy, back then, I thought. So I put on a happy face. What else could I do? They don't tell you about these things. They don't prepare you for problems like that."

"They?" I asked.

Mrs. Polk didn't answer. She just bent forward, shook her head back and forth, stunned, it seemed, by her own words. I heard Rebecca's footsteps through the house again, even-tempoed but slow. Mrs. Polk looked up toward the ceiling, huffed, fighting back more tears. "Who do you tell? I wasn't going to tell anyone. You do the best you can. You know what happens when you have children? Your husband never looks at you the same. I blamed myself, you know. I ate too much. And Mitch didn't find me attractive anymore. We hadn't been together in years before that started, with Lee. Then it just became habit, the way things went. I was alone all day, you know. I was a housewife. I had nobody else, you understand. Mitch didn't talk to me, just came home, ate his dinner, drank, and I was just a stranger in the room, a nuisance. He could barely stand me. But after he went to bed with Lee, he'd come to me. And it was like a big burden had been lifted. He was relaxed. And it felt good, how he'd hold me. He loved me then. He was tender. I knew he loved me. He would show it. He'd whisper and kiss me and say nice things. It was the way it had been before, when we were young and happy and in love, and it felt good to me. Is that so wrong? To want to feel that way? I even got pregnant once, but I lost it. I didn't care. I had my husband back. You wouldn't understand," she said, looking up at me. "You're young. You haven't had your heart broken."

But I understood her perfectly. Of course I did. Who wouldn't?

She began to cry again, solemnly this time.

"There, there," I said, the first time in my life I had ever sincerely tried to comfort anyone. We sat in silence for a moment. Then we heard the door open, footsteps. We both turned to watch Rebecca float down the stairs, carrying a pad of paper and a pen.

"Will you untie me now?" Mrs. Polk looked at me. "I've said everything."

Rebecca looked at me suspiciously. I nodded. "It's true," I said, all my rage now gone. Mrs. Polk's eyes darted nervously from Rebecca's face to mine, then down at the gun on the floor.

"We'll untie you once you agree to our terms," Rebecca said. "And sign a contract. Eileen," she looked at me incredulously. "What did she say?" I wasn't going to repeat to Rebecca what Mrs. Polk had said. There was no polite way to phrase it. Rebecca grunted in frustration. "Eileen," she whined. To Mrs. Polk she said, "You'll have to write it all down, or else our deal is off."

"What deal?" Mrs. Polk was now clear-eyed, flushed more with anger than fear.

"The deal is you admit what you've done and we don't kill you." Rebecca was angry now, too, at Mrs. Polk and at me, it seemed. "Hand me the gun, Eileen," Rebecca said gruffly. I did as I was told. I didn't want her to turn against me. She stood back looking down at Mrs. Polk, as I had done earlier. "Tell me what you told her," she insisted, holding the gun awkwardly, her elbows bent outward, her fingers closed over the barrel. Mrs. Polk looked at me, as though I could save her.

"Be careful," I told Rebecca. She rolled her eyes.

"Rita," she said. "Don't be stupid."

"Shoot me," the woman cried. "I don't care anymore." I could barely breathe under my wool scarf. I lowered it from my face and wiped my sweaty cheeks with the cuff of my coat.

"I know you," said Mrs. Polk suddenly, dismayed. "You're the girl from Moorehead."

Rebecca turned to me, shocked. "What are you doing, Eileen?" I fumbled to pull the scarf back up.

"She already knew my name," I said in my defense. "Rebecca."

What happened next is still unclear, but as far as I could tell, Rebecca took one hand off the gun to pull back the cuffs of her robe, and when she gripped the gun again, her hands shook, she fumbled and the gun fell and fired as it hit the floor. The blast stopped us all from breathing. I crouched down and froze. Rebecca hid her face in her hands and turned away from us. Mrs. Polk was silent, drew her fat legs up to her large chest, exposing her fleshy calves and knees. Outside the dog began to bark again. And then, the blast still echoing in my ears, we three looked at one another.

"Shit," said Rebecca. She pointed at Mrs. Polk's right arm, a quickly spreading darkness seeping through her quilted housecoat.

"You shot me?" Mrs. Polk asked, her voice suddenly childlike with disbelief.

"Shit," Rebecca said again.

Mrs. Polk started to scream again, struggling against her restraints. "I'm bleeding!" she cried. "Call a doctor!" She became hysterical, as anyone would.

"Hush," said Rebecca, going to Mrs. Polk's side. "The neighbors will hear you. Don't make it any worse. Quit fussing," she said, covering the woman's mouth with her hand. I had warned Rebecca about the gun. Mrs. Polk would be fine, I assured myself. A superficial flesh wound was all I thought she'd suffered. Her arm was wide and fatty. No great harm had occurred, I thought. But the woman could not be soothed. She panted like a crazed animal and shook her head violently against Rebecca's hold, trying to scream for help. I picked up the gun, and feeling the strange heat through the grip, I was struck with an idea.

You can think what you want, that I was vicious and conniving, that I was selfish, delusional, so twisted and paranoid that only death and destruction would satisfy me, make me happy. You can say I had a criminal mind, I was pleased only by the suffering of others, what have you. In a moment's time I figured out how to solve everyone's problems—mine, Rebecca's, Mrs. Polk's, my father's. I came up with a plan to take Mrs. Polk to my house, shoot her, wait until she died, leave the gun in my father's hands—he would be passed out drunk—then drive off into the sunrise. Yes, of course I wanted to run off, and all the more if Rebecca would come with me. And yes, I thought killing Mrs. Polk was the only way to save Rebecca and me from the consequences of Rebecca's scheme. If Mrs. Polk were dead, no one would know that Rebecca and I had been involved, I figured. We'd be free.

But I was also thinking of my father. Nothing I could do would ever inspire him to dry out for good, get straight, be the father I wanted. He couldn't even see how sick he was. Only a massive shock would wake him up. If he believed he'd killed an innocent woman, that might be enough to shake him. Then he might see the light, accept the truth of his condition. He might have a change of heart. If they asked my father why he shot Mrs. Polk, maybe he'd mutter something about me and Lee, suggesting he thought that Lee was my boyfriend. The police would see he'd really lost his mind. They'd put him in prison maybe, but more likely they'd take him to a hospital, treat him well, nurse him back to health. I'd be long gone, of course, but at least he'd have the presence of mind to miss me, to regret what he'd put me through, to wish he could somehow make amends.

And as for me, I'd put off my escape from X-ville for long enough, my desire to leave always outweighed by my laziness and fear. If I killed Mrs. Polk, I'd be forced out of X-ville once and for all. I'd have to change my name. I'd have to completely disappear. Only fear of imprisonment, restitution, could propel me to leave. I could stay in X-ville and face hell, or I could disappear. I gave myself no choice. Shooting Mrs. Polk was the only option.

But how would we get Mrs. Polk to my house without her screaming the whole ride long? I wondered, turning the gun over in my hands. She bucked and stomped, wailing and gnashing her teeth as Rebecca shushed her and tried to stifle the screams by pressing her hands over the woman's mouth, but it was like stopping a break in a dam—Mrs. Polk refused to quiet down. Her arm was bleeding, but not profusely. Rebecca looked at me in desperation.

"What do we do?"

I shuffled around in my purse for my mother's pills. "I have these," I said, shaking the bottle. "They're for pain."

"Tranquilizers?" Rebecca's face brightened. She grabbed them from my hand. "What else do you have in your purse, Eileen?" she asked. I didn't catch her sarcasm at first.

"Lipstick," I answered.

I watched as Rebecca approached Mrs. Polk again, this time cautiously, coolly, as she would a frightened animal. The woman twisted her neck and bucked her head as Rebecca reached out to grab her face, one fist under her jaw, holding the pills in her other hand. She wrestled with the woman's head like a farmer with a cow, pinched her nose closed. Seeing her move like that made me wonder still, where had Rebecca come from? Perhaps she was a country girl, a farmer's daughter, a rancher. Truthfully, I cared less and less to make sense of her. I watched as Mrs. Polk clenched her jaw, held her breath, stared up fiercely into Rebecca's eyes. Finally her lips parted, and Rebecca opened her fist and took the pills in her other hand and worked them into Mrs. Polk's mouth. I was crouched down at a distance, observing them. I had a strangely comic impulse to pray or sing. I thought of the rites of passage I'd read about in *National Geographic,* bizarre ceremonies where people are bound and gagged, left in the desert, trapped in cages for days without food or water, administered hallucinogenic drugs so powerful that they forget their childhoods, their names. They return to their villages entirely new people, imbued with the spirit of God, fearless of death, and respected by everyone. Perhaps this experience in the basement, I thought, was akin to that. After it was over I'd be living on a higher plane. No one could ever hurt me, I imagined. I'd be immune.

"You'll be sorry!" Mrs. Polk cried once the pills went down. "I know you now. I'll tell everyone what you've done."

"Nobody will believe you," said Rebecca, her tone not as assured or confident as it should have been.

"Like hell," said Mrs. Polk, eyeing me. There was no great heartfelt surrender in the basement that night, just the three of us, our faces shiny with sweat or tears in the quaking light. Rebecca and I sat back and waited. The stain of blood on Mrs. Polk's arm seemed to stop spreading. Her breathing began to slow. "Get out, go away," she whined. "Get the hell out of here." Her voice dragged out like a slowing record bit by bit as the pills took effect. Once she was asleep, slumped against the wall, mouth leaking, tears drying into a crust around her eyes, Rebecca and I began to whisper. It took less than ten minutes, I'd say, to convince her that my plan was a good one. "My father's a drunk," I said. "If he killed somebody, it'd be on the cops—they should have locked him up years ago. Maybe they'll find Mrs. Polk and sweep the whole thing under the rug. It doesn't matter. We'll be fine." Rebecca's face had flattened and stiffened, her knuckles white as she clutched the dirty hem of her robe. "We'll have to hide out somewhere," I added, trying to maintain my composure. "I was thinking New York City."

"How do we get her to your father's house?" is all Rebecca asked me.

"We'll have to carry her out to the car." It seemed easy.

"And you'll shoot her?"

"My father will," I said. "But we'll pull the trigger."

"We?" Rebecca's eyebrows lifted. She pushed her hair out of her face.

"I will," I assented. It didn't seem so terrible. The woman had nothing to live for anyway. Either she could die quickly and painlessly or stay and rot in that awful house of hers, her dark past weighing on her day after day. "It won't hurt," I said. "Look." I kicked at the woman's fat feet. "She's out cold."

After a few moments of biting her lip and wringing her hands, Rebecca agreed. Together we untied Mrs. Polk's hands and lifted her off the floor. Remarkable how much a human being can weigh, I remember thinking. I took her from under her shoulders and Rebecca held her feet, and we hoisted her bit by bit up the steps, me going backward and bearing most of the load. It took every reserve of energy I had, and by the time we'd reached the top of the stairs, my knees shook and my arms burned. "Let's take a break," I said. But Rebecca insisted we move quickly.

"Let's get her out of here. Then you go on ahead to your father's house. Get him ready. I'll clean up here. We can't leave any evidence behind." She grabbed Mrs. Polk's feet again. The weight of her body was like a tub of water. Her head fell back toward me, her mouth hung open. When I looked down into it, her teeth were brown, her gums nearly white. She was as good as dead already, I thought. Rebecca stopped to cover her with her robe before we carried her out the front door. We moved carefully, but it was impossible not to bump her rear end on the frozen steps. A few times Rebecca slipped and let Mrs. Polk's legs hit the snow on the path to the sidewalk. It was slapstick, ridiculous, and I remember the jubilance rising from my chest into my throat. Once the woman was in the car, I paused to exhale, looked up at the sky, the stars spangled across the darkness like splattered paint. I thought I might burst into hysterical laughter under the quiet of that night, the beautiful stillness. I could feel the entire universe revolving around me in that moment. Rebecca looked tense. I shut the car door and put my death mask on then, tried to contain my excitement. I can't tell you what I was thinking. I'm not here to make excuses.

"I'll see you," Rebecca said suddenly, turning to dash back into the house.

I called out after her. "I'll be waiting!" My voice bounded loud across the snow-filled yard. Rebecca turned and put a finger to her lips to hush me. "We can go anywhere we want," I said, hushed. "Just the two of us. I have money. No one will ever find us." I gave her my address. "A block from the elementary school. Can you find it?"

She just waved, hopped up the icy stairs, and closed the door behind her.

THE END

I left X-ville without a single family photo, so all I have are my shifting memories to go on. I remember Dad as I left him—drawn and unconscious on the bed. Joanie I think of as a young girl, sensual and pretty and mindless. Mom, as I've told you, is harder to picture. I imagine just the frothiness of her graying hair as she lay dead in her bed, me curled up beside her, waiting to catch my breath before going out to tell my father, drunk for weeks already, that she was gone. "Are you sure?" is what he asked as I stood there in the stuffy, hot morning sunlight. I remember it—that image of loneliness, looking back at the half-open door to the room where my mother was no longer sleeping. The bathroom was where I went to cry. I remember my reflection vividly, eyes swollen and red in the mirror. I took off my clothes, still shaking, my arms ropy and useless as I held myself and sobbed in the shower. She died when I was just nineteen, thin as a rail by then, something my mother had praised me for.

I never liked looking at photos of myself. I'd been a pudgy child—that pale and homely girl in grade school who could not climb the rope or run as others did in P.E. Fat, loping thighs caused me to waddle in clothes my mother bought a size too tight in the hope that I would somehow change to fit them. And as I grew older, I remained short but whittled down to a small, birdlike stature. For a while I kept a little gut, doughy and oblong like a child's belly. By the time I left X-ville, though, I was a scarecrow, hardly an ounce of flesh to pinch, which was how I liked it. I knew that wasn't quite right, of course. I vowed to eat better, to dress better when I grew up. Be a real lady, I thought. I suppose I figured that once I left X-ville I would grow six inches, become shapely and beautiful. I thought of Rebecca, imagined her in a swimsuit, narrow hips and long, elegant thighs like models in the fashion magazines. A healthy glow. Maybe Rebecca could help me somehow, I wished, guide me, tell me where to go, how to dress, what to do, how to live. The picture of my future I'd had in mind before meeting Rebecca turned out to be somewhat accurate: I'd move into some ramshackle apartment, maybe a girls' boardinghouse where I'd be free to do such wonderful things as read newspapers, eat a spotted banana, go for a walk in the park, sit in a room like a normal person. But being with Rebecca could set me on a different path, I hoped. I wanted to do something great with my life. I wanted so badly to be someone important, to look down on the world from a skyscraper window and squash anyone who ever crossed me like a roach under my shoe.

Here is how I spend my days now. I live in a beautiful place. I sleep in a beautiful bed. I eat beautiful food. I go for walks through beautiful places. I care for people deeply. At night my bed is full of love, because I alone am in it. I cry easily, from pain and pleasure, and I don't apologize for that. In the mornings I step outside and I'm thankful for another day. It took me many years to arrive at such a life. When I was twenty-four, the most I wanted was a cramped afternoon among strangers, or to dawdle down a sidewalk without my father waiting for me, to be safe someplace far away, to be home somewhere. As I've said, my disappearance was not the solution to all my problems, but it did allow me to start over. When I got to New York late on Christmas Day, I was sobered and hungry and my body was cramped and my face was swollen. I walked around Times Square all evening and went to a dirty movie because I was cold and too nervous to check into a hotel, worried that the police were after me. I was scared to speak to anyone, scared to breathe. That's where I met my first husband—in the back row of that movie theater. So you see, what came after this story ends was not a direct line to paradise, but I believe I got on the right road, with all the appropriate trips and kinks.

*I*n the quiet darkness of that cold Christmas morning in X-ville, I parked the Dodge in my driveway, left Mrs. Polk slumped in the passenger seat, and barreled through the snow to the front of the house and went inside. I didn't think to pack a suitcase, though I knew then these were my last moments in that house. My father awoke as I came down the attic steps stuffing the gun and my money, all the cash I had, into my purse. I never did empty my father's bank account, or cash my last paycheck. I wondered for a long time whether I'd stand to inherit the house after my father died, but after a decade or two, assuming he had passed away, I decided to forget about it. There was nothing in that house, no part of it that I wanted enough to go back to claim it. In any case, I am dead in X-ville, a ghost, a lost soul, a lost cause. When I found my father standing halfway up the stairs that morning, he was already drunk. He had a hat on and a coat wrapped around his shoulders over his usual robe and boxers. He looked as though he'd seen a ghost.

"Something's staking us out from behind the house," he said. "I heard it breathing all night, dug inside the snow. A hoodlum it was not." He shook his head. "Some kind of wild animal. A wolf, maybe."

"Get into bed, Dad," I told him. There was a bottle on the floor. I picked it up.

"Did you see it?" he asked, straining to lower himself down to sit at the top of the stairs, a decrepit king on his splintery throne. I sat down next to him, handed him the bottle, and turned to face him, watched him drink, his eyes milky, hands quaking.

"There are no wolves," I told him, "only mice."

It took him just a minute or two to suck all that gin down. I remember how he grew sleepy—the effect of the gin came over him like a spirit entering his body—and like a child his head lolled, mouth frowned, eyelids fluttered like dying moths. I helped him up, gripping his arms at the elbows, and he fell onto me, neck clammy against my cheek. "Mice?" he mumbled. I led him into my mother's bedroom, laid him down, kissed his spotted, swollen hand.

"Good night, Dad" is how I said good-bye, and I stood there and watched him fumble awkwardly with an empty bottle on the nightstand, squint at it, drop it on the dusty carpet, sigh, close his eyes, and drift off. I closed the door.

That was it. There was no grand finale. He was my father, and that is all he was to me. I could have sat and waited for hours for Rebecca to show up. But there was no point. I knew she was not coming. I knew she was long gone. In the end, she was a coward. Idealism without consequences is the pathetic dream of every spoiled brat, I suppose. Do I hold a grudge against her? I really don't. She was a strange woman, Rebecca was, and came into my life at an odd moment, just when I needed to run away from it the most. I could say more about her, but this is my story after all, not hers.

Before I left I used the bathroom, ran hot water over my frozen fingers. In the mirror I was a different girl. I can't explain the certitude I saw in my face. There was a whole new look in my eyes, my mouth. I said good-bye to the house from where I stood over the bathroom sink. I tell you I felt strangely calm. The weight of the gun, the money in my purse told me yes, it's time. Get out of here. I had my last moment with myself in that place, in front of the mirror with my eyes shut. It hurt to leave. It was my home, after all, and it meant something to me, each of the rooms, each chair and shelf and lamp, the walls, the creaking floorboards, the worn banister. I'd cry my eyes out over it all in the weeks and months to come, but that day I just bid a solemn adieu. I really saw myself for the first time that night, a small creature in the throes of life, changing. I felt a great urge to look at photographs from my childhood, to kiss and caress the young faces in those snapshots. I kissed myself in the mirror—something I used to do as a child—and went down the stairs one final time. I would have liked to have gone out to the car and carried back all the shoes I could hold in my arms, drop them in the foyer, a parting gift to my dying father, hoping he'd storm X-ville like a tornado, create as much havoc as his weak heart would let him. But I didn't. I couldn't. I pictured him from earlier that morning as he trampled through the snow like a little boy toddling excitedly in his big coat, only gleeless and ragged, his eyes wide with panic instead of joy on our way to the liquor store. He'd lost his mind, and now his daughter.

I don't know where we went wrong in my family. We weren't terrible people, no worse than any of you. I suppose it's the luck of the draw, where we end up, what happens. I shut that front door forever. Then, as though God himself had willed it, as I turned to face the yard, one of those icicles cracked and struck me on the cheek, slicing like a thin blade from my eye to my jaw. It didn't hurt. It just stung a little. I felt the blood well up and the cold creep into the wound like a ghost. Men would later say the scar gave me character. One said that the line drawn down my face was like an empty grave. Another called it the trail of tears. To me it is simply the mark of having been someone else once, that girl, Eileen—the one who got away.

That was a nice final ride through X-ville in the Dodge before the sun came up. All I had with me was the gun and the money in my purse and the map in my pocket. I had plotted my route from X-ville to Rutland over and over. There was no reason not to follow through with my plan, after all. I thought it would have been nice to have disappeared on New Year's Eve, lost in the bustle and revelry of out with the old, in with the new. But Christmas was just as easy a day to disappear into, as it turned out. In hindsight, the trains may not have been running at all that day. I'd never know, because I never made it to Rutland.

I sometimes like to imagine the conversation Rebecca would have had with my father if somehow he had stumbled down our cellar stairs and found her bound and frightened, as I'd found Mrs. Polk. Perhaps he'd simply untie her, ask if she had any booze, wander back up, dodging his ghosts. Or maybe he'd listen to her explain her story, her whole philosophy, then leave her to shiver and starve for a few days, or forever. Maybe he'd call the police, put the hounds out for me, his wounded daughter, using the convoluted scent of my sweat on my mother's soiled clothing to track me through the snow-covered hills. I've fantasized all kinds of scenarios. Nobody ever did come looking for me. Either that, or I hid well enough to never be found.

I told people to call me Lena. And I did change my last name when I got married that spring. That is one benefit of marriage. The woman becomes someone new.

Perhaps a week earlier I'd have pined for a normal Christmas, wishing I could knock on somebody's door, sit down at a lavish table—a turkey or ham or lamb, or roast duck being carved by a handsome and grinning old father. I may have pined for a loving mother in pearl earrings, a gentle granddad in a hand-knit sweater, a floppy-eared hound, a crackling fire. Perhaps if I'd never met Rebecca, I would have driven out of X-ville full of regrets. Maybe I would have sobbed at my failure to thrive, sworn to God I'd change, be a real lady, eat three square meals a day, sit still like a good girl, keep a diary, go to church, pray, wear clean clothes, have nice girlfriends, date boys, go steady, do laundry, and so on—anything if it meant I didn't have to forge my way alone, an orphan driving out into that cold Christmas morning.

But as it turned out, on my way out of X-ville I had no regrets, and I was not alone. Rita Polk sat limp beside me in the Dodge, almost reverent in her complete silence. Her hands—wide, blue with cold—fell onto the seat between us as I took a turn. I picked them up and placed them gently in her lap.

I drove slowly through the deserted streets, past the elementary school, X-ville High, town hall. I took a route past the police station, bid adieu to all that green copper, those large windows, the fluorescent lights and dirty linoleum floor inside. I drove down Main Street, gray and empty in the dim morning. Needles of yellow sunlight fell from the horizon through the low buildings and illuminated the interior of the barber shop, the gold lettering on the bakery window, the crystalized slush in the gutter in front of the X-ville post office. The light teased and waned on my way out of town, as though it understood that I could not look at the place all at once, but only in glimpses, in details, and the wind howled and bit at my face and said for me to remember X-ville this way, swirling in the light and wind, just a place on Earth, a town like any other, walls and windows, nothing to be missed or loved or longed for. I tried the radio, tuned it past all the Christmas carols, then turned it off again.

I wish I could feel again the brief peace I found on that northbound highway. My mind was empty, eyes wide with wonder at the passing forests and snow-filled pastures. The sunlight blared through the trees, and at a particular swerve in the road, it blinded me. When I could see again, there was a deer standing a few yards ahead, blocking my way. I slowed, watching the animal frozen there, staring back at me head-on, as though I'd kept it waiting. I pulled over and rolled the car window back up.

Mrs. Polk was sound asleep when I left her in the car, still running by the side of the road. There was enough gas left in the tank for it to run for hours. I hope she opened her eyes to appreciate where I'd left her. If I'd had to die, that gorgeous stretch of white forest lit iridescent blue in the near dawn, still and cold, was as good a place as any. I said good-bye to the Dodge as I walked toward the deer, frozen still, breath steaming from its nostrils and hanging in the air between us like so many ghosts. I raised my hand as though to greet it. It just stood there, big black eyes fixed on mine, startled but kind, face tinged with frost, antlers floating above its head like a crown. I remember that, how I crumbled before that animal, its body quaking and heavy and huge. Tears finally filled my eyes. I opened my mouth to speak to it, but it trotted off down the embankment and into the woods. That was it. I cried. I smeared my tears around to rub the blood off my face and kept walking, my footsteps crisp and certain in the frozen snow.

When I thumbed a ride a few miles up at a crossroads heading south, I told the driver that I'd had a fight with my mother. The man passed me his thermos full of whiskey. I gulped it down, and cried some more.

"There, there," he said, patting my thigh with his thick, cold-burnt hand.

I sank into the passenger seat and drank and looked out the fogged-up window. I watched that old world go by, away and away, gone gone gone, until, like me, it disappeared.